T0265679

WINNING MAURA'S HEART

Also by Linda Broday

Outlaw Mail Order Brides

THE OUTLAW'S MAIL ORDER BRIDE
SAVING THE MAIL ORDER BRIDE
THE MAIL ORDER BRIDE'S SECRET
ONCEUPON A MAIL ORDER BRIDE

Lone Star Legends

A COWBOY OF LEGEND
A COWBOY CHRISTMAS LEGEND
A MAN OF LEGEND

WINNING MAURA'S HEART

Linda Broday

SEVERN
HOUSE

First world edition published in Great Britain and the USA in 2023
by Severn House, an imprint of Canongate Books Ltd,
14 High Street, Edinburgh EH1 1TE.

Trade paperback edition first published in Great Britain and the USA in 2023
by Severn House, an imprint of Canongate Books Ltd.

severnhouse.com

British Library Cataloguing-in-Publication Data
A CIP catalogue record for this title is available from the British Library.

ISBN-13: 978-1-4483-1024-1 (cased)
ISBN-13: 978-1-4483-1032-6 (trade paper)
ISBN-13: 978-1-4483-1026-5 (e-book)

All Severn House titles are printed on acid-free paper.

Typeset by Palimpsest Book Production Ltd.,
Falkirk, Stirlingshire, Scotland.
Printed and bound in Great Britain by
TJ Books Ltd, Padstow, Cornwall.

ONE

Whispers, dark and ugly snaked along the stone walls of the makeshift hospital in St Anthony's Church, mixing with the low moans of the sick and dying from an epidemic that had began in the summer, four months prior. Fall had thankfully brought some relief from the constant tolling of the church bells that kept a tally of those souls who'd succumbed.

Who knew whether the cooler temperatures had any bearing on the epidemic or not.

Rays of an orange morning sun fired the colors of the stained glass and a heavy weight filled the place of worship as though the old building heard and offered sympathy.

Maura Taggart shifted uneasily. Whispers and low murmurs always accompanied her and her sister Emma. At twenty-eight years of age, it seemed she'd be used to them by now. They shouldn't affect her after all these years, yet they still had the power to hurt.

Still, even worse than the whispers were the dark, open stares. A few folks appeared anxious as if the sisters might harm them in some way if they got too close, but most were the kind to make chills run up her spine. She wouldn't want to meet these people in a pitch-black alley.

No one spoke to the hangman's daughters or offered a kind word.

No suitors had ever dared call.

No invitations to town dances or church socials.

They were alone. Outcasts. This was the hand she and Emma had been dealt and nothing would change it. Their father still went right on hanging criminals, still riding each time he received a telegram from a judge.

A committee of concerned citizens had only come to them this time when another round of yellow fever broke out. The townsfolk probably figured it a blessing if the dreaded disease killed the hangman's daughters.

For sure, they wouldn't see it as any big loss.

Though they'd lived outside of San Antonio for most of their lives, not a soul would mourn their passing. Maura straightened her spine and dribbled water into a woman's feverish mouth and clutched her feeble hand. 'I wish I could take this sickness from you, Mrs Clark.'

'You . . . you won't leave me,' she begged, fear in her eyes. 'I'm afraid.'

Before she could reply, quiet footsteps sounded and she turned to see the mayor, a height-challenged man, leading a gaggle of men and women. They shuffled toward her and stopped.

The mayor cleared his throat, evidently finding his task a bit distasteful. 'Miss Taggart, I've come to inform you that we no longer have need of you and your sister's services now that the scourge of yellow fever seems to be waning.' He stopped, wet his lips, and glanced at those behind him. 'We request that you leave town by day's end tomorrow.'

'I see.' Maura kept her face a blank mask. 'It might take us a day or two to figure out a destination. As you know, our home suspiciously burned immediately after we arrived here.'

Mr Mayor's face reddened. 'Are you accusing us?'

'Merely stating facts, sir. No more. No less. We have nowhere to go. If we could stay and work long enough to earn some money, we'd be grateful.'

'Impossible.' A tall, thin woman with dark hair swept back in a severe knot stepped forward. 'We're unable to give you longer than what we've stated. It's not . . .' She paused. 'It's not good to have you lingering around. You must know what I'm trying to say.'

'Yes, ma'am,' Maura answered in a quiet voice, swallowing hard. She met and held the woman's spiteful gaze. 'I suppose I do.' She'd heard it before, but it stung all the same.

The group offered no word of thanks for working to the point of exhaustion, trying to save the sick. Or even a pat on the back. She and Emma were just tools when they needed them.

Maura forced a tiny smile, squeezing out the words. 'If you'll excuse me, I must find my sister.'

'I believe she's with those wretched orphans,' a man offered with a smirk.

With a nod, Maura took a few steps and turned. 'Do you have a plan at all for those homeless children?'

The mayor stiffened and stretched, as though trying to make himself taller. 'We have yet to determine their sad plight. We'll have to call some meetings and discuss it, but we'll likely ship them to some kind of children's home. If they'll take them.'

They too were unwanted, a blight to the good citizens of San Antonio.

'Then you won't mind if my sister and I take them off your hands?' Maura asked softly.

Mr Mayor wore a stunned look. 'Of course not. But why would you? You girls can't even take care of yourself. And your poor excuse for a father . . .' He paused, his gaze faltering. 'Well, it's best that we leave that unsaid.'

There it was again. Everything boiled down to Lucius Taggart.

'These orphans are precious little souls and can't help what's happened.' Her gaze swept each face and as she did most looked away. 'Everyone deserves kindness, to know they matter to someone. Even though it will admittedly be a hardship, Emma and I will assume their care and see that they grow up strong and healthy. And loved.'

'Well, in that case,' the mayor hedged, 'us townsfolk will pitch in some food for you to take along when you ride out tomorrow.'

'It's the Christian thing to do,' the thin woman threw in.

How ludicrous. There was nothing Christian about any of this. Maura glanced around at the sick, wondering how many would end up in a mass grave like hundreds of others. When the epidemic had struck in May, it hadn't taken long for grave diggers to stop shoveling individual burials and dig one long trench. That also had filled quickly, prompting another, and yet a third.

It seemed rather odd to her that these epidemics only arrived during the late spring and summer months, but then smarter people than her were trying to figure it out.

But for now, she had to decide where exactly to take sixteen

grief-stricken orphans. Who would give them refuge? They'd
have to keep quiet about being the hangman's daughters.

Yet people always found out. Somehow.

No, they needed a place away from everyone. Isolation was
the only way for them to live in peace.

Still wracking her brain, she found her pretty auburn-haired
sister outside the church playing games with the children. Emma
held a toddler, no older than two, calling for her mama. Another
little boy around four or five was curled up alone by the wall
sobbing his heart out. Maura watched for a moment, sorrow
choking her. Some days it was too much. How could anyone cast
a blind eye?

She turned to the ones kicking a ball, listening to the laughter
that hopefully made them forget if for only a second that their
parents had left them all alone in the cold world. When she
got Emma's attention, she pulled her aside and gave her sister
the news.

'I can't believe this!' Emma spewed, her emerald eyes flashing
behind wire-rimmed spectacles. 'How ungrateful! We've worked
hard to try to save the sick, almost wrecking our own health, and
now to be cast out like lepers. We can't help what our father
chooses to do.'

'I know.'

Emma's voice trembled. 'Where will we go? Who will
want us?'

A boy around eight or nine must've heard and ran over, worry
etched on his face. Tears pooled in his eyes. How soon laughter
turned to sorrow. 'What's wrong, Miss Maura?'

She quickly forced a smile and put an arm around his shoulders. 'Honey, you don't need to fret about anything. Miss Emma
and I are going to take you and the others to the most wonderful
place where you'll be loved and cared for.'

Where that would be she had yet to figure out, but one thing
was for sure, she wouldn't let these children suffer the sting of
being mistreated and unwanted.

Later, in the room she and Emma shared, they packed their things,
all the while trying to think of where to go.

They had faced a lot of adversity together. They were all each other had. Sisters, united and standing as one. The oldest by three years, Maura was also taller and her hair had a shade more brown to her russet than Emma's. Maura's eyes were blue to Emma's green, but they looked strikingly similar.

'It's going to be hard caring for so many children,' Maura said at last with a sigh.

'True.' Emma folded her nightgown and put it in the trunk. 'But we can do it. We can do anything we have to when it comes to making a difference.'

'It's what we always do.' Life had kicked them around plenty, but they'd never given up. And they never would if Maura had any say in the matter.

Emma seemed unusually pensive. Suddenly she spoke. 'There are a lot of old abandoned Spanish missions around here. What about one of those?'

The thought stunned Maura. Of course. One of those could work. Some were still in pretty fair shape. 'Sister, that might be the solution. I don't think anyone owns those and they're simply falling into ruin.' She mentally began a list of things they'd need. Beds of some sort, although she guessed they could put blankets on the floor for a while. 'Remember Uncle Max?'

'We haven't seen him in what? Nine or ten years?'

Emma's snort filled the small airless space. 'I recall Father speaking of his fondness for liquor quite well.'

'He once mentioned that Uncle Max is living in Mission San Francisco de la Espada outside of San Antonio.'

'How would that benefit us?' Emma asked.

'Maybe he'll help us.'

With an unladylike snort, Emma crossed her arms. 'Not likely. If the fondness for liquor is true, he probably can't stay sober long enough.'

'I always loved Max. He has a good heart,' Maura said in his defense.

Emma, always the practical one, countered, 'Wouldn't that be adding more headaches to the ones we already have?'

All true. Still. 'If Uncle Max is still there, I'll talk to him.'

'Suits me fine.' Emma clasped her hands together. 'I'm not proud of it, but I have little patience with his sort. Sounds like he's wasting his life living in a drunken stupor making extra work for everyone around him.'

'I know, but I think he may be doing the best he can. As are we all. Don't judge. Do you want to be closed-minded like the folks of this town?'

Emma's answer came quickly. 'Of course not.'

'I'll get the wagon. If the mission fits our needs, we'll come back for the children.'

Maura had long suspected that Max turned to the bottle to escape the fact his brother was a hangman. She didn't know for sure, but Max probably suffered the same barbs that people flung at everyone associated with Lucius Taggart. They cared not that hanging criminals was honest work and perfectly legal. In fact, hangmen served a vital purpose.

The profession just seemed so dirty, so ugly, so distasteful.

Ever since she was a little girl, she wished her father did something else. She'd cry that she had no friends. In school she faced bullies who called her father a killer and worse and would run home sobbing. Her mother would pull her into her lap and sing or tell funny stories. Anything to let her and Emma know they were loved beyond measure.

Then her mother had taken sick and died, leaving them to face the world with no one to guide them or offer encouragement.

Emma shrugged, removing her spectacles. 'I agree it might be a longshot but checking the mission out can't hurt. The structure would certainly be large enough and I personally have nothing against Uncle Max. Beggars can't be choosers.'

'That's the spirit.'

'However, there's no use in us both going.' Emma chewed on the earpiece of her eyeglasses. 'I should stay behind and begin getting the children's things together. No matter where we go, they'll have to be ready.'

'That's a good idea.' Maura hugged her. 'I'll be back soon. Wish me luck.'

With a spark of hope curling around her heart, Maura hurried to get the wagon. This could work. It had to work.

Because they had no other options.

TWO

The thickness of night closed around Cutter Calhoun as he listened intently to the men chatting around a campfire beyond the brush where he crouched. One low rumbling voice in particular made his ears perk up. He hadn't heard it in a long time, but he knew it like his own.

This man was the reason he'd come. He'd made a deathbed promise to get his brother out of Rupert Donavan's outlaw gang.

And he meant to deliver on the vow. No matter the risk and however he had to do it.

Jonas Calhoun had broken his mother's heart when he'd ridden away from their Texas farm and never returned. Then when they'd discovered he rode with the murderous Donavan Gang, she'd become a shell of a woman and lost the will to live. Their father had died shortly after Jonas left, which he guessed was a blessing although they hadn't seen it at the time.

Well, Cutter was here at the outlaw hideout. Now for the hard part. He was glad he wasn't a betting man because the odds of succeeding were long.

He cursed the thick darkness that hid danger and death. Cutter carefully brushed the fall leaves out of his path and inched closer, slowly parting the brush. Jonas sat across from Rupert Donavan, the flames showing his twin's relaxed features. Other men were stretched out here and there next to the fire, passing a bottle.

Six members including Jonas made up the gang, but none were more ruthless than Donavan the leader. Plain and simple, the man got a thrill out of killing and often shot someone for no reason except to feel power over them.

Jonas didn't belong here and had thus far hadn't become a killer. Cutter knew that would change the longer his brother stayed with Donavan. It was bound to, either by accidental circumstances or continued association with killers.

A spurt of laughter drifted to his hiding place and two men

got into a play scuffle. After a few minutes, Jonas rose. 'I'm going to check on the horses. They seem a bit jittery.'

'Don't be long,' Rupert barked roughly. 'We're getting a card game together.'

The rumor that he kept a tight rein on his men appeared to be true. The leader seemed to trust no one and didn't let them out of his sight often.

Why Jonas had tied himself to such a man was beyond Cutter.

As his brother strode toward the shadows, Cutter hurried as fast as he dared in that direction. The wind had kicked up a bit scattering the dead cottonwood leaves which aided greatly in covering the noise of his movements.

Cutter remained hidden in the darkness and spoke in a whisper. 'Jonas, we need to talk.'

His brother jerked his gun from his holster in a lightning move. 'Who's there?' he squinted, speaking low. 'Speak or I'll blow a hole in you.'

'It's Cutter. Put that Colt away.'

Donavan yelled from the fire, 'Who you talking to Calhoun?'

'The horses!' Jonas hollered. 'I told you they're jittery.' Jonas returned his weapon to the holster and edged between a buckskin and sorrel and lowered his voice. 'Show yourself.'

One heartbeat then two and Cutter tapped his brother on the shoulder. Jonas turned and stared for a long moment. Coming face to face with his twin after three years shook Cutter to the depths of his being. He noted the hardness in his brother's face, the new scars, the touch of gray in his dark hair that hadn't been there before. It was a funny thing, they thought they shared no resemblance and laughed when others were unable to tell them apart.

Memories of how they used to switch places as kids and no one ever knew – not their teacher, classmates, or friends. Cutter and Jonas found it amusing that even their parents struggled to tell them apart and often got them wrong.

When they were born, each parent named one, agreeing not to match the names.

'You were too much alike as it was,' his mother had told him. 'I knew you'd want your own independence.'

So, their mother bestowed Cutter on him, honoring her father. Their dad chose Jonas in remembrance of his.

Now, Jonas hesitated for a moment before a wide smile broke across his face. He enveloped Cutter in a hug then hurried him a little farther from the gang's camp. When they were out of earshot, Jonas spoke, 'I've missed you. How's Mama?' Thick emotion filled the whispered words.

'I hate like hell to break the news to you this way.' Cutter struggled with the words he knew he must say. 'She passed three months ago.' A second passed before he added, 'Her last words were of you.'

Jonas released an oath, turned away and lowered his head, clearly shaken. 'I never got to see her again.' His twin swung back around, blinking hard. 'I never got to tell her I love her. I've been trying to find a way. The only thing is, Donavan won't let anyone leave once they're in the gang and pass muster.'

'I heard that. It's why I've come. I'm going to get you out.'

'And you decide if I go or stay?' Jonas's tight voice held anger. His brother had gotten touchy.

'Didn't mean to sound so highhanded. Just came out wrong. Sorry, brother.'

Jonas sighed, shaking his head. 'Donavan will kill me if I try. He gunned down Choctaw last week in cold blood before he could get on his horse.'

'But you want to escape this, don't you?' Cutter asked softly, meeting his brother's dark gaze. 'This life isn't you, Jonas. You're better than some two-bit outlaw. We were raised to respect the law. To live right.'

A long sigh told of his brother's weariness. 'Sometimes I wake up and wonder how I got myself mired down in this. It's like quicksand pulling me under. No matter how hard I try to get out, I go deeper and deeper.'

'Then there has to be a way.' Cutter took a deep breath and set his jaw. 'I made a deathbed promise to Mama and I mean to make good on it.'

Muttering, Jonas hooked a thumb in his gun belt. 'You still a lawman chasing murderers and scalawags?'

'Getting God Almighty tired though. Trying to find a way to

hang it up because a man doesn't live long in this kind of life.'
He was quiet for a moment. 'Got myself caught up in something
bad too.' A half beat later, he added, 'I've made an enemy of a
powerful rancher and he's holding a favor I did for him over my
head. They want more. Don't see any good way out of this mess.
I expect to lose my job.'

'Having right on your side isn't enough. Doesn't seem it's
ever enough.' Jonas turned to face him, running a hand across
his unshaven jaw. 'What's become of us?'

'I don't know.' Cutter glanced away. 'I just don't know.'

A strand of silence stretched between them. Cutter tugged up
the collar of his shirt against the night chill.

Finally, Jonas spoke. 'Why did you always try to pretend you
were the better son and I could never measure up? Why, brother?
Answer me.'

The rush of air Cutter sucked in hissed through his teeth. 'Do
you want to waste our time hashing out old slights?'

Thick tension sliced the air.

Finally, Jonas raised his hands in surrender. 'You're right.
Forget it. We oughta forget this kind of life and settle down with
a good woman, have us a mess of kids.' He rubbed the back of
his neck. 'We're getting too old to ride all over hell and
creation.'

'I agree. Look, let's get you out of here. Between us we'll
outsmart Donavan. We can make a break for it right now.'

'You're crazy. You don't know who we're dealing with. They'll
cut us down before we can blink.'

'Maybe so, but I'm not ready to roll over and play dead. We
have to try.'

Thick silence enveloped them as Jonas searched Cutter's eyes.
'Fine. I'll meet you back here around midnight. The men will
have a snootful and be dead to the world. I'm hoping they won't
hear a thing. We'll ride to that abandoned mission that's close.
Called something Espada.'

'OK. Don't bother collecting your belongings. Keep quiet
and move fast.' Cutter rested a hand on his brother's shoulder.
'I have your back just like when we were kids. Remember how
I bloodied George Crenshaw's lip for spitting in your face?'

Jonas chuckled softly. 'Yep. And I recall when he pushed you through the ice on that frozen pond and I made him help pull you out.'

'I also recollect you knocking him on his butt and sitting on him until he apologized.' Cutter's mind filled with so many times when the two of them worked side by side for some common goal. 'We can do this. Together. Just like we always have.'

Tears filled Jonas's dark eyes. 'For Mama.'

Midnight came and as expected, the gang went out like a light. Cutter remained mounted on his gelding next to the string of horses, ready for the escape. Doubts that their plan would work rushed through him like molten lead, but he knew they had to try.

Ten minutes later, Jonas emerged from the darkness with a whisper, 'So far, so good.'

'Come on,' Cutter hissed.

Jonas stuck a boot in the stirrup and froze. 'I have to go back.'

'Don't have time. Let's go.'

His brother stepped down. 'No. I'm going back for the loot from our last job.'

Curses blistered Cutter's brain. 'Forget that. We have to go.'

But Jonas wouldn't listen, hurrying back to the gang's camp. Dammit to hell. Was his brother so entrenched in lawlessness that he couldn't leave ill-gotten goods? Hopefully, Jonas was thinking of turning the loot in and winning his freedom. Yes, maybe. Time crawled. Something hit the ground with a huge clang. Cutter jumped a mile and gripped his Colt. Hell!

'Let's ride!' Jonas hollered, appearing from the gloom. He struggled with two burlap bags that were tied together.

'What are you doing?'

'Help me.'

Cutter dismounted and they slung the sacks over a third horse, then leaped into their saddles. Gripping the reins of the pack horse, they lit out.

The thought that they should've untied the gang's mounts sprang as stinging regret and a sight too late. Now, it came down to outrunning them.

All hell broke loose behind them. Men yelled and released a volley of shots, running and cursing. The gang scrambled for their mounts and probably wouldn't bother with saddling up.

Cutter's heart pounded as his big bay roan ate up the ground. They rode side by side with the pack horse in the middle with bullets peppering the air around them.

The night would be their friend if they could put a little distance between them and their pursuers.

Why didn't they just leave? Why did Jonas go back for the loot?

The question lingered in both their minds as they drew every ounce of strength from their horses. They just needed to reach the old mission.

Bullets tore into both men. They returned fire blindly, unable to see a target in the pitch black. The hammering of the gang's horses' hooves against the ground drowned out everything as they gave chase.

The brothers raced side by side through shallow creeks, across flat pasture, up one hill and down the other with one singular goal driving them forward.

Escape.

Two more miles. Searing pain enveloped both men. They had no choice but to keep riding straight through hell and hoping to come out on the other side.

All of a sudden one brother was no longer there and sent a rush of overwhelming despair through the survivor.

Immense pain, scorching and hot, made it difficult to stay in the saddle. He slipped sideways at times, but he clung to the pack horse's reins with all he had.

This was supposed to have been easy! Their escape should've gone smoothly.

Through the night he rode, his vision becoming dimmer and dimmer until no longer able to hold on to the reins. He fell from the bay.

How long he lay there breathing in the moist ground, he didn't know. When he came to, he pulled to his feet to find the horses gone. The pack horse must've bucked off his load because the loot lay nearby. Slinging the heavy loot over his shoulder, he put one foot in front of the other, stumbling along.

Half of him was dead. They'd been one heart, one body, one mind for so long, tethered to each other by love, thoughts and blood.

Theirs had been an impenetrable bond that was stronger than steel.

Gone. All gone in an instant.

Now, he was adrift.

Muttering a curse, he glanced down at the heavy bags of loot, wishing he'd never seen them.

Going back had been stupid. And costly.

Exhausted, his heart pounding in his ears, he sucked in cool fall air, trying to block the searing pain in his side that burned like a roaring blacksmith's forge. Inky night pressed closer and he struggled to get his bearings. Nothing looked familiar. He ran his good hand over his eyes and leaned against a tree for a moment.

Not long enough. The crashing in the undergrowth behind him wouldn't allow for dallying. The burlap sacks weighed him down, but he struggled onward, looking for a hiding place where he could stash the loot. A thin fingernail moon overhead offered little light.

The surroundings looked nothing like he remembered. Where was the old mission where they'd planned to hide until morning?

A nightbird called in the trees overhead. If only it could tell him where he was. One fact remained: he was lost and dying. The bullet in his side and arm shot searing pain that stole his breath. As blood dripped from his fingertips, he tried to raise the arm that hung lifeless, but clutching the burlap sack with the good hand made it impossible to help.

How many times had he been shot? From the throbbing, searing, teeth-gritting pain, he knew he had more than two bullets in him.

So many men, so many guns, all blazing at once.

His breath coming in hard, raspy pants, he swept the area for something familiar. His vision blurred. Blood loss made him weaker and he was far from safety. He dragged another breath of air into his lungs and pushed away from the tree.

Then a group of boulders caught his attention. A space left between two very large rocks was covered by a smaller, flatter one that acted much like a lid. He removed his shirt and used it to scoot the small rock aside, thus keeping blood from marking it for any followers. Quickly jamming the sacks into the crevice, he slid the stone back in place. There. Unless Rupert Donavan knew exactly where to look, he'd never find the loot.

Satisfied he'd done his best, he wadded his shirt up and managed to stick it under his dangling arm, leaving nothing behind.

The thrashing of brush filled the air. Feeling the breath of his pursuers on his neck, he lurched through the thick gloom. He had to get away. For his brother's sake if not his own. They'd risked everything and the dice had come up snake eyes.

A vow crossed his lips that he'd not let his brother's death be in vain, if in fact he'd met his Maker.

Each stride took him farther from Donavan. *Focus on escape. Don't let him catch you. Just a little farther.*

Was that the old stone mission through the trees? Hope soared. Maybe. He couldn't tell. Maybe he was only seeing things.

An unexpected snarl came from close behind. 'Over here. I think the low-down thief is just ahead.'

'Get our money back!' Donavan yelled. 'Nobody steals from me.'

'We got him now!' yelled another. 'I smell the rat.'

His heart plummeted and he searched frantically for a hiding place, a cave, a tree with low branches he might climb – anything.

Nothing caught his eye and he was fading fast. A few more halting steps and his vision dimmed to a black circle. He gritted his teeth. With safety of the mission within reach, he couldn't get any more out of his shot-up body. He cursed himself for not getting far enough.

It was clear that he wasn't going to make it.

Reaching the end of the line, he dropped under the nearest tree and drew the dense foliage around him as best he could. Releasing a shuddering breath, he closed his eyes, the unmistakable odor of blood climbing up his nose and sliding down his throat.

This was it. A gurgle choked him.

As he waited for death to claim him, a smile curved his lips. They might find his body, but they'd never find what they sought.

His brother would've been happy about that.

THREE

Gray clouds hung over them the entire ten-mile journey, cloaking Maura with gloom. The silence allowed her to try to think up a new plan in case this one didn't work out. Yet despite her efforts, nothing else came to mind. They had no money so were forced to depend on charity. Still, she'd beg, not for herself, but for those innocent, heartbroken children who'd lost their whole world.

She'd do whatever it took to make them a safe home.

After the children's parents had passed on, two elderly women had done their best to find other kin and succeeded in contacting half a dozen who came to collect their young relatives.

Those had been the fortunate ones.

The top of the stone fortress of Mission San Francisco de la Espada showed through the cottonwood trees just ahead. Maura's stomach lurched as she steered the wagon around a large dip in the road and turned down a narrow lane that didn't appear to get enough use to keep the weeds knocked down.

The sprawling stone structure and numerous outbuildings looked deserted. She stopped the wagon in front of the church and walked through a tall gate into a large compound. A woman in a nun's habit hurried from a covered walkway that stretched between the chapel and a line of smaller structures at the side. A large brass ring of keys dangled from her waist. The sun peeked from the clouds as though blessing them.

'Hello,' Maura called, setting the brake.

The petite woman smiled. 'Welcome.'

It was difficult to place the accent wrapping the words. Definitely not the predominate Spanish of the area. It was very common to hear nuns speaking other languages as many came from other countries.

Another nun, a much taller one followed. *'Bonjour!'*

Ah, French.

The mystery cleared, Maura climbed down. 'I thought the place was deserted. How long have you been here?'

'Five months maybe. I am Sister Angela.' The petite nun with wrinkles shook their hands then motioned to the second. 'And this is Sister Bernadette.'

In contrast to Angela, Sister Bernadette bore a youthful face, perhaps shy of her twenties. She also shook their hands. 'We see no peoples.' She colored. '*Excusez* English. Still learn.'

Maura shook her head. 'Please don't apologize. You're doing well, Sister. How many of you are here?'

'Us and one more. Sister Anne-Marie is hiding.' Angela clasped her hands and sighed. 'Frightened of everything. Be patient.' The nun glanced toward the stone chapel. 'Come.'

'Thank you.' Maura fell in behind the nuns. 'I'm actually wondering if my uncle might be here. Max Taggart?'

Angela stopped and turned, her expression grim. 'He is here. Very sad.'

'I take it, he's liquored up most days?' Maura asked. Darn it, why couldn't he be sober for once?

Bernadette wrinkled her nose. 'He like strong drink.'

Maura offered no apology but followed the two sisters into the cool interior. She glanced up at the tall ceilings and thick walls, hoping to convince the nuns to let them run an orphanage.

They moved through the worship area, down a corridor into a kitchen.

Before they could sit at a long table made of thick wood, a voice came from the doorway. 'Visitors I see.' Max rested his weaving body against the frame, his shoulder-length brown hair hanging in disarray. 'More to try to save my rotten, worm-eaten soul.'

'Uncle Max, come and have a seat.' Her heart heavy, Maura hurried to catch him.

He perked up. 'Ah, my lovely niece. What brings you to my purgatory?'

She yanked out a chair and he fell into it with a grunt.

'A long story. But first you need coffee.' Maura swung around. 'Sister Angela, would you have a bit?'

'Yes, a small sack,' Angela answered. 'I get water.'

As the woman shuffled toward the door, Bernadette stopped her. 'Sit down, Sister. I'll get it.'

In no time they had a pot on the wood stove. While they waited, Maura learned the nuns tended a pitiful garden and had little other food. They'd been sent with orders to open the mission back up and teach Christianity to all who would listen. They hadn't known the difficulties and how unforgiving the land could be. In fact, they'd been ill-prepared for Texas. In France, they'd had forests and trees and a much cooler sun.

Max slept, his chin on his chest, a hank of hair hanging in his face. Maura's heart ached to see him so broken. Could they in all fairness bring a group of children here?

But had they little choice in the matter.

At last the coffee was ready and they began the process of sobering Max. When he became more aware of them and his surroundings, Maura laid out their dire situation.

'The sanctimonious lot of them!' Max ranted, pounding the table. 'How dare they run you girls out after helping them!'

The people of San Antonio dared a lot more than that, but Maura didn't voice opinions that would serve no purpose.

'We need a place of refuge for ourselves and those orphans. Can we bring them to safety here?'

The nuns were quick to consent, their eyes lighting up. Maura imagined this would give them purpose and to feel they were accomplishing their mission. Max stared silently into his cup.

'Max?' Maura prodded. 'What about you? You were here first.'

He raised his gaze, his haunted eyes clearer. Though he was younger than their forty-eight-year-old father by five years, Max's features bore the results of hard living. Silver had stolen the color from his temples and short beard and wrinkles carved deep lines around his mouth and eyes.

Finally, Max spoke. 'Me and kids don't mix well, but I'll manage. Sure, bring them on. Me and the sisters will find a place for them to bed down. I'll move out to one of the other buildings where I can do as I please.'

Tears welled in Maura's throat. 'Thank you for taking us in. All of you.'

A noise sounded from behind a door that Maura assumed was the larder. Round eyes peeked out through a crack.

'Sister Anne-Marie,' Angela said gently. 'There is nothing to fear, child. Come out and meet our visitor. She is going to bring children.'

This third nun, with large darting eyes and cowed head, reminded Maura of a mouse quite sure she was some wild thing's prey. Like Sister Bernadette, Anne-Marie was quite young.

Maura stretched out a hand motioning to the empty chair beside her. 'I'm so happy to meet you. I think our little ones will be quite excited to have you taking care of them.'

'*Oui, Mademoiselle*,' Anne-Marie murmured, sliding into the chair, a hint of a smile on her lips. Except for her eyes, her features were small, her figure slight. It was going to take some doing to bring her out of her shell, but Maura would definitely make an effort.

They talked of the arrangements, then Maura rose. 'I'd like to see the buildings and grounds.'

'*Oui*.' Sister Angela pushed back her chair, the ring of keys clinking at her waist. Uncle Max helped her to her feet. She wasn't as spry as at first glance and seemed to favor her right leg. '*Merci*, dear Max. *Pardonnez ces* . . . uh . . . how you say old bones.'

'What do you mean, Angie? You're just a young girl.' Max's gruff voice held tenderness. No one seemed to mind him dropping the sister from her name. But then he'd always been a charming rounder.

A little giggle sprang from the elderly sister's mouth.

Love for their uncle swelled in Maura's chest. Despite trying to wash his brain away, he cared about these ladies living in a foreign country. This was going to benefit them all, not just the children.

Tolerance, kindness and acceptance had to be learned and cherished.

Maura followed the black-clothed figures while Max stayed behind. Maura worried he'd return to the bottle, but that was his choice. They couldn't make a grown man do as they wished any more than fly to the moon.

The mission complex was large. In addition to the chapel,

there were the two-story priests' quarters, workshops, storage facilities, a friary where the nuns stayed, a stone granary and a line of quarters where workers had once lived. The covered walkway ran from the sanctuary to the priests' quarters and would make a perfect place for the children to live.

Max, it seemed, had claimed the room off the sanctuary. Maura was glad he hadn't put up a fuss about moving because they couldn't allow the children so near him.

But surprise greeted Maura when they returned to see that Max had already gathered his things and set them outside his door. 'Where do you want me?' he asked.

'Any of the line of workers' quarters are in good shape and will be excellent to keep watch from.' Maura patted his arm. 'Thank you for being amiable to this.'

Max shrugged. 'It'll be nice hearing the sound of children's laughter ringing through these old buildings. Might rid them of ghosts.'

'Ghosts, Uncle?'

'Laugh if you want but I hear them all the time. This was the site of a battle for Texas Independence. Jim Bowie himself put up fierce resistance here. It's rumored that he buried some treasure around here. Some silver ore from his mine.'

'That's interesting.' She hadn't heard that. It seemed that what happened at the Alamo must've stolen all the attention. She looked at Mission Espada through new eyes. 'Any truth to the rumor?'

He snorted. 'Probably started by a bunch of drunks sitting around a campfire.'

Still, it would be nice to find treasure. They sure could use money to help the kids.

'Are you a fan of history, Uncle Max?'

'Your grandfather Taggart fought and died here.' His quiet words silenced the teasing poised on the tip of Maura's tongue.

'I didn't know,' she managed. 'Father never told us.'

Max snorted. 'Figures.'

She glanced out a window. 'He never brought up our grandparents' period. I always wondered why. Maybe you can tell us, Uncle.'

'You'll have to ask him.' Max picked up a bag of his belongings.

The nuns minus Sister Anne-Marie joined them. 'It will do, no?' Sister Angela asked.

'It's perfect.' Maura hugged her. 'Thank you for opening your hearts to us.'

The petite woman's eyes misted with tears. 'We went through much to get here. Then find all in vain.' She shook her head. 'So hard to see no . . . how you say . . . purpose.'

'Now we teach *les enfants*,' Bernadette said, beaming with happiness. 'God give us de gift. He knew.'

'And we are truly grateful. I need to get back. We have much to do to get ready by tomorrow. And we've been promised food.'

With wide smiles, the nuns clasped their hands together. '*Très bien.*' Bernadette beamed.

Max walked them out to the wagon and his words came out gruff. 'You may not know it, but you're the answer to those women's prayers.'

Maura patted his hand. 'So are you, Uncle.'

'Ah hell. I just care about 'em. You know?'

'I think I do.' She accepted his hand up to the wagon bench. As she wound down the narrow lane, she turned to look back. The gloom had lifted. It seemed they'd found a home.

FOUR

Late afternoon shadows had fallen by the time Maura returned to San Antonio. She hurried to unhitch the horses from the wagon and lead them inside the small barn behind the place where they'd been staying. The wagon was one of their few possessions, so she took pains to leave it against the side of the building where an overhang offered a little protection. Then she lengthened her stride, in a hurry to give Emma the result of her trip.

Quiet sobs reached her outside the room assigned to her and Emma. She paused, her hand on the knob. The sorrow came from an adult, not one of the children. Prickles of alarm raced up her spine.

She pushed inside and stared in shock, sucking in a strangled cry.

Emma huddled on the floor while children pressed around attempting to console her. Long strands of her beautiful auburn hair lay scattered on the rough-hewn planking.

'Emma!' Maura hurried to envelop her sister in a gentle hug. 'Emma! My beautiful, kind, sensitive sister. Tell me what happened. Who did this?'

Eight-year-old Sunny, a deep red bruise on the side of her face, burst out, 'Mean people come and cut it all off. I kicked one hard. He slapped me. I hate them.'

She needed to admonish the girl but couldn't find it in her because rage had dug into her own heart. She struggled to keep it out of her voice. 'I'm so sorry, Emma. I shouldn't have left you here.' Maura rocked her sister. 'We're leaving this place and the despicable people, and you'll never see them again. I only wish we could leave right this minute.'

The five Johnson brothers looked as though they'd fought a buzz saw. They loved to fight and would be a challenge to keep in check. Stair-stepped in age from five to twelve, nearly all had torn shirts, bruises and angry scowls. The same from the eight-year-old Harrison twin sisters who'd hidden under the bed until it was all over.

It'd be a job calming everyone down, but first she had Emma to console.

Chopped hair of uneven lengths framed Emma's face as she raised teary eyes. 'It's only hair. It'll grow back and I'll be fine. I'm alive and so are the children and that's what's important.' Her stoic demeanor vanished when she picked up a long length of auburn hair from the floor and tears bubbled over again.

'What did they say and who exactly was it?'

'It was a group of men and women from the church. They said they didn't appreciate our kind here. Said we're dirty and low class and the mayor sanctioned their decision.'

'Probably the same ones with him when they came to tell me we had to leave town.'

Four-year-old Amos spoke up. 'Them say . . . them say . . .'

Sunny rescued the boy. 'They said we're not welcome and they'll make sure Miss Em learns a lesson.'

That vicious, ugly people invaded their living space and attacked her sweet sister and the children filled Maura with such fury she shook. How many times would they have to face such prejudice? She lifted the hem of her dress and wiped Emma's tears.

'There. Children, will you see if you can find Miss Emma's spectacles?' Had the committee stomped on them like they'd done Emma's heart? For once, Maura wished she'd been born a man. Men had ways of settling these things.

'Here's her spec'ables.' Henry handed them to Maura.

'Thank you, Henry.' At least they weren't broken. She straightened the bent earpieces and slipped the glasses on Emma's face. 'Now, can you get me the broom?' While two of the boys went for that, Maura helped Emma to her feet and over to the bed. 'After I sweep up this mess, I'll even up your new hairdo. I think I rather like your hair short. It's impish, like you.'

A smile tried to form on Emma's lips but quickly vanished as she felt her shorn head. 'I appreciate trying to make me feel better. But it's going to take a while to get used to this.'

'I'm sure you're right.'

Once Maura swept the room, she sat Emma down and evened up the ungodly hatchet job. Emma's tears had dried, and she sat staring into space, her expression hard. Maura could imagine the thoughts going through her sister's head. She'd been violated as surely as they'd stripped off her clothes and leaped on her body. Hair was a woman's crowning glory.

The women who'd cut it had been jealous of Emma's beauty. With pursed lips and disapproving eyes, they wore ugliness like a second skin. Their scorn still seemed to echo in the room.

Dirty?

Low class?

Not hardly.

'There.' She handed Emma a hand mirror and stepped back to view the results from one angle then another. 'I like it. I really do. It suits your personality.'

The short auburn hair curved around her sister's face framing her striking features. Her green eyes and long dark lashes were even more beautiful with this becoming hair style.

Emma sighed and turned her head this way and that, looking. 'I'd prefer to have it long, but I do think you're right.'

'You're real pretty, Miss Em,' Henry said, patting her hand.

Sunny clutched her doll that had become a permanent fixture. 'What if those mean people come back?'

Maura caught Emma's horrified expression and winked. 'Don't you worry. I have a plan.'

'You do?' Emma's voice held quiet fear. 'Mind sharing?'

'For one thing I'm going to bar the door and slide the dresser in front of it. Then, I'll sleep with that old pistol of Father's under my pillow.' Maura tightened her jaw. 'I won't hesitate to shoot anyone who tries to bother us.'

The children's worried faces told her to change the subject. 'Let's get ready for bed and I'll tell you all about Homer the donkey and a squirrel named Pete.'

'Yay!' the pint-sized group hollered in unison.

'Does Homer wear spec'ables?' Henry asked, giggling, the gap in his mouth showing where he'd lost two top front teeth.

'Well, you never know, he just might.' Maura tweaked his nose.

*   *   *

Later in the dark room they would vacate come morning, Maura told Emma about Uncle Max and the nuns. 'The mission suits our needs perfectly and we'll have the nuns' help.'

'How about Uncle Max?'

'He hasn't changed much, but he won't stand in our way. He truly has a soft heart for the three sisters. You should've seen him.' The memory of him calling Sister Angela by Angie swept into mind. 'I'm extremely encouraged. I feel he just needs someone to care.'

'We all do,' Emma replied, a sob hanging in her throat.

Soon after, Sally began sobbing her heart out for her contented little world that had been all she'd known. The three-year-old sobbed for her mother and father. Maura wrapped her arms around her and murmured soothing words, hoping she'd soon exhaust her tears and go to sleep.

Maura gently smoothed the silky blonde curls. 'There, little one. Get some sleep. I've got you. One day this will all be a bad memory.'

Over in the next bed, Emma was cuddling with two five-year-old brothers, trying to bring solace to their aching hearts. So many kids in the same situation. Tears sprang into Maura's eyes. Doubts rose that she and Emma could do this. What if they failed? What if they couldn't save these sweet children?

They knew nothing about raising little ones. They were lucky to have survived their own childhood. School had been a nightmare. Parents had threatened their kids if they played with the hangman's daughters. Their mother had done her best to shield them from the worst of it, until she'd gotten sick and died.

Then Maura and Emma had learned what it was to be utterly alone.

As the traveling hangman, their father had rarely been home, and it had fallen to Maura to take care of Emma. Even when Lucius Taggart spent a little time at home, he was a cold stranger. She and Emma hadn't had a kind word, a gentle touch, or warm nights around the fire in so long. His thoughts had always been on his work. And a bottle of some strong drink. He'd sat with a rope in his hands, testing the strength, the pliability, the ability to snap a man's neck.

Now Maura and Emma were taking on the task of raising lost children when they knew nothing of the challenges ahead.

Emma reached across the narrow space that separated their beds and patted Maura's arm. 'It'll be all right, Maura. We can do this. We can do anything we have to. We're strong and we're able. Besides, we'll have the nuns and Uncle Max. We don't have to do it alone this time.'

'I know. Worry just got to me.' Maura squeezed her sister's hand. 'I love you, Emma. I'm not sure I tell you that enough.'

'There's no need to say what I already know, Sister.'

The warm exchange seemed to bolster them both and Maura's worry eased. Soon she was asleep.

Morning's dawn brought a red-tinged sky. They got the children up and fed them biscuits and apples that two kindly gray-haired women had brought. Maura thanked them for their kindness as one who could barely hobble wished them good luck.

Emma threw a shawl over her hair. A second passed. Then she defiantly lowered it and went out to face the world with her shoulders back and head held high. Maura had never been prouder of her.

They glanced around for any sign of the group who'd shorn Emma's hair, but didn't see anyone lurking about. She'd bet any amount of money they were watching though. How interesting that the mayor, for some odd reason, hadn't been with the attackers even though the group had told Emma he sanctioned their actions.

As they loaded the children, the mayor delivered a ten-pound sack of flour, one of sugar and another of dried beans. 'This is all I could scrounge up.' The worm glanced down to keep from meeting Maura's gaze, but kept giving sidelong glances at Emma.

'Take a good, long look, Mr Mayor.' Emma raised her chin. 'Your friends did this. I see they're too chicken to face me in the daylight and on the street where people can see.'

He ignored her, instead turning his attention to Maura. 'I heard you're moving into the Mission Espada.'

'That's right,' Maura answered. 'It has the space we need.' She gave him a cold stare. 'How unfortunate if your name got linked to Emma's group of attackers. Now that would sure be a *real* pity.'

He coughed and red streaks started up his neck. 'You can't pin that on me.'

'Maybe not, but my sister and I aren't fools. You condoned it and they mentioned your name. What does it say about their character to jump one measly woman and a bunch of little kids?' She snorted. 'That's *real* brave. Almost makes me wonder what they'd do facing a grown man. But I already know.' She cleared her throat of the choking anger and motioned to the pittance of what they'd been promised. Determined to be grateful, she took the high road. 'Thank you for bringing these supplies.'

'Well, if things improve here, we might see our way clear to bringing more later. But don't hold us to that.' He glanced down at a boy patting his leg.

'Mister, I lost my marble,' the boy said.

The mayor stepped back, clearing his throat. 'These women will help you.' He tried to turn away, but the kid gripped his trousers. He sighed. 'I'll tell you what, drive down to the mercantile and I'll add some more provisions. Out of my own pocket.'

If that was supposed to impress her, it didn't. The man was a lowdown snake. He did nothing that didn't benefit him. It was nothing but a silent bribe and she wanted to tell him what he could do with it. But she wasn't stupid. They needed as much as they could get.

'We won't spurn your offer,' Maura answered. 'I'll drive down there.'

Nodding, the mayor almost sprinted toward the store. Clearly, he wanted to hurry them out of town.

Emma found the missing marble and climbed into the back with the children, and they went the two blocks.

The additional increase to their supplies was worth the extra stop. And the mayor passed out licorice sticks for all.

When he handed Sunny one, he stared at the dark bruise covering the side of her face before patting the top of her head and moving on.

That he was trying to smooth everything over made Maura see red again. When he turned to walk away, she called after him, 'A few licorice sticks won't help you sleep better at night, Mr Mayor. It'll take a long time for Emma's hair to grow back. And we have a very sharp memory.' Maura climbed into the wagon box and gave the man a dose of sugary sweetness. 'Oh, I almost forgot. Tell those yellow-bellied friends of yours they can crawl back under their rock.'

The mayor's face flushed. 'I don't know what you expect me to do. Maybe you should talk to Lucius Taggart.'

Their father? So, it all had to boil down to him. Again.

Satisfied that the extra addition to their supplies would have to suffice, Maura turned the wagon toward the mission. The air seemed to smell better once they'd left San Antonio behind.

Emma certainly seemed in better spirits as she held three-year-old Sally on her lap playing and singing 'Patty Cake'.

They sang more songs and clapped as they drove. It brought a festive feel to the day and also shortened the trip.

No one had kicked them out. They'd simply decided to leave for better things.

FIVE

Strange how the sky seemed so much bluer outside of town. They sang one song then another and soon the Mission Espada came into view. Sisters Angela and Bernadette met them and clucked over each child like mother hens. Shy, terrified Sister Anne-Marie left her hiding place to join them but didn't offer a word.

Maura introduced Emma and noting the nuns' surreptitious glances at her hair, felt compelled to add, 'My sister had a nasty encounter with a group in town and they chopped off her hair.'

'I'm still adjusting to it,' Emma said quietly, tugging at the short strands.

Sister Bernadette hugged her. 'Speak no more.' Then she winked. 'I shave head.'

Maura had heard that women in the order shaved their heads upon entering a postulancy and taking vows, but she couldn't imagine herself wanting to do so. It warmed her heart though that the nun with the sparkling eyes tried to make Emma feel better.

The sisters and Emma herded the children inside to get settled in.

Rubbing sleep from his eyes, Uncle Max looked on from the doorway of his new abode.

Maura waved hello. 'Uncle, can you help unload the wagon?'

'I'll get my shoes,' he replied, slurring some of his words.

Oh dear, he'd likely spent the night inside a bottle. A pang shot through her heart. They'd make sure to steer the kids away from him. If they could just get his help for a minute, she'd hustle him back to his room.

While waiting for Max, Maura scanned the large complex for places the children might play. They'd have to knock down the weeds and such before it would be safe. And the large unkept yard extended all the way to the tree line which would require supervision at all times whenever they let the kids play outdoors.

A good portion of the landscape around San Antonio was covered with low brush, but here at the mission they had the river that provided water for tall trees. The soil seemed perfect for growing a garden or some type of crops if they came by any seeds. She eyed the aqueduct coming from the river and what looked like a gravity irrigation system the former occupants had built. Her excitement grew. They had the resources to become self-sustainable. That is if the women worked at it and got enough help from Max. And if the weather cooperated and they were able to find cheap enough mules or oxen to plow the fields.

She sighed. And if they could come up with a little money. That was the biggest obstacle and the most impossible.

'No time for wool-gathering, Maura.' Max's voice startled her.

'Looking the place over. It has lots of promise.' She touched his arm, smelling liquor. 'Are you all right?'

He met her gaze and held it without glancing away. 'I'm not drunk if that's what you're referring to. But I have been drinking.'

'Oh, Uncle Max.'

His chin rose to a defiant angle. 'I'll make no excuses for that. Don't meddle in things you have no business.'

'I'm not judging, but I'd be lying if I said I'm not a bit disappointed. These children have been through sheer hell, and I won't let you add to that.'

Max released a long sigh and it seemed the lines around his mouth and eyes deepened even more. His voice was soft, contrite. 'I am who I am. I make no apologies or excuses. This thing I'm fighting won't let go. Do you think I like being this way? To have you girls look at me and turn away? This demon is worse than any enemy I've ever fought. I'll stay away from those poor kids.'

'Fair enough.' One question had been on her mind and it needed asking. 'How do you get your whiskey? Do you go somewhere or do they bring it to you?'

'Don't worry. I go after it. I won't let that sort come here. Those nuns don't need that and now there's the little ones.'

'Good.' She kissed his bearded jaw. 'I love you, Uncle Max.'

'Yeah, well, don't get maudlin over me,' he said in a gruff tone. He shook his shoulder-length hair back and hefted one of the sacks on to his shoulder. At the door of the kitchen, he paused. 'I'm just what I am. No more. No less.'

'As are we all, Uncle.'

The plain talk boosted her admiration of him. If only they could all be so open. She picked up a smaller bag and followed.

Inside the kitchen, he stared at Emma, trying to place her. 'Who? Emma?'

'Uncle, it's good to see you.' Emma stepped forward to give him a hug.

'My God, girl! What happened to your hair?'

'While Maura was here looking the place over, I was attacked in town.' Emma lifted her chin. 'As you said coming in, you are who you are. Well, I am too.'

Anger filled Max's eyes. 'I hope they burn in the fiery pits of hell!'

'Don't waste your time on them.' Emma fingered the hair curling around her ear. 'I'm not. We have too much work to do.'

When they'd toted all of the reluctant charity inside, Max disappeared into his room. Maura wondered if Emma's attack would send him deeper into the bottle and prayed not.

The women set to work making blanket pallets on the stone floor for their little charges.

Maura sighed. 'It'll have to do for now. I hate it though.'

'Maybe some benevolent soul will make little beds for each of them at some point,' Emma said, smoothing a blanket on one pallet. 'These can't be comfortable.'

'God send bed,' Sister Angela said, smiling.

'I hope so, Sister.' Maura didn't add that the good Lord had never seemed to look their way. Or take notice of the lack.

That afternoon, Maura took Max's rifle and went hunting for meat for supper. She entered the trees that were like silent sentinels, looking for a rabbit or squirrel to make a stew with. The birds twittered happily overhead, flying from branch to branch.

A squirrel scampered up a cottonwood tree that had begun to lose its pretty yellow leaves. Inhaling, she took aim and gently squeezed the trigger. The animal fell and she hurried to collect it. As she bent over, a piece of fabric sticking from the underbrush caught her eye.

Blood had soaked the leaves and turned the fresh scent of the ground a vile repugnant odor.

Had a wild animal killed some prey? Maybe whatever it was still lived. Her heart pounding, she crept closer and gasped at a hand. This was a person. Trembling, she knelt and began to carefully uncover the victim.

Tension that stretched her nerves to the breaking point gripped her.

Her hand brushed bare skin and uncontrollable shudders took over. Inch by inch she uncovered a man's form. His shirt, wadded and dirty, lay beside him. Maura noted the horrible wounds, the blood, then the holster and gun.

As she'd been taught by a doctor, she felt for signs of life below the jaw on the man's throat. Her heart lurched.

He was alive.

A tendril of hope leaped inside her.

But she had no time to waste. He was dying with each shuddering breath.

SIX

The afternoon shadows were setting in as Maura raced back to the mission on foot for help. She prayed Uncle Max would be sober. She couldn't do this by herself.

Emma came running, her face white. 'What's wrong?'

'A man's dying! I need the wagon.' Her mouth dry, Maura shot a glance toward the small row of living quarters before running for the barn. 'I have to hurry. Max?'

'Good luck there. I haven't seen much of him,' Emma replied, keeping pace with her. 'I'll go back with you.'

'You may have to, but the stranger is much too heavy for the two of us. We need the nuns to watch the children. Hurry.' Out of breath and trembling, Maura reached the barn and yanked the door open. With Emma's help, she pulled the wagon out and went back for the horses.

The exertion had Emma huffing. 'We can't let the kids see us unloading him.'

'If he's still alive,' Maura added.

They finished hitching the horses then climbed in and first went to tell the sisters of the situation. Then they drove around to Max's. Maura pounded on the door.

Bleary-eyed, Max opened up, smelling of whiskey. 'I'm busy.'

Maura set her jaw. 'Please help.' Wasting no time, she told him about her discovery.

Without another word, he slammed the door and unsteadily climbed into the wagon bed.

Though Emma raised her eyebrows in question, Maura stayed silent and drove as fast as she dared over the uneven ground, then parked at an angle to make the loading easier.

The stranger was barely breathing but still alive.

'This poor man's hanging by a thread,' Max murmured, sucking in a breath through his teeth. 'We'd best hurry. I'll lift his head and shoulders if you girls can get the feet.'

'He's sure big,' Emma said softly. 'Well over six feet.' She moved into position next to Maura.

Between the three of them, they managed to get him into the wagon. Maura was thankful the man was unconscious, or he'd have been screaming in pain.

It didn't take long to pull up to one of the empty quarters away from the children. They hadn't had time to clean so it was very dusty. Nothing except for a narrow bed and an old trunk someone had left filled the room. A small fireplace was in the corner.

They strained every muscle getting the stranger inside. Although Max was not at his best, they couldn't have done it without him.

Max propped the man against him, holding him steady while they laid a slicker down on the ticking to catch the blood.

They'd no sooner gotten the man on the bed than Sister Bernadette hurried in with a pail of water and clean cloths. 'What else?' she asked.

'A doctor preferably. But since one probably won't come, scissors and a sharp knife,' Maura replied, unbuckling her patient's gun belt and handing it to Max. Emma helped remove the man's boots and they exchanged worried glances, the dim lighting softening her short hair.

The sister hurried out and Maura turned to her uncle. 'Do you think we should ride to town for a doctor and try to convince him to make the trip?'

'You don't have time.' Max stroked the bristles of his jaw. 'He'll die while we wait.'

He might die anyway but at least they'd stand a chance of saving him by proceeding.

'My thoughts exactly.' She gave him a searching glance. 'Do you think you can remove the bullets? I've never done it but if you can't, I'll try my best. I won't let him die if I can do something about it.'

'My hands are a little shaky, but I'll give it a shot.' Max rolled up his sleeves. 'First, I need something to tie my hair back.'

Maura ripped off a strip of her petticoat and he made quick work of the job.

'Good enough. We'll need whiskey to sterilize with,' she said. He left, and she glanced at Emma, standing silent on the other side of the bed. 'We need more light. Can you round up a lantern?'

'Sure. I'll bring candles as well,' Emma answered. 'It's so dark in here with just one small window.' With a swish of her skirts, she hurried out.

Maura stripped the stranger to his drawers and sucked in a quick breath. His waist was trim, legs long and muscular, and had a broad chest. He was the perfect example of a man in his prime. While she wished to admire his lean form, she quickly moved on to more pressing issues.

His injuries consisted of three gunshots with a side wound far the worst. Blood was pooling on the slicker, but better that than soaking the thin feather mattress. She dipped a cloth in the pail Sister Angela had brought and began to wash him. As she removed the blood, scars began to show. Some old, one fairly new that looked to be made by a knife.

Outlaws lived a violent life. But then some lawmen and bounty hunters did as well. Her own father had been shot in the attempt to hang one of his criminals.

She worked quickly and had just finished smoothing a light blanket over the man's midsection when everyone returned.

'Are you ready, Uncle Max?'

'As much as I'll ever be.' He inhaled a sharp breath and poured whiskey over the knife and scissors. 'Damn, I hate to waste this.' He hesitated just a second and took a long swig. When Maura sighed, he growled, 'You can't expect me to do this without something to settle my nerves.'

'Save some for the patient,' Emma snapped. 'He'll be in pure misery when he wakes.'

Maura wanted to add an 'if' to that but didn't. They didn't need that thought out there.

Time crawled at a snail's pace. The arm wound was easiest. Then Max wiped his forehead and moved to the place above the left knee. Maura watched the man's face as Max dug around. The lines around the stranger's mouth tightened even though he was still unconscious. The airless room smelled of blood and whiskey. She grabbed the man's hand and held it tightly.

Hopefully, he'd sense on some level that she prayed for him and know he wasn't alone.

She leaned to place her mouth at his ear. 'We're not going to let you die. Fight.'

'Are you about to get the lead, Uncle Max?' Emma held the lantern closer.

Sweat dotted their uncle's forehead. 'The damn thing is slick and I can't grab hold.'

'Want me to try?' Maura asked.

Wordlessly, he stepped aside and handed her the knife. She took it and switched places. The wrinkles on Max's face eased. He stumbled outside and the sound of retching reached them. She spared a glance at the horrible side wound and shuddered, dreading to tackle that. But one thing at a time.

Finally, her small fingers were able to reach into the bloody hole above his knee and, going strictly by feel alone, grabbed the projectile. She pulled it out and rolled her shoulders.

'Oh good,' Emma breathed. 'Just one more.'

And it was by far the worst.

Uncle Max came back in, wiping his mouth. 'Sorry,' he mumbled, keeping his eyes lowered. 'Bad whiskey.'

Maura lifted her gaze. 'It's all right. We're all doing the best we can.' She shifted her attention to their patient. 'Including this man who's trying to die. Emma, would you hold the light up a little?'

Time didn't seem to be on their side and after several more painstaking attempts at the metal fragment lodged in the man's side, Max took the place beside her. 'Rest. We've been at this for over an hour.'

'Gladly.' She moved back in relief, again rolling her shoulders and neck.

The stranger's gray face and shallow breathing told her he was fading. She gripped his hand, leaning to place her mouth at his ear once more. 'Mister, if you want to find the person who did this to you, you'd best fight harder to live. Don't let them win. You're stronger than that. Prove you're the better man.'

The next forty minutes saw a turn in their luck. Max was finally able to locate and remove the metal fragment. Maura sewed up the gaping hole.

Sister Angela ambled in on her short legs and handed Maura a large spider's web to stick in the wound. 'I search for big one in barn,' she said. 'It heal.'

'Yes, ma'am. Thank you.' Maura gently washed the blood from the large side wound then rolled up the spider web and pressed it on to the area, making sure to cover all the edges.

The natural healing agent had been used since the beginning of time for cuts and gunshot wounds. Full of a kind of antiseptic, the web had long been known for its clotting ability. Emma reached into a dark corner of the room and pulled out a smaller web that Maura put on the other two wounds before covering them all with a clean bandage.

'That's all we can do.' She stood back, wiping her hands. 'The rest is up to the Almighty.'

Uncle Max started for the door.

'We pray,' Sister Angela said. It wasn't a request.

Max turned around and Emma clasped his hand.

They bowed their heads and the petite woman with nerves of steel spoke to God. Then they removed the slicker from under their patient and everyone except Maura filed out. She sat next to the bed and laid a hand on the man's bandaged chest. He needed to know he wasn't alone.

He had pleasing features from wavy black hair to a strong, determined jaw and full lips. A deep cleft indented his chin, and she could imagine the way the cleft would look when he smiled. His brows were heavy dark slashes above his closed eyes as though someone had drawn them on in a big hurry.

Who was he? Did he have someone waiting for him? Worrying about him.

She lifted his large hand, studying the callouses that spoke of hard work, noting the corded muscles of his arms and chest. As Emma had stated, he was a large man but lean with not a bit of fat. He could protect anyone if he was the right sort to do so.

Or like everyone else would he be afraid of the hangman's daughter?

Perhaps he *was* an outlaw. The area was overrun with robbers, horse thieves, rustlers and killers.

She rose and went to the pile of his clothes where they still lay. Maybe something in them would shed light on their mysterious patient. The gun belt and Colt rested on top of the trunk where Uncle Max had left them. She picked up the heavy weapon and flipped open the chamber to find it empty save for one bullet. He must've fired back at his attackers as he ran for his life. She closed the chamber and stuck the gun belt and Colt inside the trunk out of sight.

Something struck her as odd – there'd been no body odor. The man had recently bathed. That seemed to take him out of the outlaw ranks. The criminals she'd seen had stunk to high heaven, seeming to care more about their evildoing than cleanliness.

Pondering that, Maura moved to the denim trousers she'd pulled off him. They were soft from wearing, but not frayed or torn – except for the bullet hole where he'd been shot. They had molded to the stranger's legs as though made for him. Dirt and blood were in patches, yet the pants weren't overly soiled which told her the man took pride in his appearance. The pockets revealed three silver dollars, some neatly folded bank notes amounting to twenty dollars, and a little loose change. She stuck it in her dress pocket for safe keeping.

The bloody shirt yielded no clues and was in such pitiful shape there was no saving it. The fabric was a lightweight weave common among menfolk in Texas. A tobacco pouch with just about enough for one cigarette was in one of the pockets along with papers.

In the end, there was nothing in the clothing to shed light neither on the wearer's identity or profession. Maura returned to the man lying so white and still. 'Who are you, mister? Did we bring trouble to our door?'

If the ones responsible for his condition were searching for him, they'd likely follow the wagon tracks to them. Protecting the children was paramount. She'd speak to her uncle.

The man moved his lips, but no sound emerged. He clenched his hands then opened them and appeared to be reaching for something.

Maura wet a cloth in a clean pail of water and wiped his forehead. 'You're not alone. I'm here and I won't let anyone hurt you. Rest and heal. That's all you need to do.'

The door opened and Emma stepped in, holding a cup. 'I brought you some tea. Thought you might use it.'

'Bless you.' Maura took it and sipped. 'Exactly what I need. Thank you.'

'How is he?' Emma asked.

'Fever may be sitting in. By morning we'll know for sure. I've been going through his clothes looking for anything that might tell us more about him, but I didn't find much. Everything is typical of any man.' Maura cradled her cup. 'I choose to think he's a law-abiding citizen caught up in something terrible that almost ended his life.'

Why she wanted so strongly for that to be the case, she didn't know. Maybe because he seemed to have gotten a raw deal. No one should've suffered what he had.

And he just seemed to have a kind face.

'You always like to think the best of most people, Maura dear. Even Uncle Max. One of the reasons why I love you.'

Maura shrugged. 'The world has enough judgmental people.'

'You get no argument from me.' Emma dragged another chair to the bed. 'Do you remember the little five-year-old named Alphabet?'

'Cotton-haired with big brown eyes? His father was so proud of learning to read he named his son Alphabet. Yes. Cute as he can be. Why?'

Emma nodded. 'He started crying and won't stop no matter what we do. You're so good with him I wonder if you'd go try to put him in a better humor. I'll stay with the mystery man.'

'For starters, I think we should nickname the boy Alphie. He'll fit in better with the other children and it's easier for them to say. And him too.' Maura finished her tea. 'Yes, I'll go. I want to get my knitting to help fill the time. And I need to stretch my legs anyway and see if we have some willow bark for this gentleman to help with the pain when he wakes up.'

'So, you think he'll make it?' Emma asked quietly as though any louder would seal the poor man's fate.

'I can't say. I just know his chances are far better now.'

Maura walked to the door and turned, praying they wouldn't have to add a grave to the small plot next to the chapel this soon after arriving.

They wouldn't even have a name to give him.

SEVEN

Maura's thoughts whirled after leaving the patient. So many questions and no answers. The wind whipped up as she crossed the compound, blowing, twisting her skirts. Golden leaves scattered this way and that, landing in piles as though by some unseen hand. By the time she reached the mission, she was a little out of breath and found Alphie in the play area the nuns had made that sat adjacent to where the children slept. It was a bright, sunny room that needed to be filled with laughter. Yet there was little of that so far. But the grief was very fresh, and she didn't expect it to go away overnight. She feared they had a lot of hard times ahead.

The boy jumped up and ran to Maura sobbing. 'I want Papa. I wanna go home.'

She sat in a rocker with him. 'I know. I wish I could take you to them.'

'Are they in heaven with mine?' Sunny asked quietly, clutching a ragdoll. She rested her weight against the wooden chair arm.

'Yes, honey.'

'And my big brother? And baby sister?'

'That's right. They're all in heaven with the angels.'

Large tears filled her eyes and she whispered, 'Can I sit in your lap, too?'

'Absolutely.' Maura made room and the girl climbed up next to little Alphie. The boy had stopped sobbing and watched Sunny curiously. 'Do you know Alphabet? We've shortened his name to Alphie.'

'I like Alphie better. Would you like to hold my dolly?' she asked the boy. 'It helps when you feel sad.'

Alphie took it and clutched it to his body.

'That's sweet of you for sharing, Sunny. Does your dolly have a name?' Maura asked.

'Missy. She likes carrots and sweet potatoes and she's real

good and never cries. Missy likes to be rocked and sometimes I sing to her.'

'What a lovely idea. Would you like to sing, Alphie?' Maura asked.

He nodded. '"Mary Little Lamb".'

For quite some time, Maura sang and her audience grew until all the children crowded around, including the nuns. The singing appeared to be a magic solution toward helping to heal.

Afterward, she took the three sisters aside. 'Let's make singing part of the children's daily routine.'

'*Oui*. Singing good for de soul.' Sister Angela's eyes twinkled. 'Very good. *Oui*.'

'Anything to help keep their minds busy. Painting might be another way.' Maura glanced toward the children who seemed in better spirits. Sweet Alphie held Sunny's hand, still clutching the doll that didn't have much holding it together. 'I have some brown paper that the man at the mercantile gave me for the children to draw on and it'll be perfect.'

'*Magnifique*! Maybe paint rocks too.'

Bernadette clapped excitedly. '*Oui*.'

'Sister Angela, that's a great suggestion.' An idea took shape in Maura's head. 'The children can put them around their play area outside.'

'Make pretty. Sister Anne-Marie paint.' Sister Bernadette rested a hand on a child's shoulder. The children all seemed to love the light-hearted sister who always wore a smile.

The shy youngest one blushed and mumbled, '*Pas très bien*.'

'She says not very good,' Angela translated. 'But don't believe. Hide light under bushel, that one.'

Maura patted Anne-Marie's shoulder. 'We're all guilty of that sometimes. But painting and creating is fun. We don't have to be very good to paint what's in our hearts.'

Nodding in agreement, Sister Bernadette asked in broken English, 'The patient?'

'Sleeping. I need to go relieve Emma and check on him.' Maura glanced around the room and found little joy among the children. Hopefully, that would soon change. Grief was still oozing from their broken hearts.

She did notice one change, however. Shy Sister Anne-Marie

had snuck in and was sitting in a corner with Sally in her lap, braiding the young girl's hair. Such a sight made Maura's heart smile. Since their arrival, she'd not seen Anne-Marie venture from hiding except at mealtimes. This was definitely a welcome improvement.

Maura met Bernadette's glance and motioned with her head. They smiled and nodded to each other.

'Sister, if you have need of me, you'll find me with the patient.' With that, Maura hurried out into the gathering darkness to relieve Emma who would help feed the children the supper meal.

Her sister glanced up from a book as Maura entered the room. 'Any change in him?' she asked.

'He hasn't moved a muscle. If his chest didn't rise and fall, I'd think he was dead.' Emma closed her book, rose, and stretched. 'Did you see to Alphie?'

'I did. He found a sweet friend in Sunny. The girl let him borrow her doll to hold. That seemed to help. I think we should make them all a doll of some sort to help soothe their immense grief. And singing more.' She told her about how they all crept closer when they heard the music.

'How wonderful. We'll have to make singing part of a daily routine.'

Maura nodded. 'I've already spoken to the sisters about it. And painting as well.'

Emma's eyes lit up. 'We're going to do this, Maura. We'll make a go of this place.'

'Yes, we will.' Maura lifted a bag. 'I brought fabric scraps and yarn to make more ragdolls. Every child should have one if they want it. And I have more than enough time on my hands. I need to stay busy.'

'I'll help.' With hope in her step, Emma moved to the door. 'I'll bring you a plate for supper.'

'Thanks.'

Fading light spilled in when Emma opened the door and gasped softly. 'Did we get a couple of new horses you didn't tell me about?'

'Horses? I don't think so.' Maura looked over her sister's shoulder. Two strange mounts were grazing peacefully on the grass in front of the stone chapel. One bore a saddle and the other

was bareback. 'Where do you think they came from? We haven't
had any visitors.'

They went to check the horses out and Uncle Max joined them.

'Uncle, do you know anything about these horses?' Emma
asked.

From Max's disheveled appearance, he'd been drinking
again. He ran a hand across his eyes. 'You see them too? I thought
I had conjured them up.'

Maura ignored his slurred words and moved closer. 'No, they're
real.'

The animals stared at them but didn't move as they checked
them over. Only the saddled one wore a brand. It clearly
belonged to someone. The bedroll tied behind the saddle told
of a traveler as did a burlap bag tied to the pommel. Inside the
bag were a tin plate, cup and beat-up coffeepot with a tin of
Arbuckle's.

'Well, I'll be damned,' Max mumbled.

'What?' Emma asked. 'Do you recognize them?'

'Might. 'Course my memory ain't what it used to be.' He
peered hard at the brand again and straightened. 'Nope, I'm
mistaken. It's close to a former trail buddy's horse though.'

'Well, we'll keep them and see if the owner comes looking
for his animals.' Emma grabbed the reins of both mounts. 'I'll
take them to the barn. Maybe someone will come.'

Maura watched for a moment then noticed Max weaving and
took his arm. 'Let me help you back.'

It took time from her patient, but she got him back into his
room.

Max stretched out on the small bed, his feet hanging off the
end. 'I'm sorry. I'm a sorry piece of cow dung,' he mumbled.

'Hush that kind of talk. You're a good man.' She covered him
with a light blanket and left.

When she returned, the mystery man hadn't moved. She
checked for fever, encouraged at finding none, and changed his
bandages. There was some seepage but that didn't overly worry
her. The seriousness of his wounds assured there would be blood
escaping.

Wetting a cloth, she bathed his face in cool water. 'I wish
you'd wake up but it's way too soon. Sleep and heal.'

Sitting down, she lifted his right hand, studying it again. The back of it bore a three-inch scar. There was hardly a place on him that hadn't suffered a wound, either from a gunshot or knife. She pushed aside the thought that he was an outlaw, shaking her head. Lawmen lived just as dangerous a life.

Just then, the door opened. Emma entered. 'Guess what I found in those saddlebags.'

'I haven't a clue.'

Her sister handed her a silver badge with the words: Deputy US Marshal. 'Do you think those horses belong to our patient and he's a lawman?'

Maura turned it over, staring at it. She couldn't deny the sense of relief washing over her. 'They sure could. I guess we won't know until he wakes up.'

'I don't think our man is an outlaw,' Emma blurted.

'What's convinced you?' Maura waited for the answer. Nothing had really changed. All they had was a badge and that didn't prove anything. It might not belong to him.

'Well, he doesn't have the appearance of a dirty old outlaw. This man takes pride in himself. Someone has cut his hair recently and he's bathed. Shaved also within the last two days. His bristles tell us that much. Then there's this badge. I realize we don't know if it came from him, but I choose to believe it did.'

'Is that so, Miss Pinkerton?' A smile curved Maura's mouth. She loved watching her sister work through something. Emma had a methodical mind and enjoyed laying out her findings. She'd adjusted better to her short hair and Maura burst with pride for her. 'Was there anything else in the saddlebags?'

'A wanted poster for a bank robber named J.A. Cody. It doesn't have a picture.' Emma unfolded a piece of heavy paper and handed it to Maura.

The sheriff in a Missouri town called Panther Gap was offering a five-thousand-dollar reward for the capture of Cody for bank and stagecoach holdups.

'I wonder who this Cody fellow is,' Maura mused. 'And if they caught him.'

'Of course not. Otherwise, why keep the poster? I think our patient is a deputy marshal and he was tracking Cody. That's probably who shot him.' Emma took off her spectacles and let them dangle from her hand by the earpiece. 'But I can't figure out why he removed his badge and hid it in the saddlebag.'

'A riddle for sure. One we might never solve if this man dies. Then again, he could be that Cody guy on the run.' Maura cast the man a glance. 'All of this speculation could be in vain and the horses aren't even his to start with.'

'I know.' Emma sighed. 'But it's fun to play detective.' She chewed her lip. 'This last thing really puzzles me and I don't know what to think of it.' She pulled a thick bag from her pocket. It was large enough to hold quite a bit.

Right away, Maura could tell it was empty. Her stomach knotted at the lettering across it: Frost National Bank of San Antonio.

'What do you think this means?' Emma whispered. 'Wasn't that bank held up last month?'

Folks had a field day with that, speculating about the identity of the bandits. Maura had watched the sheriff run willy nilly with little accomplished. The culprits had covered their trail good. The bank had been forced to close its doors for a week since the robbery had wiped them out and they'd had to wait for a money shipment to come in on the stagecoach.

'Yes, it was.' And she was holding the empty sack. She met Emma's crestfallen features and had to cheer her up. 'But honey, the marshal could've found it and stuck it in his saddlebag to study later.'

Emma brightened. 'That's right. He only found it while he was on the trail of Cody.'

A light tap sounded at the door. Maura opened it to find Sunny standing there clutching Alphie's hand. She gave them a stern look. 'What are you doing here? Shouldn't you be with the sisters?'

'We was lookin' for you.' Sunny tried to help Alphie inside and ended up grabbing the back of his shirt and yanking.

Unable to resist a grin at the unlikely pair, Maura kept the boy on his feet. 'Why do you need to find me? You should stay with the others and not go wandering off in the darkness. It's way too dangerous.'

'They's a man asleep, Miss Mo.' Alphie pointed toward the door.

Sunny pursed her mouth. 'He ain't even in a bed. I think he's dead.'

Emma looked out and groaned. 'It's Uncle Max.'

'Passed out?' Maura went to see for herself. Sure enough, Max was laying several yards from his quarters. 'OK, why don't you get Sunny and Alphie back to the others and I'll see to Max.'

'I don't understand him.' Emma took the kids' hands and set out across the compound.

Sadness filled Maura as she went to the still form and shook him. 'Wake up, Uncle Max.'

'Go a-away,' he slurred.

'Can't do that. The children will see you. Two already have. Come on, I'll help you back to bed.'

Sister Angela came hurrying out as fast as her short legs would carry her. 'I help.'

'Thank you.' Relief sped through Maura. 'Let's see if we can get him up. You take one side and I'll take the other.'

Max groaned. 'Wha's that?'

'Come on. Get up now.' She and Sister Angela pulled on his arms, but he was much too heavy. 'Uncle Max, you're going to be the death of me yet. Come on. I mean it.'

'W . . . where are we going?'

'To your quarters to bed. Now move.'

Instead of following her instructions, he rolled over. This was useless. Seeing nothing else to be done, she went inside his small room for a blanket and spread it over him. She met Sister Angela's sad eyes. 'He'll just have to lie here. There's nothing more we can do.'

'God take care. Goodnight.'

'Goodnight, Sister.'

Her heart heavy, she went back to her other unconscious patient who just might turn out to be the easiest to help.

EIGHT

The next morning, the children had thick oatmeal without a drop of milk to thin it. They sat silent and stared at the elder sister, her black habit already stained although the day was young.

Sister Angela made the sign of the cross and said quietly, 'In God's time.'

Maybe so, but Maura wasn't sure God listened to the hangman's daughters.

After helping clean up the breakfast dishes, she gathered the children around. 'We have to give this new home a name. This is where you'll live until you get old enough to leave. So what would you like to call it?'

Sunny raised her hand first. 'House for Kids.'

'No . . . uh . . .' Betsy squirmed, with a finger in her mouth. 'I like . . . uh . . . The Happy Place.'

'Aw, that's so sweet, Betsy.' That touched Maura's heart that she'd find happiness this soon after coming. It spoke of the spirit of the old mission. There was something about it.

Six-year-old Henry raised his hand. 'How about The Children's Lighthouse?'

Silent up to now, Alphie grinned. 'Heaven's Door. We can walk through and be with our mamas and papas. And they can open the door and watch us.'

Maura was at a loss for words. She blinked hard. Heaven's Door. What a concept. 'I love that, Alphie. Any more suggestions?'

When no more raised their hands, she said, 'We'll take all of these into consideration and decide. Thank you for helping us with this difficult task. Now, go play and have fun.'

She watched the three sisters herd them outside to play, separating them into groups their own age. The women had a system that worked smoothly, and she wasn't about to mess with it.

An old saying came to mind. If it's not broke, don't fix it.

She went outside and gathered the women. 'We need to decide

on a name for this place.' She went over the list of suggestions. 'Do any strike your fancy?'

Emma's eyes filled with tears. 'Heaven's Door.'

The three nuns nodded, and Sister Angela voted. 'Heaven's Door.'

'That settles it. It was my favorite too. OK, I need to check on the patient.'

No more than three hours later, two farmers appeared on foot. Maura watched them through a window. One man led a pair of milk cows. The other herded a half dozen goats. Again, Sister Angela, along with Bernadette and Anne-Marie, made the sign of the cross and gave thanks.

Maura hurried out. She'd give anything for their deep faith and not question God.

It suddenly occurred to her that each person had something to teach and shouldn't hold back. The sisters taught faith. Maura's strength seemed to be patience. She never fretted over too many things and took her time. Emma always wore herself out trying to change people, but she had such a spontaneous spirit. There was a great deal to be said for grabbing every second of life and finding joy. And Max, he made no excuses for his shortcomings. People shouldn't try to explain faults away but admit them with honesty.

'Come,' Sister Angela told the farmers. 'We give.'

'Please,' Maura added. 'We'd like to show our thanks.'

A tall, skinny one rubbed his head. 'No, ma'am. We won't take anything. The children need a lot more than this. We're just happy to help.'

After adding her thanks, Maura left the group tending to the new livestock. A smile curved her lips at the kindness of strangers who opened their hearts. Humming a soft tune, she went to relieve Emma who was with the marshal. Or outlaw.

Toward the end of that second day, the mystery patient's eyes began to flutter. Maura put aside her sewing, rose from the chair next to the bed and leaned over him. 'Mister, can you hear me?'

He tried to lift an arm but was too weak and it flopped back on to the bed. Chills enveloped him. Maura put his arm back beneath the blanket and piled on a second. As he warmed, the fluttering movement stopped and he descended back into unconsciousness. Sleep was best for a healing body. She checked his bandages and saw no sign of redness or puss seepage that would indicate infection. Breathing a little easier, she returned to her chair and passed the night keeping watch.

And making dolls. Her project was coming along nicely.

Uncle Max had remained to himself ever since the kids had found him passed out in the compound. He was probably more than a bit ashamed to have let that happen and embarrassed to show his face. Sister Angela left plates of food outside his door which he ate.

'Max fight demon.' The sister shook her head. 'Bad.'

'Do you know about these kinds of demons?' Maura had asked.

'Father. Brother. Very sad.'

'Yes, it is.' Maura wished she had a magic elixir that would take away Max's desire for the rotten stuff. Only there wasn't.

The following morning, she was with the gunshot victim, straightening up the room when he opened his eyes and stared at her. She smiled. 'Hi there. I'm glad to see you returning to the land of the living. You gave us quite a scare.'

His cracked, dry lips moved but no sound emerged. She wet a cloth and dribbled water into his mouth then gently dabbed salve on to his lips.

'You must wonder where you are. This used to be the Mission San Francisco de la Espada but we're turning it into an orphanage. The children named it Heaven's Door. It's kind of sweet.'

His coal dark eyes flickered. He must be trying to figure out how he got here.

'Someone shot you three times. I found you unconscious and bleeding at the tree line. I'm Maura.'

Just as she thought he might speak, his eyes closed and he went back to sleep, evidently satisfied and worn out from that small exertion. He'd get stronger as each day passed.

Maura hummed as she rocked, keeping watch on the marshal. Despite telling Emma not to let her fanciful nature run away with itself, Maura was already latching on to the marshal theory. Inside her head, he was becoming a lawman.

'Well, I have to call him something,' she muttered to the room. And she rather liked that he was on the right side of the law.

His black eyes had bored into her so intently but not in a frightening way. Confused and lost, he was just trying to make sense of where he was.

Emma came to relieve her, and she relayed the incident adding, 'I think he'll wake up soon and we'll find out his name.'

'I think he'll have a nice, strong name to go with his marshal's badge,' Emma's green eyes twinkled behind her spectacles. 'Maybe Joseph or Thomas. I always thought if I should marry, I'd want his name something similar.' She lowered her lashes. 'Of course, that was a pure waste of time.' Her voice dropped to a whisper. 'I lie awake and wonder what it might be like to kiss a man, to feel his arms holding me.'

Maura pulled her morose sister into a hug. 'I have also and there's nothing wrong with it. We're not harming anyone.' A moment's silence enveloped them, then Maura added, 'I do think your short hair is so becoming and I'm rather envious of the ease of fixing it. One shake of your head and it falls into place while I spend so much time on mine.'

Emma stepped back, fingering her short locks. 'I do kind of like it. Makes me look sassy.'

Their laughter evidently disturbed the patient because he moved restlessly.

'Do you think he has a wife?' Emma asked softly.

'He might and children too, so don't go letting yourself daydream about him.' Maura gave her sister a smile to offset the needed lecture. It was her job to keep Emma from getting hurt.

No one would marry the hangman's daughters and that was the fact in a nutshell.

There was no use letting her pretend a man ever would. She would only get her heart broken again. The first time was with Daniel Mahoney when Emma was sixteen. Oh how she'd had her sights set on marrying that boy. And then he'd told her that he couldn't tie himself to the hangman's daughter for fear of too much retaliation from his family and friends. It turned out Daniel's father had told him that he'd disown him if he persisted in traveling down that path.

All of Emma's hopes and dreams had been brought to a swift end.

Emma cried her eyes out for days on end. No, Maura would see that didn't happen again. Somehow or another.

Light from the oil lamp bathed the small room. She glanced at her sister who'd moved to the bed to straighten the covers. She had so much love to give. At least the orphans would benefit from Emma's mothering ways.

As far as Maura was concerned, she'd not let herself get sucked into those intent eyes and handsome face. She'd had enough heartache to last the rest of her life.

The marshal might as well understand that.

On Sunday, they put the children in their best clothes and Sister Angela held a service in the chapel. The sixteen children in their clean clothes, their hair combed, wearing solemn expressions lined the pews. The sight touched Maura. She knew what many prayed for and refrained from telling them it was impossible to bring back the dead. No matter how fervently they cried and begged.

The service wasn't long, but her heart felt lighter as she hurried back to her patient.

Another day passed with the man opening his eyes for a longer period of time, yet he still hadn't uttered a word. He just looked around and went back to sleep.

The children were very curious about the stranger in the little room and Sunny and Alphie sneaked in to stare at him as much as they dared. Maura had to sternly forbid them to make the trek across the compound. She threatened to shut them in their room if they came again.

On the fourth day, the marshal opened his eyes and spoke in a weak voice. 'Water.'

'Thank heavens, you decided to join us, Marshal.' Maura filled half a glass from a pitcher on the bedside table they'd moved into the room.

'Marshal?' he asked, barely above a whisper.

'Pardon me for calling you that. While you were asleep, two horses wandered up and there was a marshal's badge in one of the saddlebags. My sister Emma decided then and there that the

badge belongs to you and we began to think of you as a marshal.'
She lifted his head and put the glass to his lips. 'Drink slowly.
You might choke.'

Considering everything, he managed pretty well, and she set
the empty glass back on the table. 'If you don't mind, can you
tell me your name and where you're from?'

Lines formed on his forehead as he knitted his dark brows
together, staring. 'I uh . . .'

He seemed unsure of his identity or else the hesitancy was
due to weighing the balance between a lie or the truth.

'You do know your name, don't you?' she pressed.

'Uh, can I have more water, please?'

'Sure.' She poured some into the glass and held it to his mouth.
'Do you have any objection to us calling you Marshal?'

'No. That's fine.' He lay back against the pillows. 'Where did
you find me?'

'At the tree line here. We've recently turned the Mission San
Francisco into an orphanage. My sister and I, along with our
uncle and three nuns, care for sixteen children who lost their
parents to yellow fever.' She sat down in the chair next to the
bed. 'I went out hunting for food about dusk and found you lying
under a cottonwood tree. Someone had shot you – three times
to be exact. We brought you here and removed the bullet
fragments.'

'How long ago?'

'Today is the fourth day.'

'Did you see anyone else nearby?'

'No. If you were traveling with anyone, I don't know what
happened to them.'

Anguish filled his eyes.

'I'm sorry, Marshal. Would you like me to give you some
privacy?'

'Yes.' He ran a hand over his eyes. When he looked up, his
expression was grim. 'Then I'd like my gun.'

The sharp breath she sucked in seemed loud in the small
room. 'You're not well enough.'

'I have to be able to defend myself. My Colt, please.'

This had been coming and she'd known it. He was yet too
weak to even fire a weapon, but she couldn't deny him. He was

right. A lawman needed to be able to protect himself. She wasn't of a mind to argue however much she wanted. She'd try to stall him a little longer.

'Very well, I'll go fix you something light to eat. I'm sure you're hungry.' When he didn't say anything, she moved to the door. 'I'm Maura and I'll be back soon.'

'Bring coffee, Maura. Please.'

She nodded and shut the door, glad that their patient had turned a corner. Someone had clearly been with him during his ordeal, and they were more than a casual acquaintance. Emma was in the kitchen with the smaller children when Maura entered and gave her the good news.

'How wonderful that the marshal woke up.' Emma's smile stretched across her face. 'Did you ask him his name? Where he lives?'

'I did, and he was not forthcoming at all, but he doesn't mind us calling him Marshal.'

'See? I told you he's a lawman.'

Yes, she did. But that didn't make him one. He was simply grasping at anything to keep from giving his identity. Men with secrets troubled her. A lot.

And this one was hiding something.

The part that worried her was not knowing what he was going to bring to their door. They had the children and the sisters to look out for and protect. And until she knew what to look for, everything represented a threat.

She'd speak to Uncle Max in the morning. He seemed to recognize those horses and then tried to cover up his reaction. Why? She meant to get to the bottom of that, if possible.

Morning came and Maura met it with new hope. The marshal had slept well and wouldn't need anyone to stay at his side from here on as she'd done.

Now that he had some food in him, his color had improved significantly. He'd eaten the light meal of toast, broth, and coffee for supper then managed two soft eggs and a biscuit, washing it down with coffee for breakfast.

Although he was still a long way from riding out and getting back to his life, Maura couldn't be more relieved at his progress.

Yet, in the back of her mind, change was coming. And he would leave for wherever and whatever was waiting.

Uncle Max wrapped a sheet around the marshal and helped get him into a chair.

As Maura changed the bed covers her glance kept straying to the man who'd cheated death. He sat with his head resting against the high back of the chair, his dark eyes following her every move.

'I need my gun,' Marshal said, his jaw set. 'Now.' A beat later, he added, 'Please.'

She exchanged a look with Uncle Max and nodded. He reached into the trunk and pulled out the holster and Colt, handing it to the weak man.

With trembling fingers, he flipped open the cylinder and checked the chamber, seeing only one round. He reached for his holster and tried to pull extra cartridges out only he kept dropping them. It was excruciating to watch him struggle.

Finally, Maura had enough. 'Let me do it.'

Taking the Colt, she filled each slot with a fresh cartridge until the cylinder was full. 'There.' Her mouth set, she handed it back.

A look of relief eased the lines of his face. 'Thank you. Now, my clothes.'

'You can't leave yet. I won't have it. You're too weak and your bandages have to be changed twice a day. I doubt you can even sit on a horse.' She shot her uncle a look for help. 'You men are a stubborn lot. I didn't – we didn't – patch you up for you to fall on your face.'

'No?' he replied weakly.

Uncle Max pushed away from the door frame. 'There'll be no talk of leaving. But a man does need his dignity. That I understand. There's a slight problem though. We had to throw your shirt away. There was no saving it.'

'And my trousers? Did you toss them as well?' the marshal asked, irritation in his voice.

Maura pushed back a reddish-brown strand of hair. 'They needed scrubbing, but we didn't get around to it today. As soon as they dry, I'll bring them. Maybe Uncle Max would have a shirt. You're pretty close in size. The next time someone goes to town, we can pick you up another.'

'You should've found a little money in my trousers.'

She nodded, gathering up the dolls she'd made and putting them in a burlap bag. 'I did. I'll bring it when I return with the rest of your clothes.'

'What is that you're gathering up?' he asked.

'Ragdolls. I made them while I sat by your bedside.' At his quizzical expression, she added, 'The children need something to cling to that brings comfort. Only one or two of them have dolls, so I used the time to make something useful.'

'I see you had a lot of time on your hands.'

'That's true but I'm not complaining.'

Just then the frantic voice of Sister Bernadette called, 'Miss Maura, come quick!'

Oh, dear God! What had happened now?

The blood froze in her veins.

The morning dew had yet to burn off under the early sunrise and some new problem had arisen. Had one of the children been injured?

Maura's heart pounded against her ribs as she picked up the bag of dolls and raced to face the next crisis.

NINE

Maura was out of breath by the time she reached the grim-faced sister. 'What's wrong? Who's hurt?'

'No one. Sister Angela find infant.'

They fell into step, taking long strides to the chapel. 'Tell me everything,' Maura said.

'Sister opened door and see babe on step. No note. Nothing.'

'Was it wrapped up in a blanket?'

'*Oui.* In de basket.'

Maybe the mother had just left it there for some reason and would return. They weren't equipped to care for an infant. But then they hadn't been any better prepared for a dying man with gunshot wounds. Her panic settled. They'd manage. Somehow. She just had to have faith and do her best. The good Lord would take care of the rest.

Sister Anne-Marie came toward her, a babe clutched to her chest. Sister Angela strode at her side carrying a woven basket.

Children crowded around all clamoring to let them see. The sister who was terrified of everything stopped and bent to show the children the miracle left on their chapel step. Sister Anne-Marie's face held no sign of fear. In fact, a happy light filled her mud-brown gaze.

Maura stopped to watch for a moment. The fear would likely return but Anne-Marie had stepped from her dark closet again for a little while at least.

Old Sister Angela glanced up and saw Maura. 'Come. God has blessed us.'

Not one word about the work ahead in caring for a babe. Angela only saw the positive.

'I see that.' Maura joined the happy circle and took the infant. Warmth and such a feeling of love washed over her the moment she put the little bundle to her chest. The child's happy cooing resembled that of a mourning dove.

Who would've given up this precious new life? Or even left

it for a moment where a wild animal could've gotten it. Before she was aware, she was crooning softly and swaying to and fro.

Emma rushed from outside. 'Let me see.'

Maura cradled the babe in her arm and moved the blanket aside.

'Oh my goodness! Such a sweet little mouth and perfect face. Who would've left this angel?' Tears sparkled in Emma's green eyes as she leaned in.

'No one knows. There was no note.'

'Maybe the mother died or is bad sick.' Emma took the infant whose eyes were cloudy with it being only a day or two old. 'The sweet thing's not squalling its eyes out and seems very satisfied, so someone had to have fed it recently.'

'It would appear that way.' Maura lifted Alphie up so he could see.

'Sweet baby,' the five-year-old murmured.

'Yes, it is.' Maura kissed his soft cheek. 'We need to unwrap it and see if it's a boy or a girl.'

'I was just about to suggest that.' Emma smiled. 'And we can give it a name.' She carried the infant to the kitchen and laid it on the table. All the nuns and Maura crowded around.

The first thing Maura noticed was the fresh umbilical chord with a bit of blood caked around the string tying it. 'The little thing isn't more than a day old,' she murmured.

'*Oui*,' Sister Angela agreed.

Emma untied the thick layers of a towel that someone had used for a diaper and announced, 'It's a girl. A sweet baby girl.'

'Juliette,' whispered Sister Anne-Marie. 'Name Juliette.'

'That's so pretty, Sister.' Maura hugged the shy nun. 'I think it fits her just fine.'

'You like?'

Tears stung the back of Maura's eyelids. The love shining from Anne-Marie's face was startling. 'Yes, indeed. It's a lovely name for a beautiful baby girl.'

It was funny how a baby could change a person in an instant. Change an entire household in fact.

Everyone sprang to life, finding cloth for diapers, milking one of the cows, then milking a goat just in case Juliette preferred one over the other, and making her a soft bed. The children clamored to hold her and one by one each got their turn for a few minutes. Just a simple thing, but it eased their sorrow and put a big smile on their lips for a while.

This was what caring for others could do.

Maura and Emma handed out the homemade dolls and the girls and boys snatched them up in nothing flat, thanking her. Then for no reason at all, Maura made a pot of coffee and carried it and three cups out to finish her bed-making.

Crossing the compound, the sight of the children clutching the dolls filled her with warmth. She was making a difference – in small ways and large – and it gave her such joy.

Uncle Max had fetched a checkerboard from his things and he and the marshal were playing. Their eyes lit up to see the coffee. It shocked her a little to see the marshal wearing a pair of faded long johns. Max must have gotten them for him.

'You don't know how welcome that is, Maura honey.' Max hopped up to take the pot from her. He kissed her cheek. 'You're an angel.'

She laughed. 'Don't get carried away. Many would dispute your word.'

His unusually good mood had her glancing around for a whiskey bottle. None was in sight. And his breath carried no smell either.

'Thank you.' The marshal's quiet words let her know he meant it.

His deep voice carried a hint of the Old South. He was educated, at least to some degree, and he had manners.

'Both of you are very welcome. I'll join you then finish making the bed.' She filled the cups and told them about baby Juliette. 'She's such a sweet little thing. I fear it'll break a lot of hearts here when and if the mother does return to claim her child.'

'A babe needs its mother,' the marshal said softly.

'That's a fact.' Uncle Max winked at her. He seemed about to say something else when the marshal spoke.

'Someone should look for tracks. Find out the direction they went after leaving the baby and the size will show if it was a woman.'

The man spoke with authority and knew what he was talking

about. But then, a lawman would. So would an outlaw, though. Or anyone who'd ridden a trail.

She gave a silent groan. 'That's an excellent idea. Uncle Max, will you take a look?'

'I'll see what I can find and let you know.' He grinned at the marshal. 'You and me had best stay out of sight. These ladies are far too busy taking care of all these kids and I fear they'll press us men into babysitting.'

Maura glanced at him over the cup. 'Is that why you've been hiding? We haven't seen much of you lately.'

'I've been working on something if you must know.'

'Oh? Care to tell me what?'

Was he trying to cover the fact he'd been passed out?

'When the time's right.' He put his fingers to his lips and twisted like he was turning a key.

'I'm sure it'll be welcome whatever it is.' She turned to the marshal, aware of his dark gaze that seemed to peer deep inside. Heat rose to her cheeks. 'Your trousers will be dry soon. I checked on them while I was gone. When they're dry, I want Uncle Max to bring those two horses over and let you look at them, see if they belong to you.'

'I'll like having my clothes on.' He made a wry face and gave her a flicker of a smile, running a hand across his chin. 'A man feels a bit peculiar sitting with a pretty lady in his underwear.'

This talk about clothes and the lack of them once again sent heat into her face. She was aware of him as a man – a very handsome one at that. Her attention kept straying to his chest.

'You have a good excuse.' She reached into her pocket and pulled out the marshal's badge. 'Now that you have something to pin this to, I'm sure you're anxious to put it on.'

An odd look crossed his unshaven features bearing at least four days of stubble as he slowly took the shiny piece of metal. 'No rush. I don't need it to know who I am.' He laid it on the checkerboard.

'Of course not.' She sipped on her coffee. 'Something else was in those saddlebags.'

'Oh?' A hood seemed to cover his eyes. He glanced down, the cleft in his chin deepening.

'A wanted poster for the outlaw J.A. Cody. Seems he has quite a price on his head for bank and stagecoach holdups, but then you must already know that.' For some odd reason she didn't mention anything about the bank bag. Maybe she didn't want to see his reaction to that.

He remained silent, finally lifting his dark gaze.

She leaned closer, wishing she could touch his face, smooth the deep lines around his mouth. 'Is he the one who tried to kill you?'

Again, he didn't speak. After a long moment, he finally said, 'I really can't say who shot me. Everything about that night is a bit hazy.'

'That's understandable,' Max said. 'Mine gets that way sometimes.'

'Just one more question. We have to protect these children at all costs. Are we in danger? Is the man – or men – going to come looking for you to finish the job?'

TEN

Maura's question hung in the thick air. The marshal blinked hard. Outside, the sound of playing children drifted into the small room.

'Please answer,' she pressed. 'I . . . we need to know if we're in danger.'

'I wish I knew. With any luck, they'll assume I'm dead.' He rubbed his eyes. 'I need to get back to bed.'

He'd used the word 'they'll' which meant there was more than one shooter.

'Of course. I'm sorry for the questions.' She rose and moved to finish putting the sheets on the bed.

'Like you said, you need to know if danger's coming. Wish I could say.'

Uncle Max gathered the pot and cups. 'I'll take these back to the kitchen. Maura, let me know when you want me to get those horses. Meanwhile, I'll take a look at those tracks.'

'Can you wait a moment and help get our patient back to bed?'

'I ain't in no hurry.'

She finished up and her and Max helped the marshal stretch out. Maura spread a light blanket over him and left with her uncle.

The noon hour came and the marshal didn't wake up so she didn't bother him. She had his trousers folded with the money back in the pocket, waiting to be taken over. She collected a basket of darning and went outside to watch the children while she repaired the used clothing. The marshal's socks also had a hole. She picked them up first and turned them inside out.

Who knew when the man would take a notion to simply up and leave?

Emma wandered outside to sit in the warm sunshine with baby Juliette. 'It's peaceful here, isn't it?'

'For a fact. This place has welcoming arms that wraps around us, shielding us from harm. I love the feeling. Wish I knew what spell it's woven over us.' Maura glanced up at the sky and the fluffy clouds floating along. She took a deep, cleansing breath.

'Me too.' Emma gently patted the baby's back. 'If we hadn't been here, I don't know what would've happened to this child.'

'But we were. We're meant to be here. We're doing so much good.' She threaded a needle with black thread and set to work.

'Aren't those the marshal's?' Emma asked.

'They are.' She told her sister about the odd way the marshal had acted when she asked the needed questions.

'It's not strange at all.' The baby gave a loud burp and Emma lowered her. 'Often these lawmen go undercover and can't give away their identity. That must be the case. Don't ask him anything else. He'll say what he wants us to know. He's a smart man.'

Maura laughed. 'And you know this how, Miss Pinkerton?'

'I read. Besides, I've never seen a dumb federal lawman.'

Maura gave an unladylike snort. 'You haven't seen any kind, dear sister, except from a distance.'

'Laugh all you want. You'll see.'

Companionable silence settled between them. Suddenly, Emma squinted toward an old workshop that sat toward the back of the property. 'Would you look at that? I wonder what our uncle is up to. I thought he didn't have much use for kids.'

Maura followed her sister's stare. Uncle Max knelt working on something and Alphie squatted down beside him. 'It's a bit odd to see the boy with him.'

'I'll say.'

'Maybe Max reminds the kid of a family member. Our uncle told me he's working on something but not ready to share it.'

'Alphie doesn't need to be with him. Our uncle isn't exactly a good role model.'

'Stop it, Emma. Are you worried about that five-year-old suddenly developing a hankering for whiskey? I say if Uncle Max is sober and can bring the boy some bit of happiness what's the harm?'

'You're not getting my point. He drinks a lot and Alphie doesn't know when to stay away. He could get hurt.'

'Sister, give Uncle Max some credit. He knows when he's not fit to be around. I think these kids might be good for him. Relax.'

Emma threw up her hands. 'You were the one saying we needed to keep the kids away from him. What's changed?'

'Being here and seeing with more than our hearts is different. Alphie has lost everyone in his life. I won't take Uncle Max from him, too. They're good for each other. It's early, but I sense healing starting to take shape.' Maura put an arm around her sister. 'Will Uncle Max still drink? Probably. But I'm betting these kids might replace the desire to make him drink. If I'm wrong, I'll be the first to admit it. This is learning for all of us.'

'I know.' Emma sighed. 'I just worry we'll mess up with these children and it'll give folks another reason to hate us.'

'We can't fret about that every second of every day. I won't live that way.' Maura stared at their uncle's lean figure and added softly, 'We all need someone to believe in us. We're all Max has, and I won't let him down.'

Uncle Max stood and pushed inside the workshop with Alphie on his heels. It was nice to see him doing something productive, whatever it was.

'I forgot to tell you. I don't know how this slipped my mind.' Maura snipped her thread. 'Uncle Max looked at the tracks in front of the chapel and he said they were small. A woman left this baby.'

'Oh, dear God! I was hoping . . . I'm afraid I haven't been very sympathetic toward the mother.' Emma glanced down at Juliette and lovingly cradled her head. 'What kind of woman abandons her child? I wonder who she was. What else did the tracks say?'

'They came from the main road and returned that way as well.'

'I wonder if she came from San Antonio? She likely left her horse or wagon in the brush at the entrance to the lane, not wanting to wake us.'

'Yes, she did. Uncle Max found the spot. But I don't know how you do all this reasoning, Miss Pinkerton.' Maura grinned at her little sister. 'You should be a detective.'

Emma shrugged. 'I just use my head. I'm glad Uncle Max looked at the tracks.'

'The marshal mentioned it and said Max needed to check them.'

'A marshal would know to do that.'

'So would an outlaw,' Maura pointed out, raising an eyebrow.

Shy Sister Anne-Marie came out to take baby Juliette. Emma wasn't happy to relinquish her bundle, but she didn't put up a fuss.

Juliet became the darling of Heaven's Door immediately but that was no surprise to Maura. Such a sweet baby was easy to love and care for. Everyone young and old quickly fell in love with her.

'I think I'll look in on the marshal and see if he's awake.' Emma stood. 'I can't wait for him to see the horses. I hope he claims them, but if he's working undercover, he might deny ownership.'

'He might,' Maura agreed. 'We'll soon find out.'

Marshal woke at the dawn's rays working through the window. Although he'd been awake a little the previous day, his brain had been mush. But today, he seemed more like himself. A good sign. He pulled himself into a sitting position on the thin feather mattress that smelled of mold and sweat. No telling how long it'd been there. The mission had been vacated for some time.

'Marshal,' he muttered. 'Guess it's as good a name as any. For now anyway.'

Miss Maura had caught him by surprise when she'd pressed for what to call him. Truth was, he needed a little time to think. Was his brother alive or had the gang killed him? He wished he knew. The hope he'd turn up here was fading. Maybe after he saw the horses that had wandered up, he'd get a better answer.

He ran a hand over his bristles. A shave was in order when he felt up to it. He touched the bandages where Miss Maura and her uncle had removed the metal bullet fragments. The large wound in his side still burned like a raging fire.

By all rights, he should be dead and would be if not for Maura hunting that day.

She was a beauty with those cornflower blue eyes. When she bent over changing his bandages, the ends of her reddish-brown hair brushed his chest. He'd gotten a whiff of the timeless scent of the deep woods with a hint of lily of the valley.

That flower had always been his mother's favorite but that's where their similarities ended.

Maura was in a class by herself. Her sister Emma was pretty, but Maura was something real special. Maybe one day he'd tell her how she stirred tender feelings inside and made him dream.

He couldn't afford to get distracted. Rupert Donavan would come sooner or later, and he had to be prepared.

Dear God, just let him be well enough. That's all he asked.

Her question rang in his head. *Are we in danger?*

Why hadn't he told her the truth? That the gang would kill

her and everyone around in a heartbeat. It had been the fear that would darken those cornflower blues that had stopped him. Still, he knew he hadn't done her or any of them any favors.

Someone knocked, slid breakfast and coffee inside and quickly left.

After eating and downing the coffee, Marshal felt renewed enough to try dressing. He stood on wobbly legs, wrestling with the clean trousers, trying to get them on. With no one around, he cursed a blue streak.

He was struggling one-handed with the fastener when the two sisters came through the door. He gave them a wry grin. 'I can't quite get this with my bum arm.'

'I'll help you.' Maura closed the space to him and took hold of the gaping waist.

Her touch did funny things in his belly. That damn lily of the valley. She stood too close yet not close enough. Her soft breath penetrated the wanting inside him that twisted him up. The ends of her silky hair made him forget everything except the sudden yearning to kiss her.

'There.' She lifted her gaze and time stopped.

He noted a subtle shift inside her and the awareness dawning of how near she stood. Yet, she didn't step back. Maybe she couldn't any more than he. Marshal could almost hear her heart beating and it seemed to skip a few – or maybe that was his wishful thinking.

Seconds passed but he couldn't have said how many. Holding her gaze, he lifted a hand to touch her cheek and her breath hung suspended.

In anticipation?

No, more likely something else. Fear maybe.

Why had she never married? What was wrong with the men around here? Were they blind?

Before his hand reached her, he let it drop.

Emma cleared her throat, the sound breaking the spell. Maura released the breath she'd been holding and quickly put space between them. Her voice had turned a bit husky. 'I brought one of Uncle Max's shirts for you to try.'

'Sure.' The word came out raspy. Dammit.

'I'll help you,' Emma volunteered.

Thank goodness. Anymore of Maura's nearness and he'd be

a ragged mess. Her, too, most likely. He glanced at the shirt Emma held open.

'I'll be real careful with your wounded arm. I think we should get it in first,' Emma said.

He'd heard from Max about the group who'd held her down and cut the younger sister's hair. She still seemed a little self-conscious about it, tugging on the ends at times. One day he hoped to meet up with the yellowbellies and teach them how to respect a woman. The kind of lesson he had in mind would stay with them for the rest of their miserable lives. Max had talked about trying to find them. Someone should.

With painstaking care, the younger sister got the shirt on him and buttoned it.

'Appreciate it, Miss Emma.' He winked. 'Looks like I'm ready.'

'The light blue of that chambray looks good on you.' Maura's gaze held him speechless.

When he unglued his tongue, he managed, 'Glad you think so.'

'Uncle Max will be here with the horses any minute.' Emma went to look out. 'Here he comes now.'

Anticipation crawled up his spine. Soon he'd know if his brother had made it. Unless . . . The gang could've captured him. There was that possibility.

The morning held a slight breeze that came through the door. Supported by Maura and Emma, Marshal hobbled toward the door. Beads of sweat had formed on his forehead from the immense effort.

Emma chewed on her bottom lip. 'Maybe we're rushing things. Would you rather wait until you're stronger?'

'She's right,' Maura said. 'You don't have to do this now.'

'Let's get it over with before I pass out,' he grated through clenched teeth. 'I want to see them.'

Max held the horses where he could see them without having to go outside, which was good seeing as how he was barefoot.

Breathing hard, he studied the two mounts, a slim spark of hope dancing inside him that his brother might've survived that hail of bullets. 'They're mine.'

Emma met Maura's gaze. 'At least we know that much.'

Yet, he really knew no more than she did. Still, miracles could happen. Just because the horses had wandered up didn't mean his twin had died. Maybe he'd been captured. All this speculating was wearing on him.

His leg gave out and he sagged against Maura. 'Can you get me back to the bed?'

They were all out of breath by the time Marshal fell on to the mattress. 'Just let me rest.'

'I'll be back with a tray in a bit.' She rested a light hand on his chest.

He stared up at those cornflower blues. A shaft of sunshine spilled through the door encircling her and he'd never seen anyone so beautiful. 'Sounds good. Maybe tomorrow you can rig me up a place to shave where I can sit? I'll try my hand at doing it myself but I might need a little help.'

She nodded. 'Just say the word.'

'I'm sorry I've taken so much of your time. You have an orphanage to run and I'm not making it easy for you.'

'I'm making it just fine. Is there anything else before I go?'

'You can answer a question that's bugging me.'

She straightened the blanket on his bed. 'What's that, Marshal?'

'Why isn't a pretty woman like you married?'

Freezing, she lowered her gaze and red colored her cheeks. 'I suppose I didn't meet the right man.'

'I think they must be blind as bats to overlook you and Emma.'

Suddenly, she was a flurry of movement and at the door. Her voice was stiff. 'Someone will bring your supper.' Then she was gone.

The silence was loud in his ears.

Dammit, why had he pried? He should've known marriage would be a sensitive question to any woman. Much less one who'd lost the bloom of youth. Though he was no good at guessing women's ages, he'd say she was late twenties judging by the faint lines beginning to show around her mouth and corners of her eyes. She wore a look in her eyes that told she'd pretty much seen more than her share of what life could throw at her. Her lot had been anything but easy.

He'd have to apologize when she came back.

With the promise of tomorrow washing through him, he closed his eyes, letting exhaustion take him where relief from pain awaited.

ELEVEN

That night, Maura tossed and turned, trying to make sense of the feeling that had come over her when she'd helped fasten Marshal's trousers. The way he'd looked at her had stirred embers inside that she'd thought long dead. And each time he spoke in that deep rumbling voice of his, warmth flooded her senses until she could barely get her tongue to move. It had happened frequently ever since he'd woken, but the incident with the trousers had been the worst.

Could it be that she'd developed an attachment because she'd saved his life?

But then, she hadn't felt this way about any of the men she'd nursed through the yellow fever epidemic.

She must be a fool to think he had one bit of interest in her. The way he stared at her, he probably thought she suffered from some affliction.

When she'd found no one willing to take his supper, it had fallen to her, but she had avoided looking his way. She'd set his supper down and hurried back to the door when he spoke.

'I apologize for prying, Miss Maura. I deserved a good slap.'

'You're just curious,' she'd replied, keeping her back to him. 'No harm.'

'You're too kind.' Something odd had crept into his voice. 'Forgive me for saying so, but you're about the most beautiful woman I've ever seen. It comes from inside you. It's in your voice, your blue eyes, every touch and action.'

He'd given her the best compliment of her life and all she'd done was mumble something and rush out.

With a groan, she pulled the pillow over her face.

Emma spoke from her side of the bed. 'What's the matter? Can't you sleep?'

'I'm sorry to wake you.' Maura released a sigh and lowered the pillow. 'I'm trying but sleep won't come. Maybe I should take a walk.'

'Are you worried about something?'

'No. Yes. I . . . maybe.'

'Want to talk about it?' Emma sat up. 'Whatever it is, we can work it out.'

'No, no,' Maura said quickly. 'I mean it's something I have to sort out for myself.'

'I see.' Her sister yawned. 'If you want a sounding board, I'm always here.'

'I know and I appreciate the offer. I think I will get up. At least you can get your rest.' Maura threw on a wrapper and padded out, easing the door shut. She quietly made her way to the kitchen and fixed a cup of tea, then went outside to sip it in the moonlight.

To her surprise, Uncle Max filled one of the chairs on the covered walkway, smoking a cigarette and sipping whiskey. He'd tied his long hair back. He glanced up. 'Can't sleep?'

'Afraid not and I was keeping Emma awake.' She stood beside him. 'It's a beautiful night but a tad on the cool side.'

'Supposed to be. It's fall.'

'Mind if I join you?'

'Not a bit. Grab a chair.'

She settled next to him. 'Uncle Max, my excuse is I have things on my mind. What's yours?'

'Just sitting here thinking about a little payback. I'm gonna find those yellow-livered men who cut Emma's hair and give them a dose of my fists. That girl wouldn't harm a flea and did nothing to deserve that.'

'I know, but you can't think these thoughts or follow through on any plans or you'll land in jail. Leave those men alone. You can't win. They all stick together and tell the same lies. You know that. Don't do anything.' She gripped his arm. 'Promise me.'

'I'll sleep on that.' He lifted the bottle and took a big swig.

'Fair enough.' Hopefully by morning, he'd have no memory of this. She glanced toward their patient's quarters. 'Uncle Max, what do think about the marshal? Is he a lawman for true or someone else?'

'You mean an outlaw?'

'I want to think he's a lawman but there are some things that draw questions. For one, he didn't want to take the badge Emma found.' She took a sip of tea. 'Some of his actions are indeed puzzling. So, you being a man, maybe you have a different perspective. Is he good or bad? You've spent time with him.'

'Yep.' Her uncle took the last puff on the cigarette and ground it under his heel. 'I ain't much good at judging the character of a man, but I like him. I think he's keeping secrets though. They're in his eyes. I've seen men like him, ridden with a few and you never want to tangle with them.'

Cradling the teacup with both hands, Maura shivered and glanced up at the moon. She didn't know how to reply. Judging from what he'd just revealed, she guessed he'd ridden in an outlaw gang. Either that or with those kinds of men.

'I've also sensed secrets in the marshal,' she said. 'He's not being honest with us. Didn't even give us his name.'

In fact, he hadn't given them any information. Everything had come from her and Emma wanting to believe he was a lawman because they needed someone like him when trouble came. He had simply gone along with Emma's wild theories.

But she believed what she said about trouble. It'd come. Trouble always followed them.

For instance, those who had cut off Emma's hair might get in their heads to do more than that. Men with that kind of evil usually didn't stop until someone forced them. And whoever tried to kill the marshal was out there trying to find him. They wouldn't rest.

'Uncle Max, have you ever heard of the outlaw J.A. Cody? You know the name on the wanted poster we found in Marshal's bag. He robbed banks and trains.'

A guarded look shot into his eyes. 'I remember.'

'Do outlaws typically keep their own wanted posters?'

'Good Lord, no! At least not the ones I knew. They didn't want anything to draw attention to themselves.'

'But did you know him?'

'Heard of him, is all. Where is this going, girl?'

'I'm trying to sort it all out. Also in the saddlebag was an empty bank bag from the Frost National Bank of San Antonio.' Her voice dropped to a whisper. 'I really don't know what to think about that. Some men held up that bank just last month.'

'I know. If our fella is a marshal, he could've found it where the outlaws discarded it.'

'I thought of that. The marshal could've come by all three items, whereas an outlaw would normally only have the bank bag. Unless . . .' She couldn't put the last of the sentence into words. It was too horrible to contemplate.

'Unless he killed a marshal and stole the badge,' Uncle Max finished. 'That'd be a good enough reason he didn't want to pin it on.'

A shiver rushed through her at the thought they might be harboring a killer.

'Exactly. You saw how funny our marshal acted when I handed it to him.' She rose and leaned against an arched stone part of the walkway. 'And you acted strange when the horses came up. Why is that, Uncle? Did you recognize them?'

Max snorted. 'You can't pay any attention to me, girl. I was probably three sheets in the wind. I say lots of things I don't remember or have any reason for saying. You know that.'

Yes, she did. So she was pretty much right back where she started. Still, he hadn't been drunk. So what was he hiding?

'One question. If you knew our patient poses a danger to us, you'd tell me, right?'

Max pointed his finger at her. 'Listen good because I'm only going to say this once. The only ones I owe loyalty to are you women and kids here. If I knew that man would bring you one speck of harm, I'd kick him out so fast his head would swim, wounds or not. Does that answer your question?'

Relief washed over Maura. 'Yes. Thank you for putting me at ease.'

He pulled to his feet. 'I'm turning in. Got work to do tomorrow.'

'What kind of work? What are you doing in that workshop of yours?'

'It's a surprise.'

'A surprise, huh? That's all you're going to say?'

'Yep, Miss Nosey.'

'Speaking of work, I noticed Alphie tagging on your heels today.' She couldn't resist grinning. 'I thought you said you and kids didn't mix.'

'He's a cute kid, just needing male companionship. He's lonely, and apart from the ten million questions he asks, I don't mind filling in for his pa.'

'Well, it's a very nice thing to do,' she said softly.

The moonlight danced around him as he crossed the compound to his room. She pondered over the strange conversation and revelations. Or lack thereof.

Something horrible had happened to Max and if she could catch him in the right mood, he might talk about it.

She stayed a little while longer, her thoughts returning to the marshal and how he made her all hot and bothered. Then the thought hit her that she'd agreed to help him shave. With his wounded arm, he wouldn't be able to perform much, if anything, of the task himself.

That would call for more close contact. Maura groaned. Maybe she could persuade one of the sisters or Uncle Max to do it. Even Emma. Anyone but her.

As though sensing her thought, the marshal opened the door of his room and leaned against the frame using a stick for a cane. Max must've made that for him. The man stared across at the mission. She shrank further into the shadows. Confident he couldn't see her. Safe in that knowledge, she watched.

After a moment, he stepped out and took a few wobbly steps. But he was barefoot and found a sticker. Balancing on the stick, he managed to remove the menace and made it back to his room. Where had he intended to go?

Maybe just out for a walk. He had to get bored of spending so much time in that room.

Clearly, he couldn't sleep. Could he be thinking about her just as she was him?

Sister Bernadette took the marshal his breakfast the following day to Maura's relief. But when she asked everyone if they'd help him shave, they all had other things that needed doing. Grumbling, she collected what the man would need into a bag and, deciding it was best to get it over with as soon as possible, she set out.

This time instead of barging in, she knocked on his door.

'Come in,' he hollered, his voice much stronger than the previous days.

She set the pail of water down and obliged.

'Ah, there you are. I thought you'd forgotten.' He sat at the small table, fully dressed right down to his holster.

'Are you expecting a gang of outlaws?' She set the water on the floor beside him and put the bag in the extra chair. 'You look ready to let loose on someone.'

He ran a hand across his bristles. 'A wounded man never knows when his attackers will find him. I want to be ready.'

'Oh? So, you know who they are?' She kept her voice casual, acting nonchalant as she unpacked the hand mirror, razor strop and razor.

'In a manner of speaking,' he hedged.

She folded the bag and pulled out the chair. It was time for some frank speaking. 'Look, if you know their identities, you have to tell us. We have a right to know that and your name.'

'Of course. I wouldn't want anything to happen to any of you.' He leaned back. 'Who I am is not easy to tell.' He paused. 'I answer to Calhoun.'

'See? That wasn't so hard. Is that your given name or a surname?'

'I can't remember having any other.' He rubbed a weary hand across his eyes. 'Why do you always pester for more?'

Although he said it in a low tone, it still shocked her. 'I don't mean to,' she managed.

'Look, I'm sorry. I shouldn't have said that after you saving my life. I know you're curious and you don't need a dangerous man here with these little ones.' He raised his gaze. 'What more do you want to know?'

'Are you a US marshal?'

'I was once a respected lawman but not now.'

'Yet . . . you didn't object to us calling you one. Why?'

'I wasn't up to answering any questions and there was no harm done. Truth was, I liked the sound of it.'

Or he had to have time to think of a name. She hated being so suspicious because she really liked him. Still . . . she had to be able to trust him. A lot of people depended on her to keep them safe.

'So, you're not a marshal but you were and your name is just Calhoun.' It was time to spring the bank bag on him. 'I didn't mention another item that Emma found in your saddlebag.' She watched his eyes widen a bit. 'It's an empty bank bag from a holdup of the Frost National Bank in San Antonio. Were you involved in that?'

'No. I swear on my mother's grave.'

Maura studied his eyes and they seemed to confirm his words as truth – unless he was an expert liar. But . . . what was the bag doing in his belongings? She'd sure like to know.

'Folks should be looking for Rupert Donavan's gang for that,' he volunteered. 'Please don't ask me how I know. I'm not free to tell you more.'

'I've heard of Donavan's ruthless crimes.'

Her father had once said he'd be hanging the man and his gang one day.

'People are afraid of him for good reason. I hope you carry a healthy fear of the man, Miss Maura.'

'I do. For him and a few others.'

'Either Donavan or one of his gang filled me full of lead when our paths crossed.'

Now they got at the truth of the matter.

She digested that a moment before replying, 'I see. Forgive me, but it kind of sounds like you were in bed with the man to know so much about him and him ending up shooting you. Maybe you had a disagreement?'

Perhaps over divvying up the loot?

'He's no friend of mine. Never was.' Calhoun glanced out the window. 'I'm taking up a lot of your time and think I should get on with shaving. Not sure how much more energy I have left. It fades quickly.'

'You're the boss, Calhoun.' She stood. 'I have to go back for a towel I left heating.'

'I'll be here.'

Unless he wasn't. If he could get his boots on and to his horse, he'd ride out faster than a greased lightning and she had no doubt about that. He'd been reluctant and extremely sparing with his information. But at least they had a name to call him.

She'd heard it before – but where?

Had it been while she was in San Antonio?

Or maybe her father had mentioned it. Lucius Taggart had often spoken of outlaws and bank robbers. Also lawmen who drifted across the line.

TWELVE

Calhoun kicked himself. There was no fooling Maura and after bungling at giving his name she'd likely put a boot to his backside and send him down the road. And she should. Still, there were things he didn't want to share. It was safer for her this way. A silent wish rose for her to see him as someone to look up to and respect. But . . .

Maybe those days were gone. Dammit. He'd acted like a kid in knee britches.

A sound at the door drew his attention and his heart sped up. She was back.

'Don't just stand there, come on in,' he called.

But it wasn't Maura. Instead a cute, half-pint kid with freckles and sandy hair opened it and came in.

'Hi there. Come on in.' Calhoun waved an arm. 'Are you looking for Miss Maura?'

'Yep.' The small boy crossed his arms. 'I'm Henry and I'm six.'

His grin revealed a big gap in his mouth where he'd lost two front teeth. He had mischievous, twinkling eyes.

'Well, Henry, I'm right proud to know you.' Calhoun held the chair while he sat down. 'This is a pretty nice place from what I can see. Are you happy to be living here?'

'Yep.'

'Miss Maura will be back in just a minute. I'm going to shave these whiskers off. Do you shave, Henry?'

'Yep.'

'You don't say?' Calhoun felt the boy's jaw. 'That's real smooth. You do a good job.'

'Yep. If I had spec'ables I could see better.' Henry propped an elbow on the table. 'Miss Em wears spec'ables but Miss Mo don't.'

'Miss Mo? Oh, you mean Miss Maura.'

'Yep, I guess.' Henry glanced toward the door.

'Are you hiding from someone?' Calhoun asked.

He nodded. 'Rosemary.' He released a troubled sigh. 'She wants to get married but I'm tired of playing with dolls. I like playing with boys, too, running and playing leapfrog. But she says I gotta choose.'

A tear-jerking Shakespearean tale if Calhoun ever heard one. He struggled to contain laughter. The boy was so serious as though this was the worst problem he'd ever have in his life. Little did Henry know he was only beginning to learn about the complexities of relationships.

Calhoun released a long sigh. 'There's nothing worse than woman trouble.'

'Nope. Sure ain't. I'm just gonna tell her the weddin' is off. I ain't marrying her.'

'That's it. Put your foot down, Henry. A woman will respect you for it.'

'What happened to you, Mister?'

'I had a bit of an accident and Miss Mo is fixing me up.'

'Oh.' He propped his chin on an arm and sighed. 'I don't have a mama or daddy. They in heaven.'

Poor kid. Calhoun's heart ached for him and the others who had no family.

'I'm really sorry to hear that, Henry. But you live in a good place with people who love you.'

'Yep.' He scooted off the chair. 'Gotta go.'

'Thank you for coming to visit. I'm glad to have a visitor.' Even if only to give advice to the lovelorn. He released the pent-up laughter.

With no reply, Henry closed the door behind him. A moment later he heard voices outside then Maura entered.

'Did you catch your escapee?' he asked, grinning.

'I did.' Maura laughed. 'Corraling these kids is like herding a bunch of cats. Just as you get them all going the right way they start breaking off and running this way and that. It's a lot for four people. And one has to care for the newborn.'

'And me. Sorry about that.' He admired the way a reddish-brown curl hugged her neck. 'Henry's a cute kid but troubled. He talked about not having any parents.'

'All the children here lost their parents to yellow fever. They're grief-stricken and the younger ones aren't even old enough to really know what happened.' She wrapped the hot towel around his face to soften his bristles. 'We'll get this started. As you said you won't be able to sit up long.'

His words coming back to haunt him delivered another mental kick. When he wanted to avoid something, he needed to think of a better way other than saying something stupid.

'We try to keep the children away from this part of the mission but it's hopeless. Anything that's off limits is exactly where they want to go and they'll find a way somehow.'

'I didn't mind and don't worry I didn't tell him anything about my situation. Just that I had an accident.' He adjusted the towel where he could breathe. He couldn't resist teasing. 'Were you aware you have a troubling lovelorn situation on your hands, Miss Mo?'

'I guessed I missed that.'

He related the conversation. 'Things are so serious with kids. This Rosemary must be quite a pushy little girl.'

'I'd call her headstrong. She's a beautiful child but determined and always wants her own way. I'll have to keep an eye on those two.'

They filled the time while waiting with more talk about the children. The deep love and compassion Maura harbored for them showed in her every word. He wondered if she and Emma had grown up orphans. Both seemed to relate to the children's plight extremely well.

Finally, she stood and unwrapped the towel. 'Those bristles should be easier to shave.'

She bent to the task of lathering him and hovered so near the soft fragrance of lily of the valley wafted around him. 'You smell good, Miss Maura. That was my mother's favorite flower. My father planted a large bush next to the porch one year for her birthday. Made her very happy. I miss them a lot. It's strange how you think you'll always have your parents.'

'My mother passed on several years ago,' Maura replied. 'How I wish I could talk to her. She, too, loved lily of the valley and I guess that's why I like it.'

So, he was wrong. The sisters didn't grow up in an orphanage. They had parents.

'Anything to keep the memories from fading,' he said softly. 'Once they do, we'll be lost. At least I know I will.'

'I'm down to the last few drops of the perfume. It was an unexpected gift from my father one Christmas several years ago. It's the last time he ever bought me and Emma anything.'

The sadness leaked from the words. Her eyes held a faraway look.

She seemed to shake herself and poured water into a large bowl, then handed him the straight razor. 'I don't know how sharp it is. I borrowed it from Uncle Max.'

'Guess I'll find out.'

With the mirror propped where he could see, he started with the left side of his throat because he knew he could do that. He warmed under her watchful gaze. 'I'm glad you're here in case I slice my jugular.'

'Please try to avoid that, Calhoun,' she said in a droll tone. 'I don't have time for another mess today.'

'You're extremely compassionate.' He spared her a look and nicked his skin. 'See what you made me do?'

'You've had worse.' She handed him a clean cloth and some astringent to dab away the spot of blood. 'You'll live.'

'Ouch!' He met her blue gaze and came near to slicing his ear. He swallowed hard and shaved all that he could get to. Finally, he laid the razor in the water. 'That's all I can do with one arm.'

'You did good, Calhoun.' She dried the straight razor and uncurled the strop.

He watched in fascination as she expertly sharpened the blade. 'You've used one of those before.'

'I used to love doing this for my father on the rare occasions when he was home. And when he let me, which was in truth only a handful of times. But it made me feel that he cared for me. At least a little.'

'I take it your father is away a lot.'

'Yes, he has to travel where the jobs take him.'

'What kind of work does he do?'

Maura froze. After several moments, she spoke. 'I'd rather not say if you don't mind. His profession has made life . . . difficult for Emma and me.'

What did he do? Curiosity had him biting his tongue to keep from asking. If he could bear waiting until tomorrow, he'd ask Max. But whatever it was had kept both girls from having a life.

Apparently, they'd been unwelcome in town so they brought the children out here. Now it made some sense why the gang of men had chopped off Emma's hair.

They were outcasts. For whatever reason, no one wanted their company.

His blood ran cold. There were only three professions that folks had difficulty with, and he didn't like the thought of any of them. Gravedigger, undertaker, and hangman. And the first two were far more acceptable than the third.

Calhoun put the thought aside for now. Maura had gotten the blade at the sharpness she wanted it and stood ready.

'I've never done this part of shaving, but I'll try not to cut you.'

'Thanks for that.' He was already sweating. First, at the thought of an untrained person holding such a sharp instrument. But worse than that – she stood so close and would have to lean in to get in the right position. No barber he'd ever gone to had been encumbered with breasts and Maura's were quite . . . well, let's just say no one would ever mistake her for a man. Not at all. Even if they were blind as bats and deaf as fenceposts.

'Relax, Calhoun. You're not scared, are you?'

'Quit teasing. Of course, I'm apprehensive.' He took a deep breath. 'Proceed.'

'You act like you're about to be drawn and quartered like they did in jolly old England.'

'I think they still might,' he muttered darkly.

Her sleeve brushed his cheek as she made the first stroke. She leaned to whisper, 'You're in good hands, Calhoun.'

A side glance found him staring down her dress at all that soft skin. He tried several times to speak before he managed to croak, 'Yes, ma'am.'

She moved and the view disappeared. He could finally release the breath he'd been holding. Despite her inexperience, her strokes were slow and smooth with no hesitation or nicks.

But keeping her bosom away from his face was all but impossible. He kept his eyes closed for the most part but every time he opened them, there they were.

Normally, he wouldn't complain but he was trying to be a gentleman as much as he was able. When his body reacted and he was about to embarrass himself, he pictured his last fishing trip and counted the fish on his stringer. When he ran out of fish, he counted the worms, then his bullets.

'Are you going to sleep, Calhoun?' she asked.

Good Lord, he was far from that! Every nerve ending was standing on end and saluting. He folded his hands over himself.

'No, ma'am. Just thinking about going fishing.'

'I see. Do you fish often?'

'Every chance I get, but it's been a while since I last went.'

'Lean your head back and tighten the skin around your mouth and nose. A little more and we'll be through.'

He did as she asked and found his head resting on those soft twin mounds. It was like floating on a cloud.

Stop it. Just stop it. He couldn't let himself enjoy the sensation. It was wrong, wrong, wrong and he was about to lose control. And would if this went on for long. And then what?

'Quit squirming,' Maura scolded.

'I'm trying.' But all sorts of inappropriate images were running through his head.

The moments passed as she finished up, then dropped the straight razor into the bowl of water and stepped back. 'I'm done.'

Not a moment too soon. He struggled to his feet, wiping away the excess shaving soap with the towel. 'Thank you. It feels good to rid myself of those bristles.'

'You're welcome. You look . . . nice.'

He chuckled. 'You mean human. I'm beginning to feel like it, thanks to you.'

Without looking at him, she opened the door to empty the bowl of water. 'No offense, but I hope you can manage by yourself next time.'

Something had happened to her voice. It seemed a little strained. Had this affected her as it had him? When she turned, he had his answer. Her dress couldn't hide the swollen nipples, proof of her aroused state. She was in a tizzy, gathering up everything and shoving them into the bag she'd brought.

She was angry. The twin spots of high color on her cheeks

told him that much. Maybe more at herself for letting him talk her into a situation where she didn't know the rules. Then again, she probably blamed him. In truth, he'd enjoyed the closeness.

He guessed this wasn't a good time to ask for help with his boots.

'Maura, it's OK to feel like a woman,' he said softly. 'There's nothing wrong when a body responds. It doesn't mean I'm going to take advantage of you.' When she wouldn't look at him, he hobbled to her and lifted her chin with a finger, staring into her blue eyes. 'You've seen every square inch of my body and know I'm no prize. I've been through hell and back and only time will tell if I brought some with me. In a few days, I'll be ready to ride and get out of your life.' He cleared his throat and tucked a strand of hair behind her ear. 'But being here with you has been the best days I've spent in a very long time.'

He pressed his lips to her cheek and knew he'd never forget her as long as he lived.

'I . . .' Before she finished what she was about to say, she whirled and hurried out the door.

THIRTEEN

The strong need to take some time to herself pushed Maura into the coolness of the cottonwood grove. Calhoun's soft kiss burned on her cheek.

What had possessed him to do that?

He hadn't known what such a token of affection would do to a woman who'd never had a kiss of any kind or a soft touch in over ten years. It was like a drop of rain on a withering flower.

Calhoun had been there seven days. Only a full week but had managed to burrow under her defenses.

Why did this hope spring to life? Why now when she'd grown accustomed to the emptiness? To the reality of her and Emma's lot.

His gentle touch had seemed to reach down inside her and soothe the ache, the yearning, the sadness. It had awakened all that she'd tried to stomp out.

He'd called her beautiful. Oh, to be able to see that when she looked in the mirror. But she couldn't afford to let herself see because when he left, everything would return back to the reality of the life she knew.

Calhoun was standing on the edge of goodbye and she couldn't stop him.

Maura found a downed tree trunk to sit on and watched the birds and squirrels. She filled her lungs with the crisp air and touched her cheek again. She could almost feel his lips on her skin.

A man like him would be accustomed to being with women, saying what he knew they wanted to hear. Maybe he hadn't meant any of those words.

Yet, they'd rang true because she'd wanted to believe him. What would it hurt to think he'd meant what he'd said? What would it hurt?

She had to tell him her last name. That would put an end to all this speculation and, seeing as how she'd barely opened her heart, it would be easier to return to her real life and not live in this make-believe world where she didn't belong.

Yes, that's what she'd do. Today. She'd tell him who she was.

Her mind made up, she rose and made her way back to Heaven's Door. Sunny and Alphie came running the minute they spied her. Sunny carried a squirming puppy.

'Where you been, Miss Mo?' Alphie gripped her hand. 'We been lookin' for you.'

'You have? Well, here I am.' She turned to Sunny. 'What do you have there?'

'We found this puppy. God left it like He did the baby.' Sunny laughed as the excited pup licked her face. 'He keeps bringing us gifts from our parents.'

'Yep.' Alphie put a hand on the dog's head. 'They still love us all the way from heaven.'

The sweetness had her blinking back tears. No reason to spoil that. 'Of course, they do. Did you doubt it?' Maura's voice was thick.

The fur ball had the tan and white markings of a collie and was as cute as could be. But where was its mother? It might not even be weaned or if so it wasn't for long.

What was going on? She knew God didn't plop babies or animals down. Besides, they had the tracks of a human to prove a woman had left the baby. She couldn't quite bring herself to scold the children for wandering where they'd been told not to go, but they had to understand they couldn't just traipse off wherever they wanted.

'Tell me exactly where you found it.'

'On the steps of the church,' Alphie said.

She gave them a stern glance. 'You've been told to stay away from there. How did you open the gate?'

'It wasn't shut so we pushed it open.' Sunny glanced down. 'We heard the puppy yipping and . . .'

'We thought it might need us,' Alphie added with a heart-melting grin. 'It was trying to get free.'

'Free of what?'

'The rope,' Sunny answered. 'It was tied up to the sign telling what this place is. Who would tie up a puppy?'

Good question.

'Did you see anyone around?'

'Nope.' Alphie reached for the dog and Sunny let him have it.

Emma hurried to meet them. 'There they are. These two are sure fast. I turned my back for a second and they took advantage. Where did the pup come from?'

'From the church steps evidently.' She filled Emma in on the mysterious appearance.

'God left it, Miss Em,' Sunny said. 'He brought it from heaven 'cause our mamas and papas love us.'

'They certainly do and never doubt it for a second. What a sweet little dog.' Emma's green eyes sparkled. 'Let's go show the sisters and the other kids.'

Sunny frowned. 'But then they'll want it. Me an' Alphie found it. He's ours.'

'No one's going to take it away from you,' Maura assured them. 'Can I hold it a minute?'

'I guess.' But Alphie didn't look too happy about it.

'I just want to see if it's a boy or a girl.'

'OK.' Alphie reluctantly let her take the pup.

Maura turned it over. 'It's a boy. He'll make you a nice friend. But I want you to understand that whoever left him might come back so don't get too attached.'

Sunny shook her head. 'God doesn't take back gifts.'

What could she say to that?

'No, He doesn't but the person who left it might want it back.' She handed the heart-tugging ball of fur back to Alphie. 'Let's go show the others.'

Alphie sighed. 'If we gotta.'

'You do.' Emma pointed to the others. 'March.'

The sullen children slowly walked toward their staring friends standing with Sister Bernadette. She was having a difficult time keeping them from running to meet Sunny and Alphie. When the two runaways got close, the children ran hollering. They pressed around, all asking questions at once.

'He's a boy,' Alphie announced proudly.

'What's his name?' Henry asked, pressing close.

'Don't have one yet,' Sunny answered. 'God just brought him.'

Emma turned to Maura. 'I'm going to take a look at that rope and the area where someone tied the pup.'

'Good idea.' Maura took Sister Bernadette aside and told her what the kids had said. 'Something odd is going on but we'll

have to take care of the collie until someone comes for him. I'm
sure there will be a fight as to who he sleeps with.'

'*Oui*. Maybe take turns?'

Maura laughed. 'That's wishful thinking, Sister. We'll have to
find a solution though.'

'Draw straw?'

'We'll see what Sister Angela suggests.'

Movement at Calhoun's door caught Maura's attention. She
cast a look that way and found him barefoot, the sunlight bathing
him. His intense stare made her uncomfortable. She hadn't
told him how handsome he was without the whiskers. Though
fifteen yards separated them, his dark good looks were striking.
She wet her dry lips.

Maybe there was no need to tell him about Lucius. He'd be
gone soon. Leave things as they were.

And she'd deal with the emptiness and unanswered questions.
For a brief moment a spark of hope had flared to life. Yet, she
knew how silly she was for letting it.

With a deep sigh, Maura took a step toward the children, when
she saw Calhoun go down from the corner of her eye. She raced
to him as he struggled to get up.

'Wait or you'll tear your stitches loose,' she yelled with Emma
right on her heels. Reaching him, she and Emma took a side and
helped him stand.

'What happened?' she asked as they got him back inside.

'My leg just gave way.' He gave her a crooked grin that sent
heat up her spine. 'I was distracted by the sight of a pretty woman
and turned loose of my hold on the doorframe for a moment.'

Emma laughed. 'That's a pitiful story if I ever heard one,
Calhoun.' She glanced down. 'You're bleeding.'

Darn the man, now he'd pulled the stitches loose in his side.

'Look what you've done,' Maura scolded. 'I've never known
a more stubborn man. It took more than that fall to break them
loose.' She stepped over his boots lying next to the bed.

'I was trying to put my boots on if you must know. Been
trying since yesterday.' He gave a huff as he sat on the side
of the bed. Exertion had created beads of sweat on his
forehead.

Maura lifted his legs and he lay back on the pillows. 'Looks like you've gotten your arm wound bleeding as well. Emma, can you run and fetch the needle and catgut?'

'Sure. I'll be right back, and I'll bring some water.'

While they waited, Maura unwrapped the bandages protecting both wounds and examined them. Still no infection and other than torn stitches, not too bad.

'The damage could be worse.' She sat down in the chair. 'Why have you been trying to put your boots on? Do you want to leave that badly?'

Calhoun's dark eyes bored into her and his expression was one of longing. 'I want to be with people. I want to be out there with you and the others. Do you know what this silence sounds like?'

'I've heard plenty of that myself.'

'To me it sounds like the inside of a tomb, and I can't take it anymore. I hear the voices and laughter but I'm isolated from them.'

A lock of dark hair fell on to his forehead, and it was everything she could do to keep from smoothing it back. Why did he awaken such strong needs in her? She wasn't an impetuous young girl. She was two years shy of thirty. You'd think she could control her emotions better.

'I'm sorry.' And she truly meant it. He was miserable. 'Maybe we can get you over to the kitchen and you can eat at the table with us.'

'I'd like that.' He rubbed his jaw. 'Say, have you seen Max today?'

'Come to think of it, I haven't.' Was he on another bender? He could've fallen and be lying over there bleeding. She'd make sure to check on him after she sewed Calhoun back up.

'I like talking to your uncle. He's led quite a life.'

'I suppose he has.' Curiosity rose. 'Did he mention our father?' She held her breath waiting for the answer.

'No. Should he have?'

'Forget I asked. I think I hear Emma.' She rose and went to the door, breathing a sigh of relief to see her sister coming.

'What was all the commotion with the children out there?' Calhoun asked.

'Someone left a puppy tied at the front of the chapel. There was no sign of anyone.'

'First a babe and now a puppy? What's next?'

'That's what I'd like to know. Sunny and Alphie are convinced that God's leaving them as gifts from their parents.'

A strange look crossed his face. 'Is that so?'

'They're hurting, Calhoun. They miss their parents, so naturally they want to know that somewhere they're thinking about their sons and daughters.' She moved back to the bed. 'I wish I knew who left the puppy. It doesn't make any sense.'

'It could be someone feeling sorry for the kids but for whatever reason don't want to show themselves.'

'I suppose.'

Emma came inside with a pail of water. 'I couldn't remember where we'd put the needle and catgut, so it took me longer.' She took some things from her pocket and laid them on the small table. 'The children are squabbling over the puppy and the sisters have their hands full. I wish whoever left it had brought a whole litter.'

'I'll go help as soon as I finish here. Calhoun wants to come join us. That is if you and I can help him over there.'

Calhoun lifted his head. 'If you can prop me up on each side, I can hobble. I just don't think I can make it alone.'

'We'll do our best. Emma, will you help me move the table over here to the bed?'

'It will make it easier, Sister.'

The two of them brought it closer in short order, then Maura turned to him. 'Do you need something for the pain? I don't know what we have though with Max not available.'

'No. Go ahead.'

It didn't take long to sew him up again, then Emma took everything back to the mission, leaving Maura alone with him. Every breath she took was heightened and she kept busy straightening up.

'I'm curious why you get all tense at the mention of your father. I know it has something to do with why the town cast you girls out. What is his name?'

'When I left after shaving you, I'd decided to tell you. Then you'll understand.' She lifted her chin and didn't look away from him this time. 'Does the name Lucius Taggart mean anything?'

Shock lined his face. He stilled. 'The hangman is your father?'

FOURTEEN

T he quiet in Calhoun's small room echoed in his head and everything inside him stilled.

They were the hangman's daughters?

This answered everything – why they started the orphanage so far from town, Emma's shorn hair, the reason neither girl had ever married.

'Good Lord!' He ran a hand across his eyes.

'So you see why things are the way they are. Keep your pretty words and compliments and save them for someone with a use for them.'

Calhoun threw his legs over the side of the bed and sat up. 'Look here, Maura Taggart. I'm not in the habit of paying lip service. Not with you or anyone. I mean what I say, and I meant every word, every compliment. There's only one thing keeping me from courting you and it's not your father.' He gave a snort. 'I don't give two hoots about Lucius Taggart. He doesn't scare me.'

'Others have said the same thing but they all snuck away.' Maura lifted her head, her voice quiet. 'So forgive me, but I don't believe you. I'm too old to play games, Calhoun. I'm smart enough to know that life has passed me by.'

'Only if you let it. You'll never get anywhere by sitting down and giving up.'

'Give up?' she asked sharply. 'Is that what you think? We've fought hard for everything we've gotten. Fought for the right to survive, to take up room on this earth. Wiped spit off our faces and walked away with heads held high. That's not giving up. But there comes a time when a woman has to face reality.'

She had a point, but he couldn't accept it.

He got to his feet and hobbled to her in his stocking feet. He placed his hands on her shoulders. 'How's this for reality? I like you and I like spending time with you and no, it has nothing to do with you patching me up. I'm not confusing gratitude with the closeness I feel with you. The only thing that is keeping me from courting you is the fact I have some dangerous business to take care of. The kind that might get me killed. Not only me, but everyone standing close and I won't do that to you. Understand?'

'I'm trying. In the meantime, I can't let false hopes take root.' Her voice dropped to an anguished whisper. 'That would finish me. Better to have no hope at all.'

'Lady, when I get this settled and if I still draw breath, I'm coming back.'

'I can see you mean that.' She put a hand to her throat. 'You have to get well before you can ride out and that might be a while, depending on how often you fall and break your stitches open.'

'You're telling me. It's all I can do to get to the door right now.'

A teasing glint sparkled in her blue eyes. At least the sadness was gone. 'See? And you're talking about walking over to the mission.'

'That's going to be more than talk. I am going to do that, with or without your help. So there. I'll go stark raving mad if I have to spend another meal in this room by myself. I want to meet these kids, see if Henry has called the wedding off or not, and get acquainted with the sisters. I want to see Baby Juliette and the new puppy and all sorts of things you've told me.' He lowered his voice and lifted a tendril of her hair that escaped from the loose knot on top of her head. 'But most of all, I want to sit with you at the table and eat a meal. That's going to be icing on the cake.'

'Then I should get moving.' She glanced at his boots on the floor. 'I guess I'm going to have to help you get those on or you'll be tearing your stitches out again.'

'That's the God's honest truth.'

'OK then. Sit in the chair, Mr Stubborn.'

'At least I did get my socks on by myself.' He sat down. 'I'm not real sure how we're going to do this. I can pull on one side with my good right arm and maybe you can pull on the left.'

'We can try it.'

Calhoun wondered if she realized how close she'd have to get. As hard as they were to get on, there wasn't any other way.

And what would that do to his sanity?

With her fragrant scent drifting around him, Maura positioned herself on his left side and leaned over grabbing the top of his boot. Mere inches away, her nearness had him struggling for breath.

Both of them tugged but only got his foot in about halfway. Trying again, she leaned down further until she was almost in his lap, pulling and yanking as hard as she could.

His yearning body tried to betray him. He closed his eyes. *Not now. This isn't the time.*

'I'm going to get this on one way or the other,' she said, blowing back a strand of fallen hair.

Before he knew it, she threw her leg across his lap and sat with her back to him. Reaching down, she put her fingers in the loops and gave a big yank. That did it.

'Thank God for a woman who doesn't give up on boots,' he murmured. The temptation to touch her, to put his hands around her waist, rose up with a strong need that surprised even him.

However, before he could blink, she removed herself from his lap. Her cheeks were bright red. 'I'm sorry, but that's the only way to get them on.'

'Do you hear me complaining?' Damn his grin that tried its best to form. 'Only one more to go.'

'Maybe you can hop?'

'That's a long way on one leg. I might fall again,' he pointed out.

'I was afraid of that.' She grabbed the other boot and this time started out sitting backward on his lap.

Calhoun didn't have to do anything but watch and watch he did. And dream. He noticed the little tendrils of hair that curled on her neck, too short to go up in the loose knot she'd pinned on the top of her head. Sometimes she wore her hair down with all that gorgeous color spilling across her shoulders and down the front of her dress. That was his favorite. But mostly she pinned it back away from her face.

Her trim waist caught his eye now and he wondered if she was eating enough. Maybe she was giving her portion to the kids. They might not have enough to go around. When he'd been at home, he'd often seen his mother give her portion away during lean times so it figured Maura might. When he got up and around, he'd do some hunting before riding out. It was the least he could do.

Before he could look closely at any other part of her anatomy, she had the boot on, giving a triumphant yell, and was off him in a flash. Without her weight, he felt oddly strange like a boat missing its rudder.

Maura dusted her hands. 'Now that I got that done, I need to check on Max. I'm worried about him. I had a conversation with him after everyone turned in and haven't seen him since.'

'Do you think he went somewhere?'

'I haven't a clue, but I hope he'd tell one of us. I'm worried he might've fallen too far into the bottle and gotten hurt.'

'Maybe so but I hope not for your sake. I'll take a nap while I wait for you to come back and get me.'

'You probably need it.' She said goodbye and went to Max's room two doors down from Calhoun.

Knocking brought no one so she turned the knob. The sparse room was dim with nothing except a bed, a small table and a trunk where Max stored his belongings. It was clear Max wasn't there.

And more importantly she saw no sign of a whiskey bottle.

Where had he gone? After some more of the rotten stuff?

She hurried to the workshop where she'd seen their uncle. The smell of wood shavings greeted her when she stepped inside. There was no sign of him, only a row of things with tarps thrown over them.

The surprise he'd mentioned. Curiosity tempted her to look but she resisted. A lump swelled in her throat. He was making something that had to benefit either the women or the children. The sight deeply touched her. Max had more worth and more heart than anyone knew. Maura eased out and shut the door. She'd keep his secret.

But where had he gone?

After looking several other places, she gave up. He'd show himself when he got ready and there wasn't any use fretting over it. Max was a grown man.

Turning, she went into the mission. Soon she was leading the singing and wiping noses. She'd missed being with the children while she took care of Calhoun. They lifted their voices in song.

The puppy went to sleep in the space on the floor between Sunny and Alphie.

When they finished the song, four-year-old Betsy raised her hand.

'Yes, Betsy?'

'Livia and Alphie won't . . .' Breathless, she squirmed, scratching her leg. 'Won't let me . . . uh . . . hold . . . hold the puppy.'

'The puppy belongs to all of you. Here's what we're going to do. Each of you will get the dog for a full day. I'll make a chart and keep track.'

'The puppy's ours!' Sunny hollered. 'Mine and Alphie's.'

Sister Angela rose from a chair by the door that she'd slipped into during the singing. 'Must share. Belong to all.'

'That's not fair!' Sunny jumped up and ran out, leaving the puppy with Alphie.

Henry reached for it and Alphie jerked it away.

Maura had enough. 'Sister Angela, will you take the dog? I'm going to talk to Sunny,' she said quietly. She went outside and found the girl sitting against the side of the building, sobbing. Maura's heart ached for her. She lowered herself beside her. 'You know, when I was a little girl, I prayed for a dog every night before I went to bed. Then one day, one came up to our house. I was so happy. I named her Annie. She was the best dog.'

'What happened to her?' Sunny asked.

'A man came and said Annie belonged to him. He took her away. I cried and cried. Sunny, that may happen here. Someone might come and claim the puppy. Enjoy him while he's here and let the others love him too. They're hurting as much as you.'

'But I found him.'

'Honey, I know you did. Please don't be selfish.' Maura wiped the girl's tears with her apron. 'God loves each of you the same. What if one of the others had found the puppy? Wouldn't you want a turn with it?'

'Yes,' the girl mumbled, sniffing.

'You owe them an apology for the way you acted.' Maura put an arm around her. 'Please try to be happy and enjoy the sweet dog. I love you, Sunny.'

'I love you too, Miss Mo.' She rose and put her arms around Maura's neck.

'I want you to apologize, then if you'd like, we can see what we can do in the kitchen to help the sisters.'

Sunny put her hand in Maura's and they went inside. When they rejoined the others, Sister Angela was teaching the children a French song called '*Frère Jacques*'.

Then Sunny stood in front of the group and apologized for getting mad and storming out. 'We hafta share because the puppy makes us all happy. Not just me and Alphie.'

Maura smiled. 'Thank you, Miss Sunny. I'm proud of you. You have a good heart.'

'My mama said we have to be kind. But I forgot.'

'We can't always remember everything, especially when the yearning in the heart is so strong.' Like it was with her for Max. She had such a deep yearning to help her uncle. 'Now do you want to help in the kitchen?'

'Yes, ma'am.'

Sister Bernadette was taking two loaves of hot bread out of the oven. Sunny's eyes lit up.

Maura sat the girl at the table. 'Sister, my little friend here has had an awfully hard difficult day. Might she have a small piece of that with a little butter to brighten her life a bit?'

'*Oui.*' Bernadette sliced off a little piece and buttered it. 'Here, angel.'

'Thank you, Sister Bernie.' Sunny wore a big smile. 'Bread is so good.'

The girl became a chatterbox and told Bernadette about her pets that she missed. She glanced at Maura. 'Can we name the puppy, Miss Mo? Please.'

'I don't see that it would hurt, and we need something to call him.' If the owner returned for the pup, they'd tell him what they'd given it. 'We'll put all the suggestions into a hat and draw one out.'

Sunny grinned with buttery lips. 'I like Peaches. That used to be my dog's name.'

Oh dear. Maura could see the way this was going to go. Some weren't going to be appropriate for a male dog. 'Is that the name you want to put in the pot?'

'Yes.'

'OK.' Maura found a scrap of paper and began the list.

While Sunny helped Sister Bernie in the kitchen, Maura rejoined the others. 'We're going to give the puppy a name so I'm taking suggestions. I'll put them in a hat and draw the winner at supper.'

Most borrowed the names of their fathers but there were a few good ones like Roan, Wags, Rowdy, Snickers and Buttons.

'Now, who would like to paint?'

Everyone raised their hand. Sister Angela nodded and quickly added. 'We go outside.'

'Excellent idea.' Maura hadn't been crazy about scrubbing up the mess. Hearing Baby Juliette's cries, Maura went into the next room and picked her up.

'Oh, my goodness, what's got you all in a tizzy, little princess,' Maura crooned, kissing her cheek. 'Did you miss your Prince Charming?'

She changed her wet diaper, and she was all content. 'There you go.' She picked her back up. 'I'm sure you're getting a little hungry.'

Emma entered the room and spoke low. 'There's a man at the door. I don't like the looks of him.'

Something in her sister's voice shot prickles of alarm up the back of Maura's neck.

FIFTEEN

Her heart racing, Maura hurried toward what was probably another problem to solve. Maybe it was the puppy's owner wanting it back. She tightened her arms around Juliette and tried not to borrow trouble, yet the feeling persisted. If only Max were here. Where did he go, darn it?

'Did the visitor say anything?' she asked Emma.

'He was very insistent about coming in and looking around. Said he's searching for someone. Do you think he's looking for Calhoun?'

'I guess we'll find out. I'm glad you're with me.'

'It's the only way we ever face anything – together.'

They reached the front door of the chapel and Maura opened it. The stranger's long, dirty hair had a scraggly appearance and had likely not seen a drop of water in a while. He slouched against the stone wall, picking his teeth with a small knife. He wore a dark hat pulled low. His insolent attitude was the kind to make a woman back up and give him a wide berth. He showed them not an ounce of respect. At her appearance, he closed the weapon and straightened, the stench of his character striking her.

She was aware that Emma had left and wondered if she'd gone to get the nuns.

'May I help you?' Maura asked.

'Lookin' for a thief. I think he might've come here.'

'This the Heaven's Door Orphanage. There are only children here.'

'He was shot and couldn't have gone far. Me and my men found a lot of blood over in the tree line. We're thinking he might've sought help here.'

So, he *was* looking for Calhoun. Well, what he wanted and what he'd get were two different things.

'What did you say your name is?'

'Didn't.'

'What did this man steal?' She put the fussy baby on her shoulder and patted her back.

'Something of mine and I aim to find it. I need to come in and look around. He's pretty dangerous and I'd hate for him to hurt you pretty ladies.'

Maura stiffened her spine. 'I'm afraid that's out of the question. I have a duty to protect these children. Good day.' She tried to shut the door but was stopped by a large boot.

The man shoved it back open. 'I'm afraid I have to insist.'

Just then Emma returned. 'We gave our answer.' She raised their father's old gun and cocked it. 'Now leave or I'll shoot you where you stand.'

'I don't think you'll fire that. You don't have the gumption.'

'There's only one way to find out, mister,' Maura grated between clenched teeth. 'But I wouldn't bet on it. My sister and I are very committed to protecting this place and all who live inside.'

He raised his hands in surrender. 'Fine. But I'll be back.'

Maura had the feeling he was laughing at them and probably thinking he could take the gun easily from them. Maybe so, but it wouldn't be easy and someone would get shot.

'The answer will be the same next time and the time after that,' Emma said, stepping closer.

'We'll see.' He moved toward a beautiful black horse and stepped into the stirrup.

Emma and Maura stood watching until he disappeared from sight.

'I wouldn't trust anything that man said. In case you were wondering, that, dear sister, was an outlaw. Quite different from Calhoun.' Emma slid the gun into her pocket. It weighed down one side of her dress yet was out of sight. 'Did you see the bandage beneath his shirt?'

'I was too busy looking at his ugly sneer,' Maura confessed. Now that the danger was past, weakness invaded her body. The baby began to cry.

'It appeared to me that he had a chest wound and the glimpse I got of it showed spots of blood.' Emma took the baby. 'I'll go feed her. She's probably starving, poor thing.'

'Thank you.' As her sister started to walk away, Maura called. 'I'm proud of you and the courage you showed, Sister.'

'We can't afford to be weak,' Emma replied. 'Being strong is the only way for women to survive.'

Yes, it was. Maura went out into the afternoon sun and tilted her face to the warm rays. Inhaling some deep, cleansing breaths, the ice inside began to melt.

The sound of a rider coming down the narrow lane jolted her. Her heart raced. She had no weapon. Had the despicable man returned? But the rider rounding the bend was Max. Thank God, he'd returned. She hurried to meet him.

He reined up and dismounted. 'What's happened?'

Maura noticed right off that he was fairly sober. 'We just had a visitor. Some man who got insistent on coming inside and having a look around. He's searching for a thief he said but it surely has to be Calhoun.'

'The man doesn't strike me as a thief. What is he supposed to have stolen?'

'This insolent visitor just said something of his.' Her voice trembled. 'When he wouldn't let me close the door, Emma had to get the gun and threaten to shoot him. He hasn't been gone long. In fact, I thought he was coming back when I heard your horse.'

Max pulled her into a hug. 'I'm here now and I won't let anyone harm you.'

It felt so good to have someone to care. It had been so long. The scent of tobacco and whiskey on his clothes gave a hint of his whereabouts. But he was back now, and she hadn't realized how deeply she truly cared about her uncle.

She stayed in the circle of his arms a second longer before stepping back. 'Calhoun wants to take supper at the table with us all. Will you please come, too? We'll celebrate his recovery.'

'I don't know. I've had a drink and probably not fit company, girl.'

'Please? I trust and love you.' She also knew he wouldn't go deeper into the bottle since he'd be coming around the kids. Maybe she was becoming a doctor of sorts.

He studied her a minute. 'I see how much it means to you. All right. If you have your heart set on it that much, I'll eat supper at the table.'

Maura kissed his cheek. 'Thank you.' She hesitated for a

second, wanting to say more. She looked up at him, squinting. 'I won't ask where you went. It's none of my business. But please let me know when you leave next time. I need to know who I can call on when that man returns. And he'll be back. I know his kind.'

With a nod, he said, 'I rode into town looking for Emma's bunch of haircutters. I think I figured out some of them.'

'Uncle Max! I wish you hadn't. Did you accuse anyone and cause trouble?'

'Nope. Just kept quiet. But I saw a horrible sight that I won't be soon forgetting.'

There were lots of sights in town that would turn your stomach.

'Dare I ask what?' she asked quietly.

Max rubbed his short beard. 'Well, I was sitting in the saloon wetting my throat and listening to the conversations around me when this seedy looking man came in telling everyone he had a wild boy in a cage. He said we could see him for two bits.' He glanced up at the sky at the noisy geese flying overhead on their way south.

'What else?'

'Me and the others followed the man around to the alley and paid our money. He had a cage in the back of a wagon with a tarp over it.' He paused, squinting. 'Are you sure you have the stomach for this?'

'Go on before I strangle you.' Her voice was tight. Whatever it was, she had to know. 'What did you see, Uncle?'

'He pulled the covering off and there stood a boy. Probably around fourteen if I was guessing. His long hair was all matted and he started yelling and shaking the bars, trying to get out of his prison. The man poked him with a sharp stick and got him even more riled.'

Oh my God! Maura's hand flew to her mouth. Anger flooded over her. How could one human do this to another? The man deserved to be flogged within an inch of his life.

'Then what happened to the kid?'

'I started to climb into the wagon and do what I could to help him and the two-bit son of a . . .' He paused and looked at her with one eye closed before ending the sentence. 'The biscuit eater pulled a gun on me. Then he threw the tarp back over the cage and I heard the boy calling for his mama and sobbing. All of us hurried back to the saloon.'

'What about this man?' Maura's words were hard. 'Did he leave town?'

'Don't think so. Said he was planning to stay a few days.' Max grabbed her arm. 'Don't be getting any ideas, girl. That'll get you killed.'

'I can't, I won't leave him there. If I did, I wouldn't be able to look at myself in the mirror. And I'd be no better than the biscuit eater who has the boy.'

Max looked away, muttering low, then turned back. 'Then I go with you.'

'I'm going tonight after everyone's in bed. If you're not ready and sober, I'll leave without you. Those are my terms.'

'Fair enough.' He sighed then changed the subject. 'How are you planning to get Calhoun over to the kitchen?'

'I managed to put his boots on him and me and Emma will support him on each side. Hopefully, he'll be able to walk between us.'

'I'll get him over there,' Max said. 'And I'll keep watch for your visitor.'

'All right. Thank you.'

Maura headed back inside, her thoughts whirling while Max took his horse around to the barn. She had much to think about.

But one thing she knew, she had to help that poor boy in the cage.

Supper was a noisy affair with all the children around the table. After helping to seat the others, Maura found the only empty chair was next to Calhoun. Her pulse raced. His handsome features and kind eyes had an odd effect on her. Somehow, he'd managed to wash and his hair appeared clean. She bet Max took credit. He'd taken a real liking for their patient. Calhoun seemed to get better by the day – but then soon he'd leave.

She had to let him go. It was the way of life and she had to accept that. Her thoughts went back to the day she'd found him and held no hope that he'd survive his injuries.

Now the stranger was hunting him.

Goosebumps rose on her arms. Without a doubt, the man would

kill Calhoun given half a chance. She had to warn him tonight once she got him back to his room.

During supper, Maura found her gaze straying to Calhoun sitting beside her. His eyes were riveted on the children and every so often he'd chuckle. He seemed to enjoy them as he had when Henry sought him out to ask marital advice. He questioned them about the puppy and talked about shaving and everything else under the sun.

Max had planted himself near the door, probably in hopes of making an early getaway. But he was here and that's what counted. A drunk or not, he'd made an effort to please her, and it touched something deep inside.

Alphie pushed back his chair and went to sit with Max. Maura didn't miss how her uncle's large hand rested on the boy's back. And how he tenderly smoothed the boy's hair.

Darn it, she had to blink back the tears that threatened.

Sister Angela stood at the head of the long table. 'Bow heads.'

When the boys and girls had settled, she offered the blessing, asking God to bless them all. Then the sisters filled the children's bowls with a fragrant stew and gave them a piece of cornbread.

While they waited for the stew to come around, Calhoun leaned close, his breath tickling her ear. 'You look real nice, Miss Maura.'

'Thank you, Calhoun. So do you. I noticed someone helped you clean up.'

His lopsided grin made her stomach lurch. 'Nothing escapes you, does it? Max was kind enough to lend a hand.' He held his bowl out to Emma to fill, then continued, 'I detect a frown marring your beautiful forehead. What's wrong?'

'I have a lot on my mind. But I do need to talk to you in private.'

'If it's about the afternoon visitor, Max already filled me in.'

'I should've known he would. That's good, though. Then you should know that I expect our visitor to return. He tried to barge his way inside and Emma had to threaten to shoot him.'

'I'm sorry you ladies got caught in the middle of my mess. I should go ahead and ride out.'

'You'll do no such thing until you're well enough. Give it a few more days.' Maura didn't realize she clutched his arm until she glanced down. She quickly released him, but Henry sat across from them and was watching.

'Are you fighting, Miss Mo?' the six-year-old asked, his eyes wide.

'No, of course not.' She gave Henry a bright smile. 'We're just having a conversation. Aren't we, Calhoun?'

The cleft of his chin deepened. Calhoun crooked an eyebrow and drawled, 'Don't know about you, Miss Mo, but I'm enjoying sitting next to you. You have the most beautiful eyes I've ever seen. The centers are dark blue and the rest of them are the color of a magnificent Texas bluebird.'

Her palms sweaty, she fidgeted under his intense stare, wishing he'd change the subject. Or move back. Or find something else to capture his attention.

Instead, he leaned closer, his deep voice low, rustling over her skin, her face, like a welcome, whispering breeze.

And she took back every single thing she wished him to do.

'In fact, you probably don't know this, Miss Maura, but Native Americans see bluebirds as a sign of hope, love and renewal. Maybe you've seen some around here.'

Any closer and she'd be able to count his white teeth. Good heavens, it was getting hot in the kitchen. She cleared her throat and muttered low, 'Calhoun, we have curious, young eyes watching.'

'Right. I forgot myself.' He moved back into his space. 'All the same, think about what I said. The bluebird and I have things in common. We both have lots of hope and my body is in the process of renewal.'

And love? She didn't quite dare to ask. Not here in front of everyone. Besides, it was better not knowing his stance on that subject. For sure.

Yet, it didn't hurt to dream just a little. Did it?

She cast his dark handsome features a glance from beneath lowered lids and couldn't help the way her heart sped up.

SIXTEEN

Calhoun could barely take his eyes off Maura. He could've eaten a horse dumpling for all the attention he paid to the meal.

At the close of the meal, she stood and drew a dog's name from Max's big hat. How the light danced in her reddish-brown hair and put a glow in her cheeks.

'The winning name is Gunner. That was Betsy's suggestion.' Maura turned to the frail child who battled one illness after another. 'As the winner, go get the dog and we'll tell him.'

'I help.' Sister Angela took the girl's hand and went out.

They soon returned. All smiles, Betsy struggled to carry the wiggly fur ball that was plastering her face with licks.

Calhoun laughed. It was a very cute puppy. 'Gunner is a good name for him.'

The children clapped and their laughter rang through the old mission, rejuvenating Calhoun. He didn't want the night to end. Escaping death had given him a new meaning on what it was to really be alive.

After supper, Maura and Max assisted Calhoun outside to sit and watch the stars pop out, then Max went to his room and Maura scurried off to help ready the children for bed. She promised to be back soon. This would give Calhoun time to gather his thoughts and soak up the peace of Heaven's Door. He was in no hurry to rush back to his dismal surroundings. When he was ready to seek his bed, she'd offer a steady arm.

'I wish I could come and go as I wish,' he muttered to himself. 'I'm nothing but a stove up invalid.'

Still, there was a lot to be said for having Maura so near. His thoughts turned to the way she'd plunked herself in his lap, pulling his boots on. Embers flared to life and pooled in his belly. If she only knew the thoughts she'd aroused. No – more than mere thoughts. She'd drawn images of bare skin, heated touches and soft sheets.

He didn't give a damn about her father the hangman. If he was free to pursue her, that wouldn't stop him.

But he had to deal with Donavan before the rotten outlaw hurt – or killed – the people here. He was coming back, that was a given. Another task would be to find out about his brother and see if anyone had bothered the loot. He wouldn't rest until he did. Then he'd seek justice. Calhoun clenched his jaw tight. Oh yeah, justice would be sweet.

Footsteps sounded and a swish of fabric came from behind. Maura plopped a baby into his arms.

The kid looked as surprised as he felt.

'I hope you don't mind seeing to Juliette for a bit. We're all up to our eyeballs in giving baths and getting the children to bed. It won't be for long,' she promised. 'Be sure and support her head. Her belly is full so she might go to sleep.'

Before he could say a word, she disappeared back inside, leaving his mouth hanging open. The baby stared up at him, probably in a panic to be left with such a reprobate.

'Well, I guess it's just you and me, kid.'

She puckered up and tried to work up a cry but evidently couldn't find it in her.

What the hell was he supposed to do? He didn't know diddly about babies. She was so small and fragile.

'Do you know how to play the game Cans?' he asked.

Juliette yawned and blinked.

'I feel the same way, little one. I'll go first seeing as how you can't talk. Try not to act bored.'

She yawned big and stretched and grabbed hold of his finger as though it was a lifeline. Despite fear he'd hurt the little thing, something curled deep inside him that he'd never felt before. A protective urge rose and he touched her blonde hair that was as soft and fine as the fuzz on baby birds.

'OK, here we go. Cans is a game devised by cowboys spending winter in line camps. Each cowboy takes a turn reciting from memory the label on canned foods. Wasn't too clever but it helped pass the lonely hours.'

He glanced up at the sky in thought and listened to the voices inside for a moment. This was the peace he'd always sought and couldn't find.

Finally, he resumed, 'I think I remember the peaches can. At least some of it.' He cleared his throat. '"Lee-Hy Delicious California peaches picked at the peak of ripeness. Packed in heavy syrup. Net weight fifteen ounces. Nutrition facts: sixty calories. Made from the finest ingredients of peaches, water and sugar".' He frowned. 'I can't remember any more. I used to recite bean cans and have to say I won more times than I lost. Then there was the condensed milk cans but I've forgotten that too.'

Juliette cooed softly and tried to pull his finger into her small mouth.

'I knew you'd be impressed,' he said, winking. 'A good thing to remember is that sugar will rot your teeth, little girl. You don't want to end up snaggly-toothed.' He lifted her up and kissed her cheek. 'You picked an excellent place to come when you needed taken care of. So did I. We know a good thing when we see it.' He wrapped the blanket around her. 'Well, actually, I was in no shape to decide anything, and neither was you. I reckon the big man was watching over us. He does that, you know.'

Calhoun tickled the baby's cheek and drew a smile. 'You sure are a heart stealer. Watch out for the boys. I've heard they have cooties.'

Darn it! Why did he have to think of his sister? April had loved telling her older brothers they had cooties. Taken by a fever, she never reached her eleventh birthday. Though she'd had a home she'd been lonely for playmates. How she would've loved a place like this with plenty of kids to play with. Piercing pain shot into his heart, and he struggled to breathe.

Why now after all these years? Strange how memories could rise up from nowhere and strangle a man.

Shaking, he inhaled some deep breaths and forced the memories back down.

'Dear one, I hope you never lose anyone that you love.' His quiet words held sadness. Maybe the child felt it.

She cooed again and seemed to be trying to talk judging by the way she moved her mouth. Maybe comforting him. 'I know, sweet girl. I feel the same way.'

Just then, the puppy scampered out and scratched at Calhoun's leg.

'Hey, Gunner. Want to play Cans?' He lifted the pup into his lap. It turned in a tight circle, then laid down as close as he could get to Juliette, resting his head on her belly. Baby girl smiled, cooed once more, and closed her eyes.

That peace unlike any Calhoun had ever known again curled around him. He rested his head against the back of the chair. In a little over a week, Heaven's Door had given him what he'd sought aimlessly. He didn't know how he'd find the strength to leave. The best he could do was enjoy it while he could and maybe take a little with him when he rode out.

He had to get far away from here and try to draw out Rupert Donavan. Because of him, the gang leader had come. He couldn't let Donavan hurt them – even if he had to give himself up. If it came to that, he'd not bat an eye. They'd put themselves in an evil man's crosshairs for him.

The stars blinked overhead like millions of twinkling diamonds. The night was one of the most beautiful Calhoun had ever seen. On nights like this it was easy to imagine he'd finally found everything he'd sought.

But he knew this peace wouldn't last. It never did.

Thoughts turned to his brother and pain shot through him. Donavan's appearance here meant that his twin had indeed been killed. Had to have happened during the escape. And now Donavan was tearing up the countryside trying to find him and that considerable loot.

Everyone knew stealing from a thief led to an early grave. No one was as vicious.

Suddenly, the door opened and Maura emerged with Emma.

'Just look at that, Emma.' Maura stood grinning in front of him with arms folded over her chest. 'If that doesn't melt your heart, I don't know what will.'

'I agree.' Emma was grinning as well. 'A sleeping baby. A puppy. And a big, tall man.'

'OK, you can stop anytime,' Calhoun growled. 'At least no one is bawling.'

'Nope. You did good.' Maura took Juliette and passed her to Emma. 'We might have to write out a recommendation when you leave. In case you need a job reference.'

Her hands brushed his stomach and something jolted inside.

He tried not to react but must've, judging by the way Maura's eyes widened, and the quick breath she took.

'Do you need me to get you back to your room?' Emma asked him.

Calhoun smiled. 'Nope. I think I can manage with just Maura's help.'

'All right. Goodnight.'

They bid her goodnight and she took Juliette inside. Calhoun watched Maura carefully and it didn't take long for worry lines to appear.

Maura sat down in the chair next to him. 'I love nights like this. Very peaceful.'

'I was thinking about that. But I can see you're keeping something. Spill it.'

She sighed. 'I doubt you're going to let this lie.' She quickly shared what Max had told her. 'I'm going into town tonight and try to rescue the boy. Max is supposed to go with me but if not, I'll go alone.'

Worry for her safety sharpened his tone. 'You'll get yourself killed. It's too dangerous!'

Her temper flared. 'There's no one else to do it! I won't be able to live with myself if I don't. I can't – I won't – let that boy suffer more abuse at the hands of his captor.' She got to her feet and paced back and forth. 'I don't understand why the law will allow this. Yet, run me and Emma out of town because our father is the hangman. Something we have no control over.' She threw up her hands. 'I don't see why the law is so lopsided. Makes me furious.'

It did him too. He'd seen more than his share of wishy-washy practices where the law was concerned.

He couldn't stop staring at the high color in her cheeks and the moonlight tangling in her hair. Beauty came in many forms but this was as close to perfection as he'd ever seen.

'Everything you say is true. But if you intend to free this young boy and bring him back here, you're going to have to settle down. Danger calls for having a clear head. I wish I could go in your place and I curse myself that I can't. I can't even ride along.' He took her hand. 'Sit. I'll help you plan. At least I can do that.'

For the next hour, they planned out every step. Disguise herself. Get to town as the saloons were shutting down. Stay out of sight. Bide her time and wait until the streets empty. Then make her way to the boy.

He met her gaze. 'You'll need a gun, Maura.'

'I have one and know how to use it.'

'OK. Breaking the lock on the cage will be the hardest part. You can't make any noise. Do you know where the despicable jackass sleeps?'

'No.'

'Find out beforehand. Max can help with this.' A thought hit him. 'In fact, Max can try to persuade the jackass to let him see the wild boy again, then knock him in the head when they get around there. Yes, that'll work best, I think. But getting the lock off. That's the tricky part.'

'Maybe the man will have the key in his pocket?'

'Let's hope so. But if not, you may have to break it open with something. Do you have a short piece of iron?'

'Max might. Or know where a piece is.'

'I hope so. Once you get the cage open, don't waste any time. Take an extra horse for him. Get him on it, and ride like hell.'

'He'll be afraid to come with me, Calhoun. I might have to calm his fears and that could take a while.'

'I agree. There are a lot of unknowns, and you can't plan for everything. The boy may try to hurt you or scream his head off and alert everyone. Maybe take him something to eat. I doubt he's had a lot of food.'

'Good idea. I'm glad I have a chance to run through this. You brought up some things I hadn't thought of.' She smiled and he squeezed her hand. 'I feel more confident.'

'I hope Max doesn't disappoint you. However, I have no doubt you can rescue that boy by yourself if need be. You're very capable and not prone to rash behavior.'

'Emma and I had to learn that and many times the hard way.'

Her voice was sad and so weary. He wanted to put his arms around her and hold her until her fears settled. She needed to know someone stood behind her. He lifted a hand to her face and brushed a soft cheek. Like Gunner, she leaned into his touch, soaking it up like a rose to the sun's warmth.

There was something wrong with a world that turned its back on two compassionate women with a heart for helping people and trying to better the world.

'I can't imagine what you've been through. It would harden most everyone else but you still help the poor and downtrodden. I wish I had met you long ago.'

'Me too. I'm scared, Calhoun. What if I fail?'

'Brave people are always scared. You wouldn't be normal if you weren't. But they saddle up and ride even knowing they might die.' He smiled. 'I wish you had known my brother. He wore courage like a suit of clothes. You would've liked him.'

'I'm sure I would've.'

'The surly man who appeared at your door is the leader of a gang of cutthroats. Even though I didn't get a look at him, I'm sure about this. His name is Rupert Donavan and he wouldn't have shown up here if my brother were alive.' His voice broke. He stopped and swallowed, taking a moment to settle his emotions.

'Sounds like you were very close.' She rested her palm on his arm. 'I'm sorry.'

'Thank you.' He inhaled the night air. 'We were together the night I got shot and riding as hard as we could push the horses. Bullets were flying from all directions. I guess one got him.'

'That would've been terrifying.' She studied his eyes and he squirmed under her intense gaze. 'Who are you, Calhoun? What were you involved in?'

SEVENTEEN

The fragrant night air swirled around them. Calhoun avoided her gaze. Maura's unexpected question seemed to have caught him at a loss for words. Good. Maybe he'd tell the truth.

'I've said all I'm at liberty to discuss. The less you know the better.'

'So you're protecting us? Is that it?'

'Correct.' A moment's silence spun like fragile blown glass. The puppy's leg twitched from his comfortable bed in Calhoun's lap. 'When I leave, and it will be soon, I want you to forget all about me.'

His stricken words came barely louder than a whisper. They spoke of sorrow and regret.

'A man with no name from anywhere and nowhere. Could be either a lawman or an outlaw. Take your pick.' A sharp ache pierced her heart that one morning soon she'd wake to find him gone. Men like him didn't say goodbye and they didn't form attachments.

She forced a brittle laugh. 'It'll be like you were never here. Just a ghost that had a few holes in him.'

'There will be nothing to tie you to me and that's the way it has to be. I have to keep you and the others safe. I brought those scum here and it's up to me to take care of that.' He released a deep sigh of regret. 'Also, everything you women do has been scrutinized and criticized. I won't add to that.'

Why wouldn't he look at her?

Maura's temper flared. She snorted. 'You're nothing but a blank slate. We have to write our own conclusions. Calhoun trusted no one.'

They lapsed into a thick silence. Maura wanted to grab the stubborn man and shake him. She didn't give two hoots what people thought. They were going to twist everything and turn every circumstance and occurrence into something shameful.

Finally, he spoke. 'I should probably get back to my room so you can get ready for your midnight ride.'

'I suppose. You and I are getting nowhere anyway.' She took Gunner from him and set the pup inside the kitchen door, then helped Calhoun to his feet.

When he straightened to his full height, he towered over her, muscle and brawn, staring down into her upturned face. He held her gaze and she found it impossible to look away. The pad of his thumb grazed her cheek like the gentle wings of a dove.

He released a soft sigh. 'I've held gold nuggets in my hand and marveled at their beautiful brilliance. But lady, they don't hold a candle to you.'

Emotion sprang from all sides. She'd never been held in someone's power like this. Never been caressed under the moon's silvery rays. Never knew such gentleness. Tears sprang into her eyes as he traced the curve of her mouth with a light finger.

'Please.' A sharp ache pierced her chest and she didn't even know what she was begging for. She just couldn't let him go, for it would tear her apart.

Staring deep into her eyes, he whispered, 'Forgive me.'

Before she could speak, he pulled her against him. Her breath got lost somewhere inside her chest. Every nerve ending burst as she closed her eyes and released all the temptation, desire and hunger she'd tamped down.

His head slowly lowered and his lips touched hers. Tender. Soft. Then firmer.

Calhoun appeared a master with lots of practice no doubt and she was a piece of clay in his hands – molding, shaping, creating the woman he thought she was.

The kiss stole her breath and turned her upside down and sideways. Her knees turned to jelly. Maura clutched the front of his shirt and kissed him back. At almost thirty, her first kiss was like a dream. He was a handsome soldier just coming home from a long war. She the woman waiting and longing for him.

As he deepened the kiss, she slipped her arms around his neck, her fingers tangling in his hair. Desperation to get all she could before he turned away took hold. No matter what happened she had this moment, and no one could take it from her. This was hers. Forever.

At last, he released her. 'I'm sorry. You may hate me, but I
had to do that.'

She inhaled a deep breath. 'All my life I wondered what it
would feel like to kiss a man. You're my first and probably my
last, but I wouldn't trade it for all the world's riches. It's even
more than I thought it would be.' She met his smoldering gaze.
'Thank you, Calhoun.'

'If I have anything to do with it, this kiss won't be your last.
I have a little more time before I'm ready to leave.'

Panic rose anew at the mention of him riding out. 'You could
stay. We'll protect you. Max. Emma and me. The sisters. What
about Juliette and the children?'

'It's not a matter of protecting me. It's harm coming to all of
you that keeps me awake at night.' He lifted a strand of her hair
and rubbed it between his fingers. 'I wish things were different,
wish I could be the man you see in me.'

'I've lived my whole life with people wanting to hurt me. It
isn't anything new.'

He cupped her jaw and his words were full of regret. 'I should
get back to my room.' Then he reached for his walking stick
he'd propped against the chair.

Not trusting herself to speak, she nodded and slipped an arm
around his waist. 'Lean on me.'

They took a slow path across the compound. Thoughts were
a jumble inside Maura's head. The kiss, losing him . . . and the
danger she'd face in the next two hours.

Winning and losing. Maybe while succeeding in one area,
she'd lose something precious in another.

His lean body brushed against Maura's hip and leg with
each step, delicious friction that aroused each nerve ending to
a fever pitch. She found the closeness almost more than she
could bear.

Relief swept through her when they reached his quarters and
she got him inside.

'What do you want me to do? Remove your boots?'

'No, I'll sleep in them, so we don't have to go through the
task of putting them back on tomorrow. Besides, I want to be
ready in case I need to go out again.' He pinched the bridge of
his nose. 'Don't look at me like that. Look, if you get into trouble,

I'm coming, and I don't care if I break stitches open or it harelips the governor or I end up in a pine box. Got that?'

'You're determined to kill yourself. I'll be fine. But if you want to sleep in your boots, I won't argue. I know when to shut up. Goodnight.' She had to get out and break this spell that had hold of her before she did or said something she'd regret.

'Maura?' He took the step separating them. 'Wait.'

She took slow, shallow breaths that seemed to hang in her chest and couldn't have moved if she'd wanted. His dark gaze speaking of things they shouldn't, his movements were those of a wild animal stalking its prey.

Dear God, this man made her yearn for impossible things long denied her.

'Calhoun,' she whispered.

Not saying a word, he slid a hand behind her neck and lowered his lips. The scent of the raw land swept through the open door and blended with the smell of the coffee he'd had at supper. One hand slipped down, skimming the side of her body to her waist.

She closed her eyes as her breasts crushed against his chest drawing a soft gasp. Even though part of her knew nothing would come of this, she clung to him tightly. A larger part said maybe this time would be different. Maybe it wasn't too late.

Maybe he'd take a chance on her.

Calhoun lifted his head, ending the kiss. 'Lady, I don't want to let you go.'

He tightened his arms around her, wrapping her in a warm cocoon. She rested her head against his chest, listening to the soft beat of his heart. 'Me either, but I need to go.'

Muttering a soft curse, he released her and took a half step back. 'When you return, I want to hear what happened. I'll be unable to sleep until I know you're safe. Promise me.'

'If I have the boy, I don't know that I can, but I'll send Uncle Max.' Maura turned and hurried out while she had the strength.

Outside, she took a big gulp of air and stood looking up at the starry sky. Her head whirled with so many conflicting thoughts. She touched her fingers to her lips and smiled. No matter what happened from here, just once she knew how it felt to be kissed and held.

Uncle Max stepped from his living quarters and she put aside her thoughts.

She had work to do. A young boy's life depended on her.

Straightening her shoulders, she joined Max. His hair hanging long beneath his hat. Marveling that he was sober for once, they strode to the barn to prepare.

Though it neared midnight, the streets of San Antonio were still alive, especially around the saloons. She and Max took the horses into a dark alley out of sight. Maura wore a pair of trousers they'd found in one of the dusty trunks left by the previous occupants and a man's jacket. She'd pinned up her hair and added a hat. The disguise wouldn't fool anyone in the daylight, but she felt certain the night would hide her womanly curves.

They tied the horses to a rail and crept along the back wall of the Golden Spoke Saloon. They hadn't gone far before they spotted the wagon that held the iron cage. A tarp covered it but couldn't block the sobs coming from it.

Maura's heart broke. How could anyone do this to another human? She was trying to pull herself into the wagon when Max held her back.

'Not yet. They'll catch us,' he whispered.

Though it took all her strength to leave, she knew he was right. As Calhoun had said, good timing was the key to success. They had to be smart.

As they made their way, pressing to the side of the building, she couldn't get those sobs out of her head. They had to free him, or she wouldn't be able to live with herself.

Back with the horses, Max patted her shoulder. 'Patience, girl. I'll go see what I can find out in the Golden Spoke Saloon where I first ran into that fellow. I'll try to find out where he sleeps.'

'OK.' She grabbed his arm. 'Please remember why we've come.'

He squinted at her. 'Don't you trust me?'

'To be honest, it's a little difficult, Uncle. Don't let me down but more importantly don't let that boy down.'

With a nod, he walked away. Worry set in as she sat down on some empty crates to wait. *Please, let him stay sober and they could do what they came for.* The saloon would close at midnight.

A million doubts circled in her head. Maybe it would've been better to try the rescue while the din from the saloons would've covered the noise.

The clock in the town square gonged twelve times. Where was Max?

She walked to the end of the alley and peered around the corner. No sign of him. A night watchman began to make his rounds. She shrank back into the dark shadows. Watching. Waiting. Praying.

Somewhere down the alley came a crash. She almost jumped out of her skin. Two cats became embroiled in a squalling, hissing fight. The horses skittered nervously reflecting her own apprehension.

Maura chewed her lip as two black cats shot past her and out of the alley. Minutes passed as drunks began to stagger out. Still no sign of Max.

A rock sat in the pit of her stomach. Max had failed her. Rescuing the kid was up to her. She sucked in a deep breath of air and tried to remember everything Calhoun had said, making sure she had the short piece of steel Max had brought. Then she untied the horses and led them around to where the wagon and cage were parked.

Ice trickled down her back. The wagon and cage were gone.

EIGHTEEN

Panic burst inside her like jagged lightning.

Maura's heart thudded against her ribs and she struggled to breathe as she turned to look in all directions. The faint tracks of a wagon leading out of town caught her notice. The boy's captor must've gotten spooked and hightailed it.

Her spirits sagging, she rode back to the Golden Spoke. It looked deserted. Dismounting, she secured the horses to the hitching rail and adjusted her pants, then moved to the batwing doors and peered inside the dismal place. One oil lamp with a grimy globe sitting in the middle of a table offered dim light. Except for that, dark shadows filled every nook and cranny of the interior.

Two men sat playing cards, a whiskey bottle at their side. If Uncle Max was inside, he was beyond the weak rays of the lamp.

Had he gotten drunk and passed out on the floor? She stood trying to decide what to do.

Finally, a deep breath helped Maura find her courage. Squaring her shoulders, she pushed inside.

The sound of her footsteps drew dark stares that made her shiver.

'We're closed! Cain't you see?' The speaker with a large cigar in the corner of his mouth snapped. 'What'cha want?'

Though she wanted to run, Maura forced herself to stay rooted. She remembered to change her voice to a deeper timbre. 'Looking for someone – Max Taggart.'

'Ain't seen him, kid.' The cigar smoker removed the lit tobacco and blew a smoke ring.

His well-dressed companion leaned back sipping from a thick glass. 'I saw him leave with that fellow getting rich showing off his Wild Boy. Neither one was feeling any pain.'

Shock rippled through her. What did Max have in mind? Or was he too drunk to even know? Immense disappointment and what felt like the deepest betrayal she'd ever known brought stinging tears to her eyes. Maura blinked hard.

'Did you happen to overhear where they were going?' she asked in a quiet voice.

'No. Sorry.'

Her legs trembling, she thanked them and left. A moment later, she climbed on to her gelding. Gripping the reins of the other two horses, she went back and picked up the tracks, following them from town.

About a mile down the road, she spied the lumbering wagon, the cage clearly visible in the light of the moon. The closer she got, the louder the men's singing became.

Coming up alongside, she pulled her pistol, pointing it at the driver. 'Stop!'

The man was a sorry-looking sight with a buffalo hide thrown around his shoulders and a stovepipe hat perched on his head. Long, shaggy hair fell down his back. 'What the h-h-hell?' he asked in a drunken slur.

'Take another drink, Rooster. Maybe she'll go away.' Max passed the man a half-empty whiskey bottle.

She stared at Max, anger and disgust dripping from every word. 'I said stop and I will not tell you again. If you don't, I'll shoot you both.'

Rooster turned her way and tumbled off the seat into the floor of the wagon box.

Max took the reins and pulled. When the wagon halted, he jumped down and came to her, keeping his voice low. 'I know how this looks but I'm not drunk. I wormed my way into Rooster's confidence and have been plying him with drinks the last several hours. He's near the passing-out stage and we can get the key for the cage.'

In truth, Max didn't sound or smell drunk. Relief washed away the last of her doubts.

'I didn't know what had happened to you and imagined the worst.'

'Sorry. I couldn't come to tell you anything.'

'Wha'cha doin', Max?' Rooster hollered, climbing back on to the seat. 'Let's sing.'

'Be right there. I have some more whiskey.'

'Tha's good,' Rooster slurred.

'What's the plan, Max?' Maura asked.

'I'll get him from the wagon and say we need to camp here. I'll work on getting the key from his pocket. He's just about there.'

Max should know if anyone did. Maura patted his arm. 'You shouldn't give me such a scare.'

With a nod, Max went back to his new friend Rooster and a moment later, helped him from the wagon. Rooster seemed to have legs of thin willow branches and Max had to keep picking him up by the collar. Maura finally had to get on the other side to prop Rooster up. They found a path through a mesquite thicket lining the road. While her uncle built a fire and got Rooster seated on the ground with the bottle, Maura returned to the wagon. She climbed into the back and pushed the tarp aside. Round, terrified eyes stared at her.

'Don't be afraid. I'm Maura Taggart but the children I help care for call me Miss Mo. I've come to free you. Do you have a name?' she asked softly.

No answer. She knew he could speak because he'd called for his mama earlier. She sat down and began to talk about everything she could think of while handing him bits of the food she'd brought. As expected, the boy was starving. Who knew if he'd had anything to speak of for days?

His voice, low and raspy came quite unexpected. 'Tully. I Tully.'

He had a thick tongue and pronounced his name as Thully. In addition, he also had thick lips. Her heart ached for him and could imagine the jeering and name-calling he'd had to suffer.

'I'm so happy to meet you, Tully. I'm going to get you out of here. My Uncle Max is trying to find the key to the cage.'

'Scared.' He wiped his nose on his sleeve.

'It won't be much longer. I'm going to take you where you're safe and loved.'

'Mama?'

'Honey, who is your mama? If you can tell me, I'll take you there. She must be awfully worried about you.'

'Worry?'

His comprehension seemed a bit off.

'She's probably wondering where you are.'

Tully shook his head. 'No!'

'Honey, I'll explain what happened. You're not in trouble. No part of this is your fault.'

'People laugh. Spit. Call names.' Tully wiped his eyes with the heel of his hand.

'I'm very sorry. People are mean.' She moved closer but he shrank against the back bars of the cage. Where was Max? He needed to hurry. 'Tully, when we get the key, will you come with me? I brought a horse for you.'

The boy plucked at a hole in his dirty shirt. 'I'm scared.'

'But you know I won't hurt you, don't you? I want to take you somewhere safe.'

'No safe,' he mumbled.

'It probably doesn't seem like it right now, but I have a place where no one will ever hurt again. And there are lots of kids to play with. We'll work to get you to your mother.'

Tully rested his head on his knees. His clothes were nothing but rags and so filthy. He probably hadn't had a bath or washed his hair since he'd been taken. But then the sorry excuse for a man who'd captured him had wanted Tully to look as scary as possible. He was selling an image of an untamed animal. She had no idea of his age, but guessed thirteen or fourteen.

Maura was about to go in search of Max when he appeared.

'Sorry. It took a while to get the key.' Max handed it to her. 'Hurry and let's get out of here before someone comes along. I have a bad feeling about this.'

The night air seemed alive with strange sounds. Something was coming. Something big and dark and scary.

'I agree.' She stood and took the key and held her breath. It fit into the lock but wouldn't turn. She kept trying but it wouldn't open. 'Are you sure this is the right one?'

'Girl, I ain't sure of nothing, but it was the only one I found. Want me to try?'

'Just a minute.' She took it out and slid it in again and this time it turned. 'Got it.'

'Good. Help the boy over here.'

'No.' Tully shook his head, his eyes round. He huddled in a corner of his iron jail, gasping for air. 'No. Scared.'

The cage was so small she couldn't get inside with him. Chills went through her at having to live in these tiny confines and never being able to stand up.

All she could do was offer him a hand which she did. 'Honey, don't be frightened. I'm Miss Mo. Remember?'

'Miss Mo,' he repeated thickly.

'Yes. Come on now.'

'OK.'

She took his hand and led him to Max. 'This is my uncle and he's going to help you down. Trust him not to hurt you.'

Tully shrank back into Maura, trembling. 'No.'

Uncle Max took a harmonica from his pocket and blew gently on it. 'Does that sound nice? I'll let you play it, but you'll have to come here, son. You'll be safe.'

'Trick.'

Maura shook her head and spoke gently. 'No, Tully. It's not a trick. Max is my friend. He cares for children.'

After staring with wide eyes for what seemed like forever, the boy edged closer and took the harmonica. A smile formed. 'Pretty.'

While Tully ran his mouth across the small reeds, Max lifted him down. 'There you go. The harmonica is yours for being a big, brave boy.'

Tully nodded, still grinning.

'Let's get on the horse now,' Maura prodded. 'Time to go.'

Max had just boosted him up into the saddle when riders galloped out of the darkness from the direction of San Antonio. 'Go, Maura. Don't worry about me. My life ain't worth a tinker's dam anyway. You have those kids to care for.'

'But—'

'Now! Get the boy to safety.'

'Halt!' barked a voice.

'What's the trouble?' Max asked. 'We were helping the owner of this wagon.'

Rooster staggered toward the riders. 'They're robbing me! Stop 'em! Thieves!'

Fear inched up Maura's spine. She reached for the gun in her pocket. She was not leaving here without Tully. If it took a fight, so be it. 'Look at him. He's nothing but a drunk. He doesn't have anything of value. We were helping him after he tumbled out of the wagon.'

'That's the Wild Boy!' one of the riders shouted. 'They're stealing him.'

'You there with the boy, get off your horse!' The moonlight glinted on the badge the rider wore.

Maura swallowed hard. What could she do?

All of a sudden, Max slapped her gelding's flank and she took off, gripping Tully's reins as tightly as she could.

Weapons fired and bullets whizzed past her ducked head. 'Uncle Max!' she screamed.

Behind her, guns blazed, and icy fear raced the length of her, making every hair stand up. Max was right in the middle of it all. She had to go back. She couldn't leave him to face the trouble alone.

Yet, she had Tully to take care of. She'd made him a promise that she'd get him to safety and she had to keep it. This was the way Max wanted it.

'I won't desert you, Uncle Max,' she whispered through the tears running down her face. She'd come back once she got Tully into the sisters' hands.

But if her uncle died thinking he was worthless, unloved . . . The thought hung inside her.

She didn't know how she'd live with herself.

NINETEEN

When Maura reached San Antonio, instinct told her to skirt the town. It would take longer but was far safer. She pulled behind a deserted barn falling into ruin and dismounted, going to Tully. 'Are you all right? Did you get hurt?'

'Sleepy.' He rubbed his eyes.

It was a miracle he'd stayed on the horse and must've learned to ride from someone.

She patted his arm. 'I know. I'm sorry. Just a little farther and I'll put you to bed.' Her mind raced. Calhoun could sit with him while she went back to see what had happened to Max. In fact, she'd just take him to Calhoun instead of where the children slept. Yes, that sounded best. That settled, she climbed back into the saddle and they went on.

It must've neared two o'clock in the morning by the time they arrived. She went straight to Calhoun's quarters, but he opened the door before she could dismount.

'I was about to go after my horse.' He ran a hand through his hair. 'You should've been back long before now. And where is Max?'

'Let us get inside. Tully is worn out. I have lots to tell you.' She helped the boy down and led him through the door to the bed. 'Lay down and get some sleep.' After he stretched out, Maura gently kissed his forehead and covered him.

Tully was a dirty mess and no telling at the bugs that were crawling in his hair, but a bath would have to wait until morning. She turned to sit at the table with Calhoun.

'No.' Tully grabbed her hand, stark fear in his eyes. 'No.'

'Honey, I'm just going to sit at the table. I'm not leaving. I promise.'

'Scared.' His grip was strong.

'OK. I'll sit here on the bed.' She glanced at Calhoun. 'Want to pull your chair over here?'

'Sure thing. The boy's really scared.' He quietly brought the chair next to the bed. He looked as weary as she felt. He laid a light hand on the kid's arm. 'Rest easy, Tully. No one will hurt you here. I stake my life on that.'

Tully gave a slight nod and closed his eyes.

'He's been through so much and doesn't trust many people.' She rested a hand on the boy's wild hair. 'It took me a while to win him over, however I fear not enough. I think all his anxiety and mistrust will come back tomorrow after breakfast when I get him in a bath and wash his hair.'

Calhoun nodded. 'He does resemble a wild boy with all that hair.' His eyes darkened with worry. 'Now tell me everything and where's Max?'

'Nothing went like we planned, and I think Uncle Max is dead.' She trembled when Calhoun took her palm in his big hand. He made her feel safe and that everything would be all right. A bit of hope began to build. She really didn't know anything yet. 'But let me start at the beginning.'

She went back over their arrival in town, the long wait, the worry that Max had gotten drunk.

'By the time I caught up with the wagon, I was boiling mad. I let him have it. But when he told me it was all a scheme to get the key to the cage, I felt an inch tall.'

Calhoun nodded. 'That was smart of Max and really made it easier.'

'But then the key didn't want to work. Like I said, nothing went as planned, especially when the sheriff with three or four riders came on us and accused us of stealing, threatened to put us in jail.' She glanced at Tully. He'd finally gone to sleep, probably from sheer exhaustion.

Maura finished the rest of the terrifying ordeal. 'I didn't care about myself. I would've gladly died to save Tully. They were not going to get him. But poor Max.' She met Calhoun's eyes. 'He sacrificed himself for us.' A sob rose. 'And now, he may be lying in a pool of blood.'

Stifling back a sob, she pulled her hand free, got to her feet, and went to the door to look out into the blackness. 'Dear, sweet Max, who thinks he's worthless. I intended to leave Tully and go back for him, but the boy is far too terrified and I haven't the heart to add more.'

'Help me on one of those horses out there. I'm all you got.' Calhoun came up behind her and rested his hands on her shoulders. 'Once I get in the saddle, I'll be OK.'

The idea, too dangerous and risky to even consider, had merit. At least they might find out something.

She turned to face him. 'How? You can barely walk with help. I hate to think what will happen when you're alone. Let me go wake Emma. Maybe she can make the ride.'

'I don't need to walk. The horse will do that for me.'

'And what if you have to get off for some reason?'

'Then I'll figure something out. Look, I count Max as a friend, and I want to do this.' The cleft in Calhoun's chin deepened with the stubborn tilt. 'He'd do the same for me.'

'I know.' Sighing, she glanced at the bed. It would be better if she went. Sure, Tully was sleeping now, but if he startled awake and she wasn't here, he'd go into a full-blown panic. 'Let me see what Emma says before we consider anything else. Will you stay with Tully?'

'I'll do whatever you need.'

'I won't be but a minute. Hopefully, the boy will sleep.' Maura stepped out into the night and ran across the compound to Emma's bed.

But it was vacant. She turned to see her sister in the doorway, wiping her mouth. 'What's wrong, Emma? You look like a horse kicked you.'

'I don't know. I'm real sick.'

She weaved on her feet and Maura hurried to help her back to bed. 'I don't think it was anything you ate, or we'll all be sick. Did you eat anything else after supper?'

'No.' Emma crawled under the covers and huddled in the warmth. 'I'm puking my guts out, have chills and think I have a fever. I hope I'm not contagious.'

'We can't take a chance. We'll keep the children away from you.' Maura had second thoughts about telling her sister about Max and decided it would wait. She smoothed back Emma's hair and felt her forehead. 'You're burning up. Stay in bed and I'll check on you later.'

'So cold. I'm sorry to let you down, Maura. You must need something to come at this hour.'

'It can wait. Get some sleep.' Maura gave her a last worried look and went back to Calhoun.

She stared into his eyes. 'Emma's sick and I have no choice. OK. Finding out something about Uncle Max is more important.'

'Good.' He gently kissed her cheek and reached for his gun belt, strapping it on. 'I'm ready.'

'You need a jacket. The night has turned chilly. I'll see if Max has one in his quarters.'

'Be quick.' He reached for his walking stick. 'Let me lean on you.'

Glancing to see if Tully still slept, they went out to the horses. With Calhoun pulling and her pushing, he got into the saddle. He released a deep groan followed by an oath. His face looked pasty and for a moment, she debated whether to call off the ride. When the pain seemed to pass, she ran to Max's room. As luck would have it, an old jacket lay on his trunk. It was torn and dirty but warm. She jerked it up and ran back.

'Got one.' She handed it up to him.

'Thanks. I'll be back as soon as I can.' Calhoun waited for her to secure his rifle in the empty scabbard then trotted off.

'Come back safe,' she whispered. 'Please.'

'Miss Mo! Miss Mo!' The anguished cry came from inside. Tully had woken.

'Just a minute,' she called. 'I'm right here.'

The boy grabbed her as soon as she opened the door. Tears streamed down his face. 'Tully scared.'

Maura put her arms around him and patted his back. 'I didn't leave you. I wouldn't do that.'

'I didn't see you anywhere.'

It took a while to settle him down enough to go back to sleep. Maura sat on the side of the bed, her thoughts on Calhoun.

He had to find Max. She'd left him to die alone. Fear gripped her body and her mouth was dry with anxiety.

Calhoun rode through the night, teeth gritted against the jarring pain of the horse's strides. The days of inactivity had made him weak. He adjusted in the saddle and rode on with one thought, one single purpose in mind. He could do this. He wouldn't let Maura and Max down.

The ten miles to San Antonio dragged and Calhoun wanted to go at a full gallop except he knew he couldn't take the punishment. Thoughts whirled as he mulled over what to do once he reached town. If Max was dead, Calhoun doubted they'd bring his body in this fast. No, they'd wait for daylight. Maybe he'd survived and been arrested in which case the jail would be a likely place to look, although far too risky. Calhoun's best bet was to find the sorry man who'd captured the boy.

It seemed probable that he had remained with the wagon. There again, the sheriff wouldn't even bother with Tully's kidnapper until morning and he'd sobered. Calhoun set his jaw. He'd welcome a chat with the no-good piece of crow bait. Maura said his name was Rooster. Calhoun snorted. About right. He turned his collar up against the chilly breeze.

The town appeared asleep when he rode in at last. A lamp burned through the window of the sheriff's office but it appeared the only one on the street. He located the doctor's office at the end of the block but it, too, was dark which meant Max hadn't needed treatment.

But was he dead? That question remained stuck in Calhoun's head.

The horse clip-clopped down the quiet street and Calhoun breathed a sigh of relief when they reached the dark landscape on the other side of town. No one had woken or hollered at him.

Following Maura's directions, he rode until he saw the empty wagon with the team of horses attached still sitting on the hard-packed road with the empty cage. The sight made him want to throw up. What kind of man could've locked a boy up in that? Only a heartless one.

Another horse was tied to the side of the wagon and Calhoun bet it was Max's.

He rode his gelding up and down the side of the road and around the wagon, but there was no sign of Max. What could've happened to him?

Flickers from a low fire showed through the mesquites lining one side of the wagon. He'd have to look over there. Carefully moving his right leg over the saddle horn, he slid to the ground then reached for his stick which Maura had secured to the horse.

Although he found a path that led through the thorny mesquites, moving slowly across the uneven ground without breaking his neck seemed to take forever. At last he stared at the heartless owner of the wagon and the empty whiskey bottles lying around. Sickening disgust flared.

He poked Rooster with his stick. 'Wake up!'

Rooster batted the air, muttered something and rolled over.

'Get up, Rooster!' Calhoun poked him again. 'Get up and tell me what I need to know.'

'W-what's t-t-that?' He made no move to obey.

Calhoun reached down and grabbed him by the collar, pulling Rooster to a sitting position. His top hat came off and his hair resembled a rat's nest of long, dirty, brown strands. 'Tell me one thing and I'll let you go back to sleep.'

'W-who's R-r-ooster?'

'That's your name, you fool! Although I'm sure you're called many others.' Calhoun ignored his leg that was giving out fast and the pain shooting into his hip. 'Tell me where Max is. Tell me and I'll leave you alone. Where is Max?'

'Max?' Rooster's forehead wrinkled. He reached for one of the whiskey bottles and held it upside down, shaking it, but not a drop came out. Shrugging, he dropped it and prepared to lie down again.

'Oh no you don't.' Calhoun caught him. 'I'll ask you one more time. Where. Is. Max? What happened to him? Tell me or I'll take my gun out and shoot you simply for the principle of the thing. And because you deserve it after what you put that boy through. You oughta be horsewhipped.'

'Max stole Tully,' Rooster mumbled. 'Took him.'

'So would a dozen other men with a speck of decency.' Calhoun shook him. 'Remember the guns and all that shooting?'

'It was loud. Hurt my ears.'

'Max was here. So was a woman. Remember?'

'Two men.'

Of course. At least Rooster remembered Maura was wearing trousers and a man's hat.

'OK. Two men were here. The shooting started. Do you recall that?'

'Yep. They stole my boy.'

'Tully didn't belong to you. You took him. Remember?' Calhoun eyed him carefully. He might find out where Rooster had gotten Tully.

'He was in a yard in front of a h-house and I asked him if he wanted to see a p-p-puppy. I d-didn't have a dog but he came and I grabbed him.' Rooster reached out, opening and closing his fist. He hiccupped. 'I locked h-him in the cage.'

'And you should've been arrested. You disgust me.' Calhoun gave up and turned loose of his hold on Rooster. The man toppled over like a rotted tree in a lightning storm.

'M-Max is d-dead,' Rooster mumbled drunkenly.

Cold invaded Calhoun's limbs and his breath hung in his chest. 'What's that you said, Rooster? Is Max dead?'

'Yep. He w-was my friend.'

How was he going to tell Maura her uncle didn't make it? This would kill her. She was Max's biggest champion. She loved him like a father.

Calhoun stared at the stinking, repulsive man and finally said, 'No, Max Taggart was no friend of yours.' Then he asked again, 'Are you for *sure* he's not alive? There's no chance he didn't escape?'

'Dead. Dead. Dead.' Rooster rolled on to his back and began to snore.

TWENTY

Sick at heart, Calhoun stumbled back to his horse. He couldn't accept the fact that Max was no longer of this world. Max would never finish the secret project he was working on. How in the hell was Calhoun going to tell Maura and Emma? And those kids. Alphabet, or rather Alphie, adored the old coot.

Calhoun had asked Max why Alphie had latched on to him. Max had grinned and said, 'Because I'm so lovable.'

The man really was, despite his affinity for liquor. The three nuns thought he hung the moon and Sister Angela giggled when he paid her any attention. Calhoun had seen that at supper when Max had called her Angie and winked.

A lump blocked his throat. Sick at heart, he rested his forehead against the saddle. How was he going to get back on the horse? Or face Maura. Or face another loss. Again.

The people at Heaven's Door Orphanage had become like family. And in such a short time at that.

Moonlight glinted on the strap iron cage in the wagon. He hated that thing with a passion. If he could just get it off, he'd put Rooster in it and lock it tight.

The brush behind him rattled, alerting him. The gun firmly in hand, he turned, prepared to face the threat, whatever it was. But rising from the mass of dead foliage was not what he expected.

'What are you doing here, Calhoun?' Max asked. The man was beaten to a bloody pulp. His long hair streamed down like wet straw and his face suggested it had been run through a meat grinder.

'I was planning your funeral, if you must know.' Calhoun grinned at his friend. 'I'd offer you a hand and hug you, but I'd probably land on my butt. Couldn't you have picked a place that wasn't so rocky?'

Max laughed. 'You were worried about me.'

'Hell yes, I was. Thanks to your drunk friend over there spouting that you were dead.'

'You can't believe anything Rooster says.' Max moved to Calhoun and gave him an awkward hug. 'I think you were standing here trying to figure out how to get back on your horse.'

With a nod, Calhoun admitted it. 'And how I could get that cage there off the wagon and lock that boy's captor in it.'

'Yeah. There's that.' The kidding stopped. Max wiped a trickle of blood from his mouth with the back of his hand. 'I'd sure like to do that. I reckon Maura made it back with the kid OK?'

'She did. That boy is in pitiful shape and clinging to her. She couldn't come back to check on you and Emma is sick, so she sent me – the cripple.'

'Cripple my big toe.' Max laughed. 'Tell that to someone who don't know you.'

'What happened and how did you wind up in the brush?'

'After they beat the living daylights out of me, I pretended to be unconscious. One said he thought I was dead, so they decided to leave me here until morning and come back with a wagon. They said maybe the wild animals would take care of me. They were a lazy bunch.' Max wiped blood from his mouth. 'I thought they might come back or someone else, so I crawled into the bushes. Must've gone to sleep.'

'You are one lucky man, Max. So how about it?'

'About what? You lost me, Calhoun.'

'If there's a rope in that wagon, we can pull the cage off with the horse.'

'I'll certainly find out.' Max moved unsteadily over the rocks to the wagon and climbed up. A second later, he lifted a coil of rope.

It didn't take long to pull the cage off, then they tied the rope around Rooster and dragged him through the mesquites with him hollering and screaming.

'Hush that bellyaching and take your medicine like a man.' Calhoun found a great deal of satisfaction in what they were doing. 'That boy you locked up like an animal has a lot more guts than you do. You sound like a dying bull. When you sober up, you'll come to like your new home. I promise.'

'We'll tack a note in town at the saloon telling someone to come save your sorry hide.' Max finished pushing Rooster inside and snapped the lock. 'It might take them a while to get you out though, because we're taking the key.'

'You can't do that! This is against the law!' Rooster screamed, sounding quite sober already.

'So is capturing that boy and making him live in this cage. You took people's money and let them taunt the kid.' Calhoun reached through the bars and grabbed Rooster's shirt, jerking him close. 'Think about that when the sun bears down tomorrow and every day after for as long as you live.'

'I took good care of Tully!' Rooster screamed in defiance.

Anger gripped Calhoun and he regretted the bars between him and that lying sack of manure. 'Don't say another word or you'll get worse than this. I'd like to beat you within an inch of your sorry life.'

'And if the thought even crosses your mind to snatch another kid and do this again, we'll come after you,' Max added. 'You can take that as a promise.'

Rooster began to sob. 'You can't leave me here like this. I might die.'

'Better you than that innocent boy.' Calhoun's words held the kind of deadly calm that comes when a man wants to wound far deeper but has to be satisfied until he can do different. He leaned against Max and the man boosted him on to the horse. Then Max untied his mount from the wagon, and they set off with Rooster's yells trailing them until they got out of range.

They rode in silence back to town. Finding a scrap of paper, he wrote a note with Rooster's whereabouts and Max tacked it to the saloon door.

As they trotted off, Calhoun voiced what was probably in both their minds. 'Max, you know they're going to come looking for you.'

'I figure so. The sheriff knows where to find me.' Max released a sigh. 'I hate that I might bring trouble to Maura's door.'

'We'll caution her to keep Tully hidden. And just because the sheriff comes to call, doesn't mean we have to let him in. He has no reason to search the place.' Calhoun would stand shoulder to shoulder with Maura and give his all to protect Tully. There would be no thoughts of leaving until Maura, the women, and those kids were safe. When he could ride better, he could still scout around some during the daytime and try to first find Donavan then his twin's body. He wouldn't leave until the orphanage was out of danger. He'd draw Donavan away from them. He wouldn't rest until he did.

Max leaned on the saddle horn to look at him. 'Calhoun, the riders that rode upon Maura and me when we were saving that boy was a posse. They were looking for Donavan. I heard them talking about a killing at one of the ranches around here. The outlaw did it.'

'Nothing he does surprises me.'

'That's not all. I did some scouting yesterday and found a campsite within view of Heaven's Door. I'm pretty sure it was that gang. They're watching us so be careful and keep your gun handy.'

'I always do, Max. Thanks for the information. I'm leaving soon.'

'Figured that.' Max tested his arm and released a groan. 'Don't see as you have much choice.'

Neither did he, but it didn't make it any easier. He'd sooner face a gallows than leave the place that brought such peace to his weary soul.

The black sky had begun to lighten by the time they reached the old mission. Maura hurried out to meet them. 'Thank goodness.'

Max turned toward her. She froze. 'You're hurt. Did they shoot you?'

'No. I took a beating though. They would've killed me if I hadn't pretended to be dead.' He dismounted. 'I probably look a bloody mess, but I'll live.'

Maura hugged him. 'I hated to leave you and if it hadn't been for Tully I'd have fought by your side.'

'I didn't want you hurt, girl.' Max stretched. 'If you don't mind, I need to get to bed.'

Calhoun watched the pair, satisfaction bursting in his chest. Max parted ways and he finally dismounted and hobbled inside with Maura.

'Let me check your stitches. I hope you didn't bust any open again.' She pulled out a chair.

'I'm fine.'

'Can you let me decide that? Sit.'

Finally giving in, he collapsed on to the seat. 'How is Tully?' He spoke in low tones so as not to wake the boy.

'He slept off and on. Startles awake in a state of panic.' Her gaze went to the sleeping form. 'I was right in not leaving him. Where did you find Uncle Max?'

'There where you left him just as he said. He'd crawled deep into the brush and lost consciousness.' He brushed her face with his fingers, mostly to assure himself she was real. It had been a long night and his thoughts were muddled. They sat down at the small table. 'We got a little bit of revenge for Tully.' He told her about stuffing the man inside the cage and locking it.

Her eyes glowed. 'I'm glad. Rooster deserves all that and more for what he did. I hope it makes a difference, but I doubt he learns from it.'

'Those kinds never do.' He yawned. 'Are you finished? I told you I'm fine.'

'No worse for wear. You're exhausted. Let me get Tully up so you can have your bed.'

'No, I'll stretch out on the floor,' he protested. 'I'm getting soft from sleeping in a bed.'

Just then Tully rolled over, muttered something, then sat straight up. 'Miss Mo!'

Maura hurried to him. 'I'm right here. You're safe.'

'Scared.'

'I know but it'll pass.' She rested a hand on his hair. 'I'll bet you're hungry. Want to go help me milk the cow?'

'Yes. You won't put me in a box?'

'Honey, you'll never have to be locked in a box again if I have anything to do with it.'

Calhoun watched Tully's eyes light up and an ache filled his chest. The boy had missed so much while Rooster held him, but Maura would soon have him running and playing with the other children. Given time they might find his kin and reunite them.

Maura pulled back the covers and Tully got up. 'We have a lot to do today, young man. After you eat, we'll bathe you and wash your hair, then get you in clean clothes. The other children will be excited to meet you.'

Tully nodded but seemed unsure about the prospect of fitting

in with the others. He'd be shy to begin with. Calhoun didn't
know where Maura was going to find anything to fit the boy. He
was much bigger than the others yet his and Max's clothes would
be too large. Maybe after a little sleep he could go into town to
the mercantile. He needed some things for himself as well.

'I'll change the bed for you before we go, Calhoun,' she said.
'You can't sleep with the bugs.'

'Just take those off and I'll sleep on the bare mattress for now.
You have plenty to do.'

She chewed her lip. 'If you're sure you don't mind.'

'I'm sure.' He placed his hands on her shoulders. 'Go take
care of Tully. I'll be fine.' He paused a moment. 'Maura, keep
an eye out for the sheriff. I suspect he'll be around looking for
Max. And Tully. Might be best for the boy to stay out of sight.'

That spine of steel straightened. 'Don't you worry. We won't
let that man in here, badge or no badge. Emma and I will see to
that. Tully isn't going anywhere.' Her expression was that of a
warrior and the sheriff would have his hands full if he messed
with her.

He chuckled. 'I believe you.'

She took an extra blanket from the trunk and laid it on the
bare mattress ticking. Picking up the dirty bedding, she took
Tully's hand. 'Let's go eat some breakfast. Do you want
something to eat now, Calhoun?'

'No. Let me sleep a while.'

Saying she'd check on him later she went out the door with
Tully in tow. The quiet surrounded Calhoun. He stumbled to
the bed.

Maura led Tully to the makeshift barn and lifted the milk pail.
'We're going to milk the cow. Have you ever done it before?'

'No. I like cows.'

'Good.' She set the pail in place and moved a low stool over.
'Watch me then I'll let you try.'

As she worked, she talked to the boy, explaining every aspect
of milking and feeding the cow. 'We have to take care of the
animals.'

Tully nodded. 'Cows are my friend. And horses.'

'Yes, they are.' She filled the pail half full then let Tully try his hand. At first, he squirted milk everywhere but soon got the hang of it and even laughed some. This was exactly what would help heal him and she'd see that he got all the chances he needed.

They took the milk into the kitchen where Sisters Angela and Bernadette were busy cooking. 'We have a new addition. This is Tully.' Maura put an arm around his shoulders. 'He's had a rough time and needs lots of love.'

Both women stopped what they were doing and gave him a hug, clucking over him like mother hens. At first, he clung to Maura but soon warmed under the attention and sat at the table. He didn't seem to mind that they spoke French and grinned through it all. Sister Bernadette sliced off a bit of hot bread for him which he scarfed down in nothing flat.

Maura wiped butter from his mouth. 'I'm going to give him a bath after breakfast and wash his hair. But we need some clean clothes. Any ideas, ladies?'

Both nuns eyed him and answered no. Then Bernadette pointed to Maura's trousers. 'Might those?'

'Yes, maybe. They might be a little large, but we can make do until we get his washed.' She pushed back Tully's hair. 'I expect to have a visitor this morning. Or maybe several and I'd like one of you to answer the door. Talk in French and play dumb. No English. They're looking for Tully and I will not turn that boy over to them.'

'*Oui*,' Sister Bernadette answered, winking.

'Have either of you seen Emma? She was very ill last night.'

Sister Angela nodded. 'I took hot tea. Better.'

'Oh good. I'll check on her after I help the children to breakfast.'

Shy little Sister Anne-Marie entered with Juliette. Grinning, Tully stared and pointed. 'Baby.'

'This is Sister Anne-Marie and baby Juliette,' Maura explained. 'She's the smallest of our children here. Do you like babies, Tully?'

'Yes. They cry.'

'That about sums it up.' Maura chuckled. 'But not always. Sometimes she laughs.'

'Babies are my friend.'

'I'm glad to know that.'

The other children began running in, anxious to eat and Maura introduced Tully. 'He's going to live with us for a while and I want you all to make him welcome. He's a little shy so take it easy.'

The small gang gathered around him, all talking at once. Panic shot into Tully's eyes. Maura quickly got them seated and he settled down. She helped serve and while they ate, she slipped out to see about Emma.

Her sister sat up when Maura entered. She noted the white face. 'Sister Angela said she brought you some hot tea.' Maura sat on the side of the bed and felt Emma's forehead. 'I don't detect a fever.'

'I'm better. The tea sort of calmed my stomach.'

'Would you like more?'

'In a bit. I don't want to put too much in me.' Worry filled Emma's eyes. 'I feel so badly that I can't help care for the children. I'm putting too much extra work on you and the sisters.'

'Nonsense. We're fine. We can take care of things so quit feeling guilty. You stay in bed and rest.'

'I guess I don't have much choice.'

'No, you don't.' Maura smoothed the covers and told Emma about Tully and their midnight ride. 'They beat Uncle Max something fierce but he's safe now.'

'I'm glad you're both safe. You should've told me what you were doing last night.'

'You had enough on your shoulders just being sick.'

'But poor Calhoun,' Emma moaned. 'He wasn't up to that.'

'I think he's none the worse for wear. I checked his bandages and the wounds are fine. There was no stopping him from going to see about Max.' She told her about the men locking Rooster in the cage.

'Exactly what the man deserved. Good for them.' Emma laid a hand on Maura's. 'You're very brave, Sister. A lot more than me. You did a wonderful thing rescuing that boy. It was so dangerous though. I'm glad I didn't know last night.'

They talked a little more then Maura left to eat and get to the chore of bathing Tully.

Chore it was. Not that she did everything for him. She only hauled and heated the water then left Tully to do it himself and shut the door. He was in there so long she began to worry about him and hollered through the door, relieved to know he was fine. The poor boy was so filthy and left the water a muddy brown.

When he'd finished and was dressed, he opened the door. Maura gasped at the difference and the big smile he wore that stretched from ear to ear. 'Good,' he said.

A lump blocked Maura's throat. The boy appreciated the smallest things more than they did. Everything had been denied him, even the most basic of needs.

She covered the threat of tears by meandering around him. 'The pants are a little big, but the length is OK. You'll soon be as tall as I am. I suspect you'll fill them out better after a few meals.' She stopped to roll up the sleeves that hung past his hands. One of the sisters had found the shirt, in addition to a pair of long johns in another old trunk.

Since learning of many assaults and raids on the mission, they could only assume the owners of the clothing had met with death. But Maura gave thanks to God for providing for their needs. The three sisters were teaching her the importance of having a grateful heart.

Although she'd not quite mastered turning the other cheek and doubted she ever would. Some things were worth standing up and fighting for.

Just then someone pounded on the door of the chapel. Maura jumped. Who? Had the sheriff come so quickly? Satisfied that Tully was safely out of sight, she stuck the old pistol into her pocket and went to see who the caller was.

She slid the heavy bolt and opened the door a crack, just wide enough to see the man on the steps. He looked rough with unshaven growth on his jaw, a frock coat and vest. But he slouched like the outlaw who'd come. She didn't miss the low-slung holster and gun.

'Can I help you?'

He didn't remove his hat but kept it lowered to hide his eyes. 'Lookin' for work, ma'am. Got anything I might do?'

Maura swallowed hard. 'Sorry, I'm afraid not. Town is down the road. Try there.'

The man stuck a matchstick in his mouth. 'I can do most anything.'

Not in a hundred years would she consider having him around the children. A man looking for real work wouldn't look like a gunslinger.

'Sorry. Now if you'll excuse me, I have things to do.' Before he could reply or stick a foot into the crack of the door, she slammed it shut and bolted it.

Shaking, she hurried to warn Emma and the nuns. 'Keep a sharp eye out for trouble.'

'Since the other outlaw failed to get inside, I think he sent this one on pretense of looking for work,' Emma said, setting her mouth in a hard line. 'They can send more but it won't do them a speck of good.'

Everyone nodded in agreement and Maura went to tell Max about the caller.

'The rats! They'll try anything. Keep your guard up because they'll be back,' Max warned.

Happy to have her uncle's help, Maura nodded and went back to Tully. After giving the boy a good shearing with Sister Bernadette's assistance, she laid the scissors and mirror aside. 'Tully, let's go out and get some sun. Maybe you want to join the children playing.'

The boy shrugged. 'OK.'

They went to join the others and after it seemed to be going well, Maura checked on Calhoun who was sleeping. Satisfied everything was fine, she turned to scrub Tully's dirty clothes. Yet, when she glanced up a half hour later, he was sitting against the side of the stone dwelling looking rather forlorn.

She started that way only to have Uncle Max limp over and intercept her. 'Let me take him with me. You have plenty to do.'

He'd washed the blood off and changed clothes, but nothing could hide the deep bruises, the scratches. They told a story of pain and suffering and looked even worse in the daylight. But he'd refused to let her even look him over. The stubborn coot!

Clutching a wet shirt, Maura nodded. 'I think that's a good idea.'

Sporting dark bruises, Max ambled over to the boy. 'Tully, do you know how to hammer a nail?'

Tully glanced around in panic and shrank back against the wall, afraid to trust.

Maura hurried to help. 'It's all right, Tully, Max won't hurt you. No one here will hurt you.'

Wide-eyed, Tully looked for a place to run. 'Lock me up.'

Max squatted down. 'No, son. I will never lock you inside anything. I promise.'

'OK.'

'So, can you hammer a nail?' Max asked.

Tully nodded and some of his fear left.

'Good, because I have some work for you. Important work in my shed.' Max gave him a hand up and they moved to Max's workshop.

Maybe this was the answer to a prayer. Max needed a purpose and Tully needed to know he mattered to someone.

Maura turned back to her work, determined to have it done before Calhoun opened his door. But sudden excitement among the children brought her to full attention again.

A group of six were coming from the side of the chapel. Four of them were carrying a good-sized wooden crate that had the dog in a barking frenzy.

'Miss Mo! Miss Em! Look what we found!' Sunny yelled.

Good Lord in heaven. It appeared God had again gifted them with something else.

TWENTY-ONE

Calhoun opened his door to see what all the shouting was about and grinned at the four children struggling with the wooden crate. Sunny would be directing them of course. She was a natural-born bosser. And an instigator. If there was any devilishness about, she was sure to be in the center. Gunner was running in circles, barking fit to raise the dead.

The three nuns came running, even the shy young one who was clutching the baby. Emma was hurrying as fast as she could, the breeze ruffling her short locks.

Calhoun stepped carefully out his doorway. 'What do you kids have there?'

'God brought us chickens!' Henry answered, his missing teeth showing clearly in his excitement.

''Cause God loves us,' Alphie added. 'He really, really does.'

Sister Angela finished making the sign of the cross and smiled. 'Of course, he does, child.'

Maura, bless her, was trying her best to keep from laughing. Calhoun admired the way the sunlight brought out the reddish glints in her brown hair. And her love for the children. And her grit. And the red spots in her cheeks when she got her dander up. Lord, he loved her fire. He pretty much admired everything about her.

She looked his way. 'You might as well join us, Calhoun. It seems someone has left us a bunch of layers. We're going to need a coop. Can you build one?'

His chest swelled that she'd included him as though he was one of them. He answered in a slow Texas drawl. 'I'm the best-known chicken coop builder in these parts, ma'am. Give me a minute.'

Reaching for his walking stick by the door, he hobbled to join them just in time to hear the story of how Sunny heard clucking and found the chickens sitting in the crate in front of the chapel. Just so happened that she had a group of followers with her.

Show-woman as she was, Sunny pursed her mouth. 'I had a dream that God was coming an' bringing us something else.'

'And here they are.' Alphie waved his arm excitedly at the chickens.

'I wonder what He'll . . . uh . . . bring next,' Betsy said, twisting and turning.

Henry scratched his ear. 'I hope it's an elephant.'

Persnickety Rosemary reached for Henry's hand. 'I want a new dress and some pretty hair bows.'

Ahh, the little wife-to-be was a bit materialistic. And still determined to make poor Henry her husband by the looks of it. Calhoun had never gotten so much enjoyment out of watching children before. They were so dramatic and easily excited by the smallest things.

As he watched, Henry jerked free and ran to Calhoun. 'Can I help you build the coop, Mr Calhoun?' His brown eyes seemed to be begging for someone to save him.

'Sure, Henry. I'm going to need lots of help to finish by nightfall. We don't want the coyotes or other wild animals getting them.'

Only having six hens and one rooster would make it easier since the coop wouldn't have to be that large at first. They could add on later. It suddenly hit him that he sounded as though he'd be sticking around. But he couldn't. He had to make that clear. To them and to himself.

Henry's tense grip of Calhoun's arm relaxed. 'Thanks, Mr Calhoun. Can we start soon?'

Maura walked around the crate. 'Henry, let him have some coffee first and eat something. He just got up.'

'Gee, Mr Calhoun, you sure sleep late. Did you even know we have a new boy? His name is Tully and he's real nice.' Henry lowered his voice to a whisper. 'Tully is bigger than me.' A smile broke across his face. 'Maybe Rosemary will want to marry him.'

Ah, the life of lovelorn six-year-olds.

'You can always hope, Henry. I think you should finish growing up before thinking of marriage. It's a big commitment.'

The boy sighed and ran his fingers through his hair. 'I just want to play a while. Let me know when you need me, Mr Calhoun.' Henry called Gunner and they ran off together.

'Can you make it to the kitchen, Calhoun?' Maura asked. 'If not, I can bring you coffee and a tray to your room.'

The unexpected moment of privacy filled him with a burst of happiness.

'I believe I would like to walk. After my midnight ride, I think I can do just about anything.' Especially, if she was at his side. He offered his arm.

Maura slipped her hand around his elbow. 'I don't think that was good for you and a doctor certainly wouldn't have prescribed it, but I also notice your walk is steadier.'

'Any sign of the sheriff?'

'Not yet but I've instructed the sisters to only speak French if they answer the door to any callers. They need to play dumb and the more the better.'

He chuckled. 'I like it. You're something, you know that, Miss Mo?'

She colored prettily under his look. 'It really seems the best solution.' She glanced toward the open door of Max's workshop. 'We did have another caller this morning.'

Maura told him about the incident and her assessment of the man. 'I don't know why he was here, but I do know he wasn't looking for work.'

Calhoun tightened his jaw. He knew beyond a doubt that Donavan had sent a member of his gang to try again. 'You were right not to trust him. Don't trust anyone.'

How long would Donavan and his men hang around to threaten the women? He had to end this. Somehow.

'Enough about that.' Maura smiled and the fear left her eyes. 'Tully bathed this morning and I cut his hair. The change is astounding. As long as he doesn't speak, no one will guess he's the Wild Boy.'

'I'll have to see this miracle. But what about clean clothing?'

'The trousers I wore last night fit him well enough and we found a few more items in another trunk. I just wonder about the former occupants. They must've died or they wouldn't have left so much behind.' Concern colored her blue gaze.

He wanted to hold her, but they were in the open with many eyes on them. 'Max told me about some of the battles that took place here and it's sad to think about but a lot of them died.'

Nodding, she opened the door of the kitchen. He went in after her. She pulled a plate from the warmer and made fresh coffee. She'd just refilled his cup a second time when a pounding commenced on the door of the chapel.

Sister Angela bustled through on her short legs. Tension stretched thin in the room but neither Calhoun nor Maura spoke.

The sheriff. Had to be.

'I'm going to listen,' Maura whispered. 'It'll be fine.'

He could feel her worry though. When she moved past him, he took her hand, squeezing her cold fingers before she moved on.

'Let Sister Angela handle it,' he cautioned quietly.

'I will. But she might need me.'

True enough. One little French nun would be no match for a burly sheriff.

Maura stole forward on silent feet. Sister Angela did exactly as Maura had told her – play dumb. She was rattling off rapid fire French in a tone that brooked disapproval.

Finally, the sheriff seemed to have enough and burst out in anger. 'Well, I'm coming in whether you like it or not, lady. I need to search this place for law breakers, and I mean to do it! No one on this earth can stop me! You got that?'

Maura pulled her shoulders back and stepped to Sister Angela's side. She forced calm to her voice. 'I do apologize, dear sir, but you take your life in your hands if you come inside.'

'Is that a threat, ma'am?' the sheriff growled.

Sister Angela let loose again, her voice rising to match his, her French working to frustrate the portly lawman.

'Stop all that gobbledygook! Speak English!' The barrel-chested sheriff pushed against the door.

'Listen to me!' Maura shouted. 'We have yellow fever here. Do you want to die? Many of the children are at death's door. We cannot let you in. Do you understand me?'

The sheriff's face paled and he swallowed hard. 'Yellow fever?'

'That's correct. You know what a toll that can take on a person having just gone through that in town. Surely you're not dumb enough to risk catching it. We cannot, will not, let you inside. It's for your own safety.'

He reached for a kerchief in his pocket and placed it over his nose and mouth. 'Well, why didn't you say so?'

Just then, one of the children hollered out as though in pain. The sound seemed to come from the kitchen and it was exactly what they needed to convince the sheriff. Before anyone could speak, a second child yelled.

Maura took Sister Angela's hand. 'Good day, Sheriff. We really must go.'

'Yes, I'll return when it's safe,' he mumbled through the kerchief.

They slammed the door and listened for the sound of a horse leaving, the hooves fading into the distance.

Sister Angela chuckled. 'The man is scared.'

'Yes, he is. I don't think he'll be back anytime soon. But I feel guilty for lying. May God forgive me.' Maura returned to the kitchen to find Henry, Alphie and Sunny with Calhoun. 'I don't know whose idea it was to cry out, but it sure worked.'

Calhoun winked. 'I thought you might need a little help convincing him.'

'It was brilliant.'

'Can we go back outside, Miss Mo?' Henry asked. 'We're about to start on the chicken coop.'

'Yes, you may.' She ushered them to the door and held it open.

Calhoun grinned. 'If you need more acting, let me know. Otherwise, I've got to get busy on that coop. The kids are itching to hammer something, and I prefer it's a piece of wood.'

Maura laughed. 'Me too. Uncle Max can point you to everything you need.'

He stood so close she caught the fragrance of the land. Her heart raced like runaway horses as the awareness of his long, lean body snuggled beneath her skin, making itself at home.

For a long moment he looked at her. His voice roughened. 'You sure tempt me, Miss Mo.'

The breath fluttered in her chest. 'How exactly?' she whispered, clutching his shirt.

'You're a scandalous woman. I shouldn't.' He shot a quick glance out the door to check on the kids. 'Aw hell. I'd kick myself if I didn't.'

He pressed a hungry kiss to her upturned lips. Barely

breathing, her eyes drifted shut and at the first touch of his mouth, urgency and fiery need swept her to a place of beauty. Maura slid a hand around his neck, his hair entwined around her fingers. Engulfed by the passion and the conflicting emotions running through her, she gave herself fully to this exciting, unexpected turn in her life.

Footsteps sounded and they broke apart.

'My goodness, Calhoun,' she murmured, patting her hair into place.

His dark eyes held promises that multiplied the flutters in her chest and stomach. 'Lady, one of these days I'll find a place without interruptions. Then . . .' He paused, the brush of a knuckle like the softest feather on her cheek. 'Then, you'd better hold on tight is all I got to say.'

'Come on, Mr Calhoun!' Henry yelled. 'We got man stuff to do.'

'Hold your horses, son,' Calhoun answered with a sigh. 'See you at supper, Maura?'

'Count on it.' Her gaze followed him out to Max's shed, her hand to her tingling lips.

He'd made her a promise and given her a taste of things to come. If another kiss affected her more than this one, she didn't know how she could contain this joy bursting inside her.

Please God, for once in my life, don't yank this away like all the others. Please let me have Calhoun.

TWENTY-TWO

Afternoon shadows were spreading across the landscape, yet all were still hard at work. Maura brought in Tully's dry clothes and folded them. She was helping Sister Bernadette in the kitchen when Uncle Max stood outside the door.

'Come out here. I want to show you something,' he hollered.

Maura dried her hands on her apron, her thoughts tumbling. Had Tully done something? 'Just a minute.' She met Bernadette's puzzled gaze.

Emma entered the kitchen. 'What's going on?'

'Someone brought us some chickens earlier and now apparently something else is happening outside.' Maura shook her finger. 'What are you doing out of bed?'

'I'm feeling better and felt left out. I want to join you so don't scold.'

Maura put an arm around her pretty sister's waist and kissed her cheek. 'Let's go see what Uncle Max wants to show us.'

As soon as the three ladies went outside, little Alphie tugged on Maura's skirt. 'Look, Miss Mo. Look, Miss Em.'

Emma put a hand over her mouth. 'Oh my!'

Following the direction of Alphie's pointing finger, Maura saw newly hammered rows of beds. 'Uncle Max!' A lump blocked her throat. How she loved the depth of Max's heart. 'How?' Tears filled her eyes as she went to put her arms around him. 'You made all these?'

'The kids needed beds to sleep on.' He drew a reluctant Tully to him. 'Couldn't have finished without my helper. He's a humdinger, this Tully.'

A good bit of fear left Tully's face and he grinned. 'I help.'

'I can see that.' Maura kissed the boy's cheek. 'You are some worker. Thank you.'

'And that's not all!' Henry hollered from the new chicken coop. 'It's all done.'

Maura hurried over to see. 'This is exceptional work.' Her

attention went to the handsome carpenter. 'It's really sturdy. If we had some wire, we could enclose it and keep the wild animals out.'

'There's some in the workshop,' Max said. 'I'll get it. Tully and I will help you finish.'

Maura put an arm across Alphie's shoulders. 'I'm just so proud of all of you. For this you get a special treat.'

'Yay!' Sunny clapped and picked up a hen. 'Me an' Rosemary an' Jenny have named them all. This one is Henrietta and those over there are Priscilla and Gertrude.'

Rosemary sighed. 'I get confused. They all look alike. Why do they all have to be white? Henry, do you want to help me?'

'Naw.' Henry kicked at a dirt clod. 'I got man stuff to do.'

Maura laughed and turned toward the kitchen. There might be enough flour to make a cake. Her heart was full of thankfulness and love for all who lived at Heaven's Door and she wanted them to know it.

Emma followed. 'I can't believe Uncle Max made all those beds.'

'I told you he has worth. He's just beginning to find it. He's more than a drunk. A lot more.'

'Yes, I can see that. He must've started on them right after we arrived. It seems everyone is finding what they need here. This must be a magical place, Maura. Can I help you and Sister Bernadette with supper?'

'After you drink a cup of hot tea. You need some sustenance. You look a little white. Sit down while I make it.'

'I'm just glad to be feeling better.' Emma pulled out a chair and sat. 'Who do you think brought the chickens?'

'The same ones that left the puppy I imagine.'

Sister Bernadette smiled. 'God leave.'

'You know, Sister, I'm beginning to believe you.' Maura put the kettle on to boil and got out the flour for the cake. They had no chocolate and no eggs yet, but the kids would welcome anything sweet. Applesauce would work fine. By the time she'd stirred up the batter and put the pans in the oven, the kettle was singing. She poured hot water over the tea leaves inside a cup and took it to Emma. 'Here you are.'

'Thank you, Maura.' Emma stirred the leaves. 'Why doesn't

the person show themselves? I'd like to thank them for being so generous.'

'So would I but until they come forward, there's little we can do.' Maura turned to help Sister Bernadette peel the potatoes. 'I don't think the person who left baby Juliette is the same as the one who brought the puppy and chickens. I can't say why but I think it's two separate individuals.'

'So do I,' Emma agreed. 'But the benefactor always chooses night or early morning while we're still sleeping to bring them. There must be a reason. Maybe they don't go out in the daytime hours. Has anyone checked to see if there are any dwellings nearby?'

'I only go into the woods to hunt, and never far. I haven't seen any houses,' Maura admitted.

'Men might know,' Bernadette said. 'Max.'

'That's true.' Maura wondered why they'd never asked him.

Emma sipped on her tea. 'Could it be Max doing it?'

Was he? He'd disappeared quite mysteriously for two days and it was after that when the puppy came.

Maura glanced up. 'I don't think so. He might've found the puppy abandoned in the woods, but the chickens were in a crate. He doesn't have money to buy them, and I know for a fact he didn't have an opportunity last night when we were rescuing Tully.'

'You're right. It has to be someone else.' Emma stared into her teacup.

After that Sister Angela came in and the women worked to put a meal on the table. Sister Anne-Marie brought Juliette in to feed her and they all had to stop and coo over the baby before they called the children to wash up.

The women ended up relenting until the children finished the coop and put the chickens inside. After supper, they'd bring the beds in. They had no straw mattresses for them yet, but they were far better than the stone floor.

When everyone sat around the table at last, they gave special thanks to God for bringing them together and to Max, Calhoun and Tully for being such hard workers.

Maura glanced at each of the sixteen faces through a blur of tears, so very grateful for their little family. When she got to

Calhoun, her heart twisted with the knowledge he was biding his time before saddling up.

Just when she'd finally found what she thought was love, he was set to ride out. Deep inside, she'd known this from the start. And yet, she'd played a silly game.

Sitting next to her, he covered her hand with his large palm and lightly squeezed her fingers. He leaned close to whisper, 'You're doing a wonderful thing here, Maura.'

'You feel it, too?'

'Yes, and I'm so glad you let me be a part of it for a while.'

'However long you want, Calhoun. The choice is yours.'

'Not really. Donavan is still out there and no one will be safe as long as he roams free.' A tap on his arm directed his attention away from Maura. He smiled at Tully seated on the other side and helped him butter his bread.

Across the table, Henry wiped his milk mustache off with a sleeve. 'Mr Calhoun, do you think my papa in heaven knows about us building a chicken coop?'

'I'm sure he does. Your mama and papa watch over you.'

'Did they send you to be my friend?' Henry persisted.

'It's very possible.'

Maura watched the exchange and how Henry was desperately needing a man to look up to. Was Calhoun that someone? They still knew nothing about him. He could be an outlaw after everything was said and done.

'Do you have any little kids, Mr Calhoun?' Henry asked.

Calhoun took a bite and chewed it before he answered. 'No, I regret to say I don't.'

'A wife?'

Maura couldn't bear to hear the answer. 'Henry! Quit pestering Mr Calhoun and eat your supper so you can have cake.'

'Yes, Miss Mo.'

The boy's downcast face released a flood of guilt. He was simply curious about his hero. She felt two inches high and vowed to give him her piece of cake.

Later when she did, the boy's face lit up. 'Thank you, Miss Mo.'

'You're welcome, Henry.'

Calhoun lifted an eyebrow and grinned as though he figured out why.

'Because I'm not hungry and it was the right thing to do,' she mumbled. The baby began to cry from the next room and Maura hopped up. 'I'll see to her.'

Juliette wasn't wet and she'd just finished a bottle. She hushed as soon as Maura picked her up. 'I know what you need, little girl.'

The nuns had figured out that she hated being alone. As long as Juliette was with the other children she was fine, no matter how noisy they were.

Maura kissed a soft cheek and walked back to the kitchen. They stood in the shadow of the door where they could see the others. 'Get your fill, sweetheart,' Maura murmured, patting Juliette's bottom.

The noisy scene stirred the thankfulness inside and tears rolled down Maura's face. She'd waited so long for a family and now had one in spades. All the lonely years were forgotten. She loved and was loved back and she'd fight tooth and nail to keep them safe.

Calhoun noticed her in the shadows and winked. Then a smile formed that took her breath.

The next morning, the children ran out to see if the hens had laid any eggs and were disappointed to find none.

'Soon, children,' Sister Angela said. 'Soon.'

'She's right.' Maura looked at their long faces. 'Let them settle in. This coop is new to them, and they have to get used to it. Just like you did when you came here.'

Sunny smiled. 'But we have beds to sleep on and we're happy about that.'

Sister Bernadette rested a hand on the girl's shoulder. 'Amen. God is good.'

Emma helped herd them all inside for breakfast. Maura glanced toward Calhoun's room but saw no sign of him. They'd had a late night though with moving all the beds inside and getting the excited children into them. He'd walked too much on that leg and it had to hurt. He'd never complained though and didn't quit until all the work was done.

They hadn't had a moment alone and disappointment had wound through Maura. She'd yearned for another tender kiss.

The gentle fall breeze caught her sigh as she turned back to the stone walls of the orphanage.

Inside the kitchen, she'd just gotten the children into their places and filled their bowls with oatmeal when Sister Angela came from the direction of the sanctuary.

'We have visitor,' she announced in her French accent.

Emma gave a strangled sound.

Maura glanced at the gentleman towering over the older nun and her mouth dried. 'Father.'

TWENTY-THREE

Neither girl went to him. Maura had no feeling of gladness to see Lucius Taggart. 'I didn't hear a knock. Did you simply walk in?' The question held no warmth.

Sister Angela gave Lucius a disapproving glance. 'I find him in sanctuary.'

'I see.' Maura set the large pan of oatmeal down. 'As you can see, we have a full table but we might squeeze you in.'

Clutching a wide-brimmed hat in his hand, Lucius stood unmoving in his long frock coat, tall, thin and forbidding as ever in his black clothes. Neither had his raspy voice changed. Everything about him was cold and aloof. 'Just need some coffee and to warm up. I heard in San Antonio that you'd started an orphanage.'

'And you wanted to find out if we'd failed?' Emma asked. 'I know it wasn't out of concern that we might need something. I imagine *you* probably do though.'

The children had stopped eating and watched the exchange with frowns. Protecting them was foremost in Maura's mind. They had to get him out of here away from them where his cold manner wouldn't touch them. She poured a cup of coffee and handed it to him.

'Did it occur to you that I might want to see my girls?' He took a sip of the steaming brew.

'Maura, did it occur to you? It sure didn't me.' Emma snorted and stood. 'We're doing just fine without you. I'm taking my breakfast outside. You can have my seat.'

The silence was palpable as Emma went out. A cold swirling mist brought a taste of the coming winter into the warm kitchen.

Anger rose and Maura itched to speak her mind, but she had the children to think about. 'Sit,' she said in a tone that didn't invite a discussion. 'Are you here on business – or pleasure?'

It really didn't matter because to Lucius Taggart it was all the same in some kind of twisted way. A memory of him always smiling when he held his precious rope brought a shiver along with a sudden thought. He loved what he did.

'A little of both.' Her father's heavy steps took him to Emma's vacated chair.

'I'm not surprised.'

Sister Angela must've sensed the calm unraveling. She and Bernadette hurried the children through the meal and toward the playroom, promising them a new game they'd devised.

Maura stood glaring at the head of the long table. Now that the children had left she was free to speak. 'Where were you when our house burned, when we had nowhere to go? Where were you when the good, righteous people of San Antonio asked us to leave? When they held Emma down and cut her hair before we could ride out.' Her trembling voice rose slightly. 'Where were you all those lonely nights when our empty bellies growled? Mama had been dead for a month before you came around.'

His voice rose as well, and his dark eyes bored into her. 'I was working.'

'Go ahead and tell yourself that, Father,' she scoffed. 'Emma and I aren't stupid anymore. We've learned not to depend on anyone but ourselves. We don't need you now.'

'Do you think I like the things I have to do? To listen to the gurgles of death over and over? To hear them beg for their lives before they drop through the trap door? It's ugly and dirty but someone has to do it and I'm very good at it.' He rubbed the stubble on his jaw. 'I take pride in making it as painless as possible for those men.'

Maura snorted. 'I can't believe you. And yes, I think you like your job. You care more for outlaws and vermin than you do your own daughters. Always have.' She turned at the sound of the opening door.

Calhoun stuck his head in. 'Would you happen to have some coffee?'

'Sure. I'll get it.' She reached for a cup.

'I know you,' Lucius said, pushing back his chair. 'Jonas Calhoun. Or would you rather go by J.A. Cody? Either one is fine by me. You have a warrant out for your arrest.'

Maura sucked in a breath. No! It wasn't possible. They were lies and she refused to believe them.

Leaning heavily on his cane, Calhoun cleared his throat and entered the room slowly and calmly. 'I'm sorry but you mistake me for another.'

'Stop it, Lucius.' Maura drew herself up straight, shoulders back. 'If you came to cause trouble you can ride back out. We don't need you here spreading unfounded accusations and drumming up more business for your despicable rope.'

Calhoun glanced her way. 'It's OK, Miss Maura.' He sat down and she placed the coffee in front of him. 'Thank you.' He took a sip. 'Taggart, I'm known only as Calhoun. My brother was Jonas but forget about going after him. He's no longer of this world. We were twins identical in looks.'

Lucius pointed a finger. 'You can't fool me. You're Jonas Calhoun or I'm the governor. I'd wager any amount of money on it.'

'And you'd lose!' Maura's voice shook.

After a long pause and a great deal of hesitance, Calhoun steepled his fingers and spoke quietly, his words coming slow. 'I'm a . . .' He looked at Maura and her twisting hands. 'I'm a deputy US marshal sent to round up the Donavan Gang.'

'On whose orders?' Lucius fired back.

'Judge Isaac Norbert and Marshal Pete Thomas in Austin!'

Satisfaction bubbled in Maura's chest that Calhoun had an answer for everything. She didn't know if those men were real, but she was glad he put Lucius in his place with no backing down.

She spoke to him with anger in her voice. 'You're always trying to stir up trouble. Never satisfied to let folks be. You'll do anything to cause me and Emma grief and destroy any life we've found. I refuse to listen to any more of this rant.'

Emma came from outside with her plate and cup, a chilly wind blowing in behind her. Her eyes were cold behind the lenses of her spectacles. She stood next to Maura. 'I see you've wasted no time doing what you do best, Lucius. You're not welcome here. We can't have your kind around the children.'

'So that's the way of things?' Lucius scoffed.

Maura raised her chin. 'It is. Drink your coffee and warm up. We'll feed you the same as the children had if you're hungry. But you have no place here.'

'I see.' Lucius drained his cup and rose. 'You'll find out soon enough that this man is Jonas Calhoun. The deep cleft in his chin confirms it. I saw it with my own eyes. He stood on the gallows with me and I thought I'd rid Texas of another outlaw. But riders galloped into town and plucked him off. He ruined my record. So I oughta know what he looks like.'

Unruffled, Calhoun's deep chuckle came loud in the tension-filled room. 'Do you know how many men in Texas have an indention in their chin? Do you have other proof?'

Lucius narrowed his eyes and put on his hat. 'Not at the moment but I'll get it.'

'Then you'll be going.' Emma turned away as though unable to look at the man who'd sired her and Maura and left them to get by as best they could.

'I'll show you out.'

Lucius lifted a shaggy eyebrow that had too much gray. He was getting old. 'You don't trust me to find the door?'

'Now that you mention it – no.' Maura lifted her chin higher. 'I don't trust anything about you. You see nothing wrong in doing as you wish no matter if you have the right or not. You simply take it. Out here, you won't get your way. Make no mistake, from now on, the doors will be locked. We've been threatened by outlaws and the sheriff alike, so we have to protect ourselves.'

Lucius was quiet until she let him out. He turned to face her, his eyes hidden under the wide brim of his hat. She imagined they were the same hardened steel she'd come to hate. 'Whether you wish to believe me or not, you're harboring a vicious criminal under your own roof, Maura. That man is Jonas Calhoun. Mark my words.'

'You don't know anything, Lucius. I choose to believe him because I've seen his heart. He's kind and generous and the children love him. They can sense bad people. Did you see how they looked at you?'

'I'm a stranger.'

'So was Calhoun and they didn't treat him this way. Goodbye, Lucius.' She closed the door in his face as he was about to say something else. She didn't care what it was. He just needed to disappear.

Turning the key in the lock, she stuck it in her pocket and returned to the kitchen. Emma had gone. Probably to help with the children.

Calhoun glanced up. 'I'm sorry for the way you found out about me.'

Pulling out a chair, she sat, her gaze burning a hole in him. 'You could've been honest with me.'

Honest? She wondered if he truly was now. How she hated these doubts that plagued her.

He released a heavy sigh. 'Yes, and I should have. But I'd hoped to avoid these questions. I was supposed to keep my identity secret.'

'Why? You have nothing to hide.' Unless it wasn't as cut and dried as he'd said.

He rose and limped over to the stove, pouring another cup of coffee. 'I was under orders to keep my reason for being here quiet. If Rupert Donavan gets wind of me, he'll disappear again.' He released a long sigh. 'And then I had the bad luck to get shot.'

'Did this Donavan discover your identity?'

Calhoun sat back down. 'I don't think so.'

'You spoke of your brother Jonas before and that you think he's dead. You didn't say that you're twins.' She was trying to figure everything out and get a clear picture. But parts of it were still murky. Something didn't sit right. The puzzle was starting to take shape but important pieces were still missing.

Why was the bank bag from the holdup on his horse?

Why had he acted so strangely about the marshal badge, not wanting to wear it?

And why was he carrying the wanted poster for J.A. Cody?

Maura tried to push away the doubts. She wanted him to be the good brother. But she also wanted the truth – whatever it was. 'I take it you were together when you got riddled with bullets.'

He nodded. 'Jonas was deep in the Donavan Gang and wanted out. I was trying to help him escape, only he made too much noise and woke them up, then all hell broke loose. I'm pretty sure they got him or Donavan wouldn't have shown up here, but I have yet to see Jonas's body.'

'You said you're identical in looks?'

'Every detail right down to this indention in my chin. Our parents had a hard time telling us apart.'

How convenient, Maura mused. That would come in handy for a wanted man with a lawman brother. How she hated these doubts that kept creeping in!

But Calhoun didn't have the appearance of an outlaw with something to hide. She always kept going back to that: his appearance.

And he certainly didn't kiss how she'd expect an outlaw to kiss.

Yet, how was she to know? She'd never been kissed, held, caressed so she couldn't judge by any of that. He held secrets and that much was crystal clear. Could she trust a man who hid things?

'I see doubts in those pretty blue eyes.' Calhoun rose and pulled her close.

With the fragrance of the fall air on his clothes circling around her, she looked up at him. 'I want to believe you. I want that more than anything in this world, Calhoun. I'll need some time.'

He pressed his lips to her temple. 'I know.'

Then he reached for his cane and hobbled out the door, closing it behind him. The empty silence left deep sadness inside her.

What would be so wrong in accepting him – whoever he was?

He'd shown her tenderness and love. How could she put a price on that?

Or turn it away. Maura hadn't asked to fall for the man and had tried her best not to let it happen.

But it had and whether outlaw or lawman, he'd changed her. He made her dream.

TWENTY-FOUR

Thoughts circled in his mind like a flock of vultures looking for prey, Calhoun hobbled across the uneven compound, picking his way through a cold wind. Damn it! Of all the rotten luck for Lucius Taggart to show up. Now he was exposed, and Donavan would know for sure he was here. The gang leader was nearby. He could feel it in his bones. A stench was in the air. But he wasn't healthy enough yet to fight him. He had to get stronger.

Lingering doubts in Maura's blue eyes had killed him. But he couldn't say more than he had. In fact, he'd offered too much.

He'd not been fair to her. Not at all. He should've warned her of the perils of falling for someone like him. He cursed his luck. Beautiful and kind, Maura was everything he'd ask in a wife and her kisses were as sweet as the purest honey.

But how could a man resist when she was so right for him? His heart had called to her and she'd answered. There was no finer woman in the whole state of Texas and he hadn't shot straight with her.

Hobbling in the swirling wind that chilled him to the bone, he felt more alone than at any time of his life.

Even more alone than when he was dying in the woods with no one to care.

Somehow, some way, he had to get on with things and see what Rupert Donavan was up to. Calhoun needed to know if he'd discovered the loot. He smiled. The gang leader would be madder than a hornet that they'd stolen the money.

He had plans for that – and none included letting Donavan have it back.

But the question remained if Calhoun would remember where exactly he'd hidden it. He'd barely been alive, the pain putting him out of his mind.

Still, it hadn't been worth losing his brother over. If he could go back . . .

Tears stung the back of his eyes and he blinked hard.

Gone. His brother was gone. He'd known it before, but it hadn't really hit him until now and it did so with the force of a giant hammer. He had to find his body. Yet when he thought of leaving Maura, great pain engulfed his heart. He gasped, staggering forward, putting one foot in front of the other.

Max ran out and with a bolstering arm, helped him from the storm to Calhoun's quarters. The strain of navigating the rough terrain and biting wind had sapped him. Shivering, he collapsed on to a chair. He had to get his strength back so he could leave. 'Thanks.'

'Don't mention it. This fall rain came up so suddenly.' Max took the other chair. 'Usually our weather is pretty mild with occasional freezing rain. In a day or two we'll be in shirt sleeves. Beats me why it's so fickle.'

They were silent a moment, listening to the wind whistling under the door.

'You missed a visitor,' Calhoun said, cupping his hands and blowing on them.

'The sheriff again?'

'No, your brother Lucius.' Calhoun still couldn't believe his bad luck. 'I had the misfortune of being over there.' He stared at the door wishing he could forget the way Maura had looked – like he'd kicked her.

'That man is no brother I want to claim. We used to be close growing up but we haven't said a civil word to each other in years. What happened?'

Calhoun told him about the exchange. 'And then Maura showed him the door.'

'Damn his hide. He'll be back, that you can count on.' Max stretched his legs out in front of him. 'My brother is a horse's ass. That's the kindest thing I can say about him. Jonas Calhoun was your brother?'

'Yes, my twin. We were identical in looks so it's not shocking that Lucius claimed I was Jonas.'

'I met Jonas once. A while back, he came into my camp and we shared a meal,' Max said softly. 'Hell, I thought you were him. Came near to asking you but figured it wasn't any of my business. You think Donavan killed him?'

'I don't see how he could've survived that barrage. I plan to leave in a few days and find out if the gang is still in the same place. I want to find Jonas's body and give him a proper burial.'

'And if the gang is still there? What then?' Max bent to inspect the worn sole of his boot.

'I'll work to bring them in. They're a menace to society and I don't like the fact they're close by with the kids here and all.' Calhoun couldn't let that stand without doing something. He wouldn't be much of a man.

'So you're a deputy US marshal?'

The question took a minute to register. Max frowned and waited. Was he trying to trap him?

Finally, Calhoun smiled. 'It's what my badge says. I'll settle this business with Donavan and make him pay. I don't much care if a bullet gets him or the end of a rope.'

'I don't care either.' Max took out his cigarette makings and rolled a couple, passing one to him.

They smoked in silence for several minutes.

'Tell me about Lucius. Why is he so cold to his daughters?' Calhoun asked.

'He never wanted kids. Didn't know how to be a father.' Max barked a laugh. 'Never cared about learning either. His wife took care of raising those girls. Then she died and they had no one. Pretty much raised themselves.' He flicked his ashes on to the floor. 'Did a fine job too if you ask me. But they were eaten up with loneliness. No one would have anything to do with the poor things. Of course, there were no offers of marriage either. Just those two girls alone.'

'That's a shame. They'd both make some man a mighty fine wife.' Yes, it was a crying shame. Maura's arms were made for holding babies and making a man feel like he'd found a pot of gold.

Max blew out a smoke ring. 'You're single, aren't you?'

'Marriage isn't for me. My . . . work . . . is too dangerous. Secondly, I travel a lot.' He released a sigh, shaking his head. 'Marriage plain wouldn't work. Besides, I'm too old and set in my ways. Barely civilized. I'd probably run a wife off. I wouldn't know the first thing about being a husband. A father either for that matter.'

His mind went back to his father and the unending supply of patience he'd had for his two boys. The times his father had sat doubled in grief beside their little sister's grave. And the love their father had shown for their mother.

No, Calhoun had best leave marriage alone.

He didn't deserve someone like Maura anyway. She needed far better than him. But even as he thought about her, the soft feel of her in his arms overrode the words. His heart cried in anguish, demanding he try to make it work.

At least she wouldn't be alone thinking no one wanted her.

Why had he let things go so far? He hadn't meant to give her hope. Or hurt her.

Calhoun inhaled deep of the cigarette and blew out the smoke, then moved to the door, tossing the butt on the frozen ground. He quickly shut out the wind and sat back down.

'Max, I've often wondered about you. I've ridden the trail for a long time and met a lot of men with secrets. I know you've got something bad chewing on you.' He pulled his coat tighter.

'Talk like that could get you a bullet,' Max growled. 'A man's business is his own. Just so you know, I'm not wanted by the law.'

'Didn't think you were.'

'Someday if I get drunk enough, I might just tell you. But, I'm fresh out of whiskey and it's colder than blue blazes outside.' Max pushed back his chair. 'Gonna burrow deep in my covers and hibernate like an old bear until this blows over or summer comes. Whichever is first.'

'Sounds like a good plan.'

Max pulled to his feet and suddenly reached for Calhoun's hand. 'As I said, I met Jonas Calhoun and he wore a scar exactly like this on the back of his hand. Kinda odd. Especially knowing how he got it.'

'A lot of men have scars. Doesn't prove anything.'

Before Calhoun could say more, Max snorted. Then he dropped his hold and went out, shutting the door behind him. The silence left Calhoun uncomfortable. Hell. Everything hung on the edge and about to blow up around him any minute.

He reached for the deputy marshal's badge lying on the end of his bed where it must've fallen. Good memories and bad spun like a roulette wheel as he turned the badge over and over. The sky had been bluer than he'd ever seen it the day they'd pinned the badge on, and they'd had a drink to celebrate. Calhoun could still taste the juicy steak they'd had afterward.

Then had come the argument.

He shivered from the cold and rubbed his face. Seemed like only yesterday. What he'd give to go back, only now it was too late.

The brothers had always been together, sharing important events – except when their mother had died. But that had been the only time in memory when they hadn't shared either joy or sorrow.

A knock came at the door. He opened it to find Maura bundled up in her coat, hat and gloves. A soft rain was falling, adding to the chill.

'You never got a chance to eat breakfast, so I brought you a small piece of cured ham we'd been saving and a biscuit.' She smiled and held up the coffeepot.

His heart leaped. 'Come in out of the cold.' He took the coffee and set it on the table.

'I thought you might find it welcome.' She closed the door. 'It's freezing in here. Our breath is fogging.' She shot the small fireplace a glance. 'I can see why.'

'It hadn't been cold enough 'til now. And I have no wood.'

'Or much of a way of getting any.' She made a wry face. 'My fault. I'll borrow some from the house and we can replace it when it warms up a little.'

By then he'd be riding on. But he didn't say that. 'I'll be fine without a fire.'

'Hush. You will not. I'll be right back. Meanwhile warm up with some coffee and eat.' With those orders she hurried out.

There was no way to stop a female hurricane when she had a bee in her bonnet so he sat down and had some breakfast, thankful for her kindness.

Maura returned in short order and Calhoun soon had a fire going.

'There,' she said, holding her hands to the heat. 'Much better. It'll warm up in no time.'

As small as this room was he'd probably soon be sweating

but he was grateful for the fire. The cold had penetrated his bad leg.

Looking pretty with the fall wind coloring her cheeks, she sat opposite him. 'I'm sorry for Lucius. He's the most maddening man I've ever seen.'

'I'm fine. I've dealt with worse.'

'You shouldn't have to. Not here.'

Calhoun took a long drink from his cup. 'It is what it is. Let it go.'

'That's the problem. I've let too much go and now he just walks in like he lives here. Like he helped us find it. Like . . .' Tears bubbled in her blue eyes. 'I shouldn't let it get under my skin, but it does.'

'You're only human.' He handed her the dish towel that had wrapped the meal.

'Thanks.' She blew her nose. 'I'm such a ninny.'

'You're one of the strongest women I've ever known,' he answered softly, wishing he could take her in his arms. Wishing he could offer her marriage and a home. Wishing for the impossible. But even if doubts didn't stand between them, he couldn't give her what she wanted.

'I try to be strong, but I don't succeed very often.'

He wanted to point out that she'd shown the hangman to the door and ordered him not to come back. But instead, he let the silence envelop them.

'When are you leaving? I see it in your eyes.'

'I'll wait for the weather to clear but yes, I have to leave.'

'The children will be heartbroken. They care for you.' Maura stared into the flames of the small fireplace. 'Are you on a quest to avenge your brother's death?'

'Maybe. Quite possibly. For sure I'll rid the world of one very bad man and keep you all safe.'

'Doesn't it bother you that you might die?' She turned back to him, her blue stare searching his face. For what? The truth?

'A man can't let himself think about dying when settling a debt.'

'Your choice of words is interesting. A debt to who? Your brother?'

'Yes. I owe him more than I could ever repay. He died because of me.' Calhoun leaned forward, resting a hand on her arm. 'You have a lot of questions and are trying to understand, but I have few answers for you. Just know that I wouldn't leave unless it was necessary. I've come to love this place, the children, the peace it offers.' He dropped his voice. 'And I've come to care deeply for you. But I wish for things I can't have.'

'Me as well. Coming to know you has changed me. I'm not the same woman who found you.' Maura's voice broke and she pulled away. 'I hope you find what you're looking for.'

The words sounded odd like they were rough and bruised. Silently she rose and jerked up her coat, hat, and gloves, putting them on as she hurried to the door. He thought he heard a strangled cry but maybe it was the wind.

'I've already found it,' he murmured in the stillness of the room.

But what good was it?

TWENTY-FIVE

Her heart aching, Maura left Calhoun and crossed the muddy ground. She slipped into the empty kitchen, swallowing her sobs. Turning down the wick, she sat in the dimness thinking. The pain was almost more than she could bear.

What if she left with him so she'd be there when the next bullet pierced Calhoun's body? She could save him.

But she couldn't leave all this responsibility for Emma to handle alone.

Her place was here. Her duty. Her life.

Somewhere down the hall in the morning gloom, baby Juliette cried and someone's hurried footsteps went to quiet her.

Wiping her eyes, she listened to the sounds of life: the nuns talking softly; the patter of little feet and sweet laughter; the puppy's excited yip. All spoke of things she could never turn her back on. Finally, she rose, raised the lamp wick, and began to cook a stew for lunch.

The day passed quickly and she was glad to keep busy. Calhoun returned the coffeepot with thanks but didn't eat. He was already beginning to separate himself from them. The children asked where he was a hundred times. Her excuses varied.

'Don't Mr Calhoun like us anymore?' Alphie asked.

'Of course he does, honey. Maybe he just doesn't want to get out in the cold.' Maura distracted him by playing a fun little guessing game. Soon all the children were playing.

Henry patted her arm. 'Do you think the chickens have laid any eggs?'

'I guess we'll know by morning.'

'Can I go look now, Miss Mo?' Sunny asked.

'It's too cold right now. Let it warm up a bit first. Hopefully, it'll stop raining and the sun will come out.'

The gloomy day wore on and it was bedtime. She helped put the children to bed then she and Emma sat at the table with hot tea and talked.

'You've been quiet today, Maura. And Calhoun didn't come to eat. I found that a bit odd. Is he sick?'

'He's leaving when this rain stops.' And taking Maura's heart with him. The ache was still there.

Emma patted her hand. 'Was it because of Lucius? Did he cause this?'

'Calhoun didn't say so, but I sense that had something to do with it.'

'That man likes you. I've seen the way he looks at you.'

Maura met Emma's gaze. 'I like him, too.' She lowered her voice. 'He kissed me and oh Emma, it felt so right. So good.'

'Please don't let him break your heart. You always warn me with reminders of how men see us and I feel I should return the favor.' Emma took a sip of tea. 'Men can't get past the fact of what our father does. They simply can't. Or won't. We have to accept that and make a good life alone.'

'Calhoun is different. He's told me that Lucius's profession doesn't bother him. No, I think the secrets he carries are what's holding Calhoun back. Despite his explanation and claims of being a deputy marshal, something isn't right.' Maura put her hands on each side of her face, wishing she could rid herself of the doubts. 'I don't know what to think.'

Emma ran her finger around the rim of her cup. 'Why doesn't he just speak the truth?'

'I've asked myself that. I don't know.' Maura shared the conversation she'd had that morning with Calhoun. 'He feels he owes his brother some kind of debt that he has to pay.'

'By getting revenge?'

'I don't know. I have this horrible feeling he might die and I don't know if I can stand that.' To think of him lying lifeless on the cold unforgiving ground brought a sudden chill. He was so handsome and she'd seen the kindness of his heart. To see the life gone from his dark eyes would cause piercing pain.

The two sisters finished their tea, banked the fire in the kitchen hearth, and went to bed.

A shaft of sunlight pierced the window of Calhoun's room. He jerked awake, kicking himself for oversleeping. Again. Once he got warm, he was dead to the world until the sun woke him.

If the storm had passed, he'd planned to be gone by the time everyone rose. Just slip out. Quick and easy.

'I hate goodbyes,' he muttered, reaching for his trousers and pulling them on. Normally, there was a measure of guilt for leaving anywhere and it would be worse this time because he'd started putting down roots.

Why had he let that happen? Pain, the close bedfellow of guilt, would come when he ripped them from the ground and rode off.

But like it or not, it had to be this way.

Dressing quickly, he put on the ripped coat of Max's, threw his saddlebags over a shoulder, and limped to saddle his horse. The pack animal would be a gift for Maura saving his worthless hide.

It was a beautiful morning, though cool, with no sign of the storm remaining. The position of the weak sun told him he was at least an hour behind.

Movement at the chicken coop drew his attention. Looked to be one of the children squatted down on his heels. As he got closer, he recognized Henry.

'What are you doing, son?' Calhoun called.

'Waiting.'

Had something gotten into the coop? 'Waiting for what?'

'For the chickens to lay their eggs so I can have one for breakfast.' The big gap in the boy's grin and the freckles marching across his nose was a sight Calhoun would miss. Henry stood shading his eyes against the sun. 'Where are you going, Mr Calhoun?'

'To the barn for my horse. You really shouldn't be out yet. Does Miss Mo or the nuns know you've escaped?'

'I kinda snuck out 'cause I needed to get me an egg.' Henry ran to his side.

'I see.' Calhoun didn't stop. Neither did Henry. 'Maybe you need to go back inside.'

'Naw, there's too many others to miss me. Why do you need your horse?'

'I have something to do.'

'You're leaving?'

The pain in Henry's voice sliced into Calhoun. 'I have to.'

'I don't want you to go.' Henry's anguished voice raised in volume. 'We need you!'

Guilt climbed up the back of Calhoun's neck. Why couldn't
he have woken early and be gone before anyone got up? He kept
his head down and picked his way across the ground. The slam
of the kitchen door sounded like a bullet. He steeled himself.

'Henry, what are you doing out here? And where is your coat?'
The voice belonged to Maura, but he didn't turn around.

'Miss Mo, I ain't cold. I had to come see if the chickens laid
an egg.' Henry muttered something and kicked at a dirt clod.
He crossed his arms and stuck his hands in his armpits. 'Miss
Mo, I hafta help Mr Calhoun saddle a horse.' Silence. Then
Henry warned him. 'Huh-oh, here she comes. We're both in
trouble, Mr Calhoun.'

'Probably so.' Calhoun kept aiming himself toward the barn.

'Henry, get back inside at once.' There was a sharpness to
Maura's tone that Calhoun had never heard, but he knew the
reason why.

'But, Miss Mo. I gotta help.'

Putting their voices behind him, Calhoun reached the dim
interior that smelled of hay and leather. His horse was in the first
stall. He pulled the saddle from a rail and was in the middle of
tacking up when Maura entered.

'I didn't want to believe you'd leave so soon.' Her voice was
low and filled with disappointment. A good deal of hurt too.

'I told you I would as soon as the storm blew over,' he
answered, not looking at her.

'I know. But a day or two more would give your leg more
time to heal.'

He finished cinching the strap under the horse's belly and
turned, finally meeting her gaze. 'Look, it doesn't matter how
much time I wait, the result would be the same,' he said softly,
admiring the way a shaft of sunlight came through cracks in the
boards, spearing her face and hair. She looked like an angel
standing there, strands of russet brown hair in disarray, high
color in her face. 'You'd still want to keep me here. So would
the children.'

'Well? What's wrong with that?' She stuck her hands in her
apron pockets. 'I know your leaving will give me a chance to
figure things out in my head, but please, tell me you'll be back.
Please.'

He moved closer and ran a finger across her soft cheek. 'I can't promise that. I won't give you more false hope than I already have. Nothing can come of whatever this is between us. Find someone better than me. There are others who'll stand up to Lucius Taggart.'

'Even if there were, it's you who has my heart.' Her voice choked and she swallowed. 'Hold me. Kiss me one more time. I can't bear it if you left me with nothing.'

Their breath fogging in the cold barn, Calhoun pulled her against him and crushed his lips to hers. Her wild heartbeat kept time with his as though they were one. She tasted of tea and sweet desire and at that moment he would've given anything to stay here at Heaven's Door because it truly held peace and love.

Her body fit his like a glove of the finest kid leather. He deepened the kiss, and she clutched his coat with both fists, hanging on. Tears filled his eyes. This felt so right. So good.

Finally, she ended the kiss and murmured against his lips, 'Please don't let me go.'

Calhoun held her for several long moments, his eyes closed, soaking up the feel of her. But that too came to an end. He stepped back. 'You're the finest woman I've ever seen. Truly gentle and kind in words and actions. If there was any way . . .' With a gentle finger, he lifted a strand of hair from her eyes. 'Try to find someone else. There are hundreds of men better than me. I'm no good for you. Don't you see? It's better this way.'

'Not better for us, so no, I don't see.'

'You will.' He slid his palm slowly down her throat, feeling her racing pulse. 'Don't shrivel up and die inside like an old crone, pretty lady. You have so much to offer, to live for.'

'I laid awake all night thinking. I don't care who you are. I know the man you are now. Nothing else matters.'

'You say that now but what about six months or a year from now? Rumors will persist. Believe me, your father and others won't let it die. Then they'll turn against you, too.'

She plucked at the sleeve of his coat. 'I'm already an outcast, how much worse can it get?'

'Lots. Accept that things have to be this way.' The secrets, the truth, separated them.

'Wait while I gather some food to take with you. It'll only take a minute.'

'No, I need to get going. I won't take food from these kids.' He had to leave before he lost his nerve. His last bit of resolve was already hanging by a thread.

Tears in her eyes, Maura lifted her chin. 'I love you, Calhoun. I think I have for some time. I can do nothing about that. Ride away if you must but you'll do it with the knowledge you'll take my heart with you.'

As her words disappeared into a strangled cry, she slipped from the barn, leaving him to the emptiness deep inside.

'I love you, Maura,' he whispered. 'What I feel is eternal, not some passing fancy.'

She was everything he wanted. And more. But he couldn't have her.

Not now or ever.

A broken, empty man, he ignored the tears that ran down his face as he continued to prepare to leave.

TWENTY-SIX

With her words of love echoing inside his head, Calhoun spied his bedroll and burlap bag of supplies in the corner. He tied them to the gelding and led the animal from the dim barn. It took several tries to get his foot in the saddle and by the time he did, his leg throbbed. It had been so much easier when Maura had helped him. Sighing a deep breath of regret and sorrow, he let the horse pick its way toward the narrow road. Away from everyone he loved.

The back door slammed. 'Mr Calhoun, don't go!' Sunny cried, running out.

'Please don't go, Mr Calhoun,' Alphie and Henry yelled. 'Come back!'

All three kids were chasing after him. Just what Calhoun tried to avoid. He kept his gaze fastened straight ahead, for if he'd stopped, he wouldn't have had the strength to go on.

'We love you, Mr Calhoun,' Sunny sobbed. 'We love you.'

The kids had lost everyone in their lives and now Calhoun, too. He called himself every name he could think of and urged the horse into a gallop. Soon, he'd left the voices behind.

But not the memories. Those were a permanent part of him now.

The sun lent meager warmth to the cool air, but it was absent of moisture. That was a blessing. The pain in his leg started to ease. He'd always enjoyed riding.

Now to find where his brother lay – either beneath the ground or on top. He wouldn't go to the loot right away. If he could even find it. Too much time had passed while he was laid up and his memory was fuzzy at best. Yet, he was ready to put it to the test.

He stopped to drink at a cool stream and water his horse, wishing he had one of Maura's hot biscuits slathered with butter. He'd have to find some food soon.

After a brief rest, he set off again. The sun put him at

mid-morning. The children would be singing their hearts out by now. He wondered if Henry got his egg. Hopefully, they'd had enough for all the boys and girls.

A short time later, he tied the gelding and skirted the outlaw camp on foot, searching for movement. He didn't see any. Maybe they were all asleep. With weapon cocked and ready in hand, he sneaked closer through the trees. The camp was deserted. Someone had brushed the ground to get rid of tracks.

He went back to get his horse and stroked the animal's neck. 'I'll bet anything they're close by.'

Several places came to mind. He'd simply have to check each known hideout and that would take time. But he was a patient man with a burning need for vengeance. And sooner or later, he'd turn over the right rock.

Calhoun set his jaw. Wherever they were, he'd find them.

Before he headed to the next possible hideout, he turned his face to the sun and closed his eyes, savoring the warmth. Then, he made a fire and soon had half a pot of coffee made.

'Not as good as Maura's, but it'll do,' he murmured, tipping his cup to the horse where it nibbled on some rye grass. With luck, he'd find some game for supper and a bit of shelter.

Maybe in time, this ache around his heart would ease. He found himself thinking of what might be happening at Heaven's Door. Would more mysterious gifts appear in front of the church? For a moment he pondered that but came up with nothing about the gifter, but it was clear someone was watching the orphanage. The things he or she left were items the orphanage needed. It was quite a mystery.

It occurred to him that he hadn't hunted for large game as he'd intended. Hopefully, Max would.

He finished his coffee and put everything back in the burlap bag. Time to stalk his prey.

Calhoun was good at one thing – dispensing justice. He could make a man real sorry for what he'd done and Donavan would know the full sting of his wrath.

As he went around the back of his gelding, he froze. The frenzied whir of insects reached him. He followed the sound to a scrap of fabric near some tall brush. His hand hovered over the butt of his pistol. But the overwhelming stench didn't come from the living. With heightened awareness standing the hair on his neck on end, he inched closer. Then he saw a denim-clad leg. Bending, he moved the leaves and brush away and stared at his gruesome discovery.

A guttural cry sprang from his mouth.

The familiar face of his brother stared up at him.

Calhoun shook from the horror, unable to move. He needn't worry any longer about his brother's whereabouts. Further inspection revealed riddling bullet wounds and a rope still bound his brother's hands. It seemed the gang had dragged the body back here, tied him to a tree, and used him for target practice.

Target practice. The knowledge sent cold chills through Calhoun and a sickening whirl to his belly.

Anguished, keening cries escaped from his mouth as he rocked back on his heels. Wild creatures had been feeding off the corpse. Someone had stolen his brother's boots and hand-tooled gun belt.

Holding a kerchief to his nose, he squatted on his heels next to the body for some time, shooing away the swarm of insects. Finally, he stood, glancing around for a place to bury him and chose a spot back in the trees hidden from view.

Who knew when Donavan or his men would ride by? That always lurked in the back of Calhoun's mind. It paid to be cautious and keep his eyes open.

Bringing nothing to dig a grave with, Calhoun used his hands then a short piece of a thick branch. Unfortunately, the hole wasn't very deep so he heaped rocks on top. The effort sapped his strength and could barely move. Though he hated the delay, he decided to stay until morning. He had to have some nourishment, or he wouldn't be able to do anything when he found the man he'd come after.

One way or another, Rupert Donavan would pay dearly.

Then his brother who'd sacrificed his life would be at peace. Tomorrow would tell the tale – about Donavan. And the loot.

By morning, there was little sign of the rainstorm and the sun felt wonderful. After being cooped up for two days, the children enjoyed running and playing. Maura and Max kept an eye out for anyone who might do them harm. Both wore guns. If the outlaw gang had seen Calhoun ride out, they might see them as easy prey.

The sisters and Emma spent a busy day of overseeing the gathering of eggs and trying to make mattresses by stuffing ticking with bluestem grass and whatever else they could find. After only filling a few, they ran out and would have to save up feathers.

'Why don't we use hay?' Alphie asked. 'My papa did.'

'Because the horses need the hay to eat.' Maura glanced around hoping something else would come to mind but nothing did so she carried the mattresses they'd made inside.

The afternoon shadows were getting long when she looked around and couldn't find Tully. She grabbed Henry and went out to search. None of the other kids had seen him all afternoon. Surely no one had taken him again, but Maura knew not to underestimate the evil that people were capable of. They'd see right off Tully wasn't like everyone else and do horrible things to him.

'Tully!' she yelled. 'Tully! Where are you?'

Henry ran ahead calling the boy's name. They were almost to the river when Henry pointed, yelling, 'There he is, Miss Mo!'

Dirty and grinning, Tully came toward them holding up a big stringer of fish. 'I got supper!'

Maura waited for him to get closer so they wouldn't have to yell, then patted his shoulder. 'My goodness, how did you catch them without hooks?'

'My hands.'

Henry's eyes bugged out. 'I didn't know you could do that.'

'Yep,' Tully answered. 'You hafta be real still.'

'You really amaze me, Tully. That's quite a catch.' Maura beamed. 'You're full of surprises.'

'Wait'll the others hear this!' Henry took off running for home and was met by Gunner's excited yips and sharp barks.

A welcome committee was waiting for them. The sisters were grinning from ear to ear and the puppy's pink tongue was lolling out the side of his mouth in an odd kind of smile.

'I wish Mr Calhoun was here to see,' Sunny said wistfully.

'Me too, Sunny.' Maura had found it difficult to keep her thoughts off the man as she'd gone about her day. She prayed he was safe and finding what he was searching for.

Sunny squinted up at her. 'Do you think he'll come back, Miss Mo?'

'We will pray he does.' Sister Angela fingered the cross she wore. 'Let's clean fish.'

'Can we have them for supper?' Henry asked.

Maura smiled at Tully. 'Yes, we certainly can.'

Uncle Max joined them, admiring the stringer. 'I'll clean them in nothing flat.'

'Thank you, Uncle.' Maura didn't like that job. She'd cook them all day long but didn't want to gut and clean them.

Supper that night was very boisterous, and everyone got their fill of the delicious fish. Max brought out his harmonica and played jaunty tunes. It was a wonderful celebration and just what they needed.

Between songs, Henry sat next to Tully. 'Can I go fishing with you next time?'

The older boy shrugged. 'I guess.'

Maura leaned across the table. 'You must ask permission. Do you understand, Tully? Henry? You can't just go wandering off. It's our job to keep you safe and that means we need to know where you are. You could slip and fall into the water and get washed downstream. Or drown.'

Tully ducked his head. 'Yes, Miss Mo.'

Henry nodded. 'I won't drown, Miss Mo. I promise. And I'll ask first.'

She smothered her laughter, turning away. Henry's solemn vow came out all backward and funny. Straightening her face, she went to sit beside Max and led the singing.

In a slight pause between songs, Max spoke in her ear. 'You can't best these kids, Maura. You need to learn that right now. They're smarter than whips and pretty much do whatever they take a notion.'

'I know and that really frightens me. We can't protect them if we don't know where they are.' Maura stared down the table at the orphans she'd come to love like her own children and a mist blurred her vision. To lose even one would devastate her.

'Let's sing "Froggie Went a Courtin",' Sunny suggested.

Gunner gave a sharp bark and danced around in a circle on his back legs which brought happy laughter.

This was home; a place of love for those with no one. Heaven's Door would help these kids grow into adults with meaningful lives and true values.

That was her vow. However, she had to do it. Forget about love and a handsome man whose kisses drove her out of her mind and made her forget her purpose.

After that fine fish supper, Maura sent the sisters out of the kitchen and she and Emma did the dishes.

Emma glanced at her. 'Are you all right? Calhoun wasted no time riding out.'

'I'll be fine. I never was supposed to have a life with him. I see that. My place is here with you, running Heaven's Door.' Not riding off with the first man who'd shown any interest in her, hoping everything would magically work out.

Magic never happened in real life. The only things that did were what she'd worked for. Nothing ever came easy.

Maura turned away to hide the sudden quivering of her lip. Warmth enveloped her when Emma slipped her arms around her and laid her head on Maura's shoulder.

'I hate to see you heartbroken.' Emma rubbed Maura's back. 'Please don't give up. Calhoun's a nice man and I don't care what anyone says. He may decide he's unable to forget you and come back. If it's meant to be, it will happen.'

'I know.' Maura inhaled a shaky breath. 'Meanwhile, we have this place to run and keeping track of these kids is a full-time job.'

Emma chuckled and dropped her hold. 'Amen to that.'

Sister Bernadette appeared in the doorway. 'We have visitor.'

'Who would visit this late?' Maura asked.

'Young girl, mademoiselle. Desperate.'

'OK, we'll be right there. Ask her to wait.' Maura removed her apron and she and Emma went to see this girl. If she wanted food, they'd share what they had.

They hurried down the hallway to the sanctuary of the chapel, finding the girl huddling on a pew, shivering with cold. Her long hair hung down her back and her dress showed stains. She crossed her arms protectively over her chest.

'Hello, welcome to Heaven's Door. I'm Maura and this is my sister Emma. We run this place.' Maura sat beside her. 'How can we help you?'

'I'm sorry for coming so late, ma'am. I was hoping you might give me a job. I've left home.' The girl had pretty eyes filled with sorrow and despair. 'It gets so cold outside at night now and winter will be here soon. And it's not safe sleeping out in the open. I'll work really hard and help you do anything. I heard this is an orphanage. Surely you must need help.' She paused. 'Please,' she whispered.

'Of course, my dear.' Maura put an arm around her. 'We won't turn anyone in need away. But we have no funds to pay you. A bed and food are all we can offer.'

Hope sprang into her pinched face. 'That's all I ask, ma'am. So I can stay?'

Emma sat on the other side of her. 'Yes, you may stay. What is your name?'

'Margaret, ma'am. My mama called me Meg, but she's gone now.'

'I'm so sorry. I'm sure you miss her.' Maura smiled. 'You don't know what a godsend you are, Meg. Welcome. Come to the kitchen and we'll feed you.' She exchanged a glance with Emma. How wonderful it would be to have one extra person. She lifted her gaze to the beautiful Virgin Mary over the altar and winked.

For a second it seemed the statue winked back, but that must've been a trick of the light from the candles the sisters had lit.

TWENTY-SEVEN

S pears of sunlight pierced the naked limbs of a pecan tree, waking Calhoun the next morning. He stirred and opened his eyes. He'd placed his bedroll beside the mound of rocks on top of his brother's grave. He wasn't morbid or strange and his choice of sleeping location wouldn't make any sense to anyone else. But being near his brother had brought some measure of comfort.

After coffee, luck would have it that he shot a prairie chicken which he cooked and ate. He made quick work of putting out the fire and packing up. He set off for the first place – another old, abandoned mission in a line of them that had fallen into ruin. The last time he was there, the chapel part was still standing.

Trotting along, he kept his thoughts off Maura and wondering what was happening at Heaven's Door. Best not to even speculate. He had to put them behind him – for his own sanity.

The day was cool, but the sun was shining and that was a blessing. His leg pained him after sleeping on the ground, but there was nothing he could do about that.

'I've gotten as soft as an old widow woman.' Calhoun's chuckle brought a loud nicker from the gelding. 'Well, you don't have to agree. That's rude.'

Everything was silent and still when he neared the once bustling monastery. He crawled through the dead grass on his belly. It appeared vacant. After watching for several long minutes, he stood and, after seeing no signs of anyone, moved on to the next one. And the next.

In the space of a week, he rode everywhere he could think of that might harbor outlaws.

It seemed the world was vacant and he was adrift. Each place he went, he encountered emptiness with wind whistling through the naked branches of cottonwood and pecan trees. Finally, deep in thought, he squatted next to a little stream and an idea struck him. A hidden box canyon within an hour's ride came to mind. It had a pretty good-sized patch of sweet grass where the horses could graze and a little trickle of water meandering through the middle. Rupert Donavan had once wintered there. Maybe that's where he and the gang were laying low. Or they could be on another job.

About an hour later, he neared the destination, praying his search would be over. He tied the gelding to a low tree limb and went forward on foot. Despite trying to be quiet, he disturbed a covey of about twenty quail. Amid the rush to take flight, they created a lot of noise. Dammit! If Donavan had heard it, he'd know someone was coming. But maybe, just maybe, the man would put the disturbance down to a wild animal.

Calhoun moved ever closer and finally lay on an overhang to see the activity below. A lot more men than those comprising the Donavan Gang were building some kind of structure. Some were felling trees, some sawing, others hammering.

A different gang maybe?

A quick count came up to a dozen but there could be more. The most Donavan usually had were six. Calhoun couldn't make out Rupert Donavan from this distance. Everyone appeared the same.

The need to get closer sent him scooting backward toward cover where he could stand. He picked his way down the bluff and skirted the stream, then quietly pushed through a stand of sugarberry, pecan and persimmon trees. Finally, he lay on the cool ground, listening, watching.

Waiting.

The workers talked about how rich they'd get after doing their next bank job. So these were outlaws, no doubt remained. And the town with the bank sounded like Austin but he wouldn't swear to it.

Then he heard something about the old Espada Mission outside San Antonio and the orphanage. His ears perked up. The men had their backs to him. Calhoun judged the distance to a stack of boards near the workers. If he could run and hide behind those . . . But he had his bad leg. No way he could run. Or slide down to hide. Or any of the things he used to not give a thought to. Still, he needed to hear what they were planning. Desperation could make a man do crazy things.

He took a deep breath and said a prayer. Just then an idea hit him, and he relaxed. Pretending to be one of them just might work. He looked similar and knew how to blend in. He rose and hobbled to the pile of boards. He picked one up and put it on his shoulder, angling it where it put his face in a shadow. Whistling a soft tune, he limped slowly past the two men, keeping his head lowered.

'Donavan is sure that other figure riding out with Jonas that night is hiding there, and aims to find him. Said he plans to have the woman before he kills her,' the taller man said, chuckling. 'I wouldn't mind having the younger one. She's got sass and will fight like a wildcat.'

'Both are sure pretty. Bet we could have us a good time with 'em. Too bad their father's the hangman,' answered the other sporting a goatee. 'Still, he'll never get a chance at our necks because we'll be far away.' He paused and shook his head. 'Slaughtering little kids gives me the shivers. That's not right and I don't think I can do that.'

Calhoun's blood turned to ice. A million thoughts ran through his head. Pictures swam in his mind of the people he cared about lying in pools of blood, baby Juliette crying and no one able to see about her. Or maybe they'd spray her tiny body with bullets too.

Dammit to hell! He had to do something. His stomach churned.

'If it wasn't for the buried treasure Donavan heard about, I'd get on my horse and ride out,' Mr Goatee said. 'He promised it would be at that orphanage. Talk is, Jim Bowie had a bit of a skirmish at the mission with the Mexicans so he buried it there. Donavan says he knows just where to look.'

'Yeah, I hope he ain't lying to us.'

A gray-haired outlaw joined them. 'Say, I overheard you talking about treasure. That's why I'm here and no other reason. I've worked my whole blamed life with nothing to show. Once before I die I want to have my own plot of ground to pass down to my son.'

'Me too,' Goatee said.

Calhoun looked for someplace to lay the slab of wood.

Suddenly, Rupert Donavan stalked from a grove of trees opposite of the ones Calhoun had come through. The big boss scanned the workers.

'Hey, you with that timber!' Donavan yelled, pointing at Calhoun. 'Get that over here and quit wasting time. We don't have all day. I swear I can see dead lice falling off you.'

Act casual, Calhoun told himself, but a herd of wild horses was inside his chest. *Don't panic.*

A lower dip of his head let the brim of his hat fall across his face. 'Yes, boss. Coming.'

He changed direction and limped faster. The sooner he put the board down, the sooner he could get out of there, preferably alive.

'Are you sure you're one of the men I hired?' Donavan snarled. 'What's your name?'

Not risking being recognized, Calhoun kept his face down and spoke in a deeper voice. 'Maxwell's my name.'

'All right, move on.' Thankfully, Donavan swung to another shirker and while he was barking orders at him, Calhoun passed his load to a man wearing a pouch full of nails around his waist and slipped out of sight around the framework of the structure.

It was useless to think about avenging his brother with all the extra gunmen around. He'd get to his horse and hurry to warn Maura.

But at least he'd found Donavan. He must've gotten some new recruits. Maybe some of his men had gotten killed the night of the escape. Now that Calhoun knew they were planning on raiding the mission, he had to make sure they failed.

Saving the people at Heaven's Door took precedence over everything else. They were family and no one was going to harm them if he had anything to do with it.

Staying had placed them in danger before and going back would make it worse. But if he didn't return to warn them, they'd surely die. What to do?

He pinched the bridge of his nose. Regardless of the consequences, he had to follow his heart. It was the only way to live with himself.

*   *   *

Early that same morning, Max found two large bags of feathers in front of the chapel and brought them to Maura. 'It seems our mysterious benefactor left another gift.'

She clasped a hand over her mouth. 'Oh, my goodness. This is wonderful. How do they know what we need? Uncle Max, do you think they're watching us?'

'Just about have to be or they wouldn't know. They must've seen us trying to make mattresses with nothing to stuff them with.' Max pushed back his hat. 'They'd cleared away any tracks again so we can't follow. I think the only way we have of catching them is to hide and keep watch.'

'I think you're right. I wish Calhoun was here. With the two of you no one would've had to spend the whole night. I'm sorry, Uncle. I'll volunteer to help. When do you want to do it?'

'Well, they usually come every other night or so. Never two in a row. We could try for Friday.'

'Sounds OK with me.' Maura lifted one bag of the feathers. 'I just want to know who it is once and for all. And to thank them. They've made such a difference in our lives and those of the children.' Feeling immensely blessed, she followed Max round back and went in to help with breakfast.

Fragile and thin, Meg looked different, pretty even with her hair combed and pulled back and in a clean dress that Emma gave her.

As the children filed in, Tully took one look and stopped in his tracks. 'Meg!' He ran around the table to hug her. 'I lost you.'

'Tully, oh Tully, I'm so glad to see you.' Meg wrapped her arms around him. 'I didn't know what happened to you.'

'I was Wild Boy.'

Maura joined them and explained where they'd found Tully. 'Are you related, Meg?'

'Yes, ma'am. He's my brother. Our mama ran off leaving us with our pa and now I've run off too. Pa is a bitter man and beats us. I couldn't take it anymore. I just couldn't.' She pulled Maura away from Tully and dropped her voice. 'Pa gave Tully to a man named Rooster in exchange for a gallon of hard liquor.'

Maura laid a hand on the girl's back. She winced and pulled back. 'Do you have welts right now?'

Meg dropped her head. 'I can't lie. He beat me something fierce and that's why I left. If I got blood on the bedding, I'll scrub it.' Her brown eyes hardened. 'He'll never touch me again. I hope I can still work here.'

'Of course, you can.' Maura's heart went out to the girl and her brother. Their lives must've been completely miserable. 'You both have a home here for as long as you want.' Last night she hadn't thought to ask the girl's age. 'How old are you, Meg?'

'Sixteen, ma'am. I'm a hard worker.'

With a smile, Maura gave her a light hug, careful of her injuries. 'I don't doubt that. Come with me. I want to put healing salve on your back.'

'I would feel obliged, ma'am. I truly would.'

Telling Tully they'd be right back, Maura took her into the bedroom she shared with Emma and shut the door. 'If you'll take your bodice off, I'll get the salve.'

There was a rustle of clothing. When she turned around and found herself face to face with the bloody results of the belt, she struggled to keep from crying out. The sight left her shaken, her stomach knotted. If she'd already eaten, the food would've come back up. She'd never seen cruelty like this.

'I'll try my best not to hurt you more than you are feeling it already.' She dipped two fingers in the salve made from the aloe vera plant that grew wild in the area and wondered where to begin. Wide welts crisscrossed Meg's tender skin. The agony had to have been indescribable. The drunken, enraged man had truly tried to kill his daughter.

Maura touched her fingers to the first of the open wounds and Meg hissed through her teeth. 'I'm being as gentle as I know how.'

'I know. Keep going.'

Tears streamed down Maura's face as she applied the salve to the shredded back. Finally she stepped back and put the lid on the salve, then wiped her eyes. 'That's good enough for now. I'll put more on over the next week.' She held Meg's bodice and helped her slip it on.

'Thank you, Miss Mo. You're very kind.'

Kissing the girl's cheek, Maura smiled. 'And you have to be the bravest young woman I've ever seen.'

Meg shrugged. 'I had two options and I chose to live. I fought to live.'

'You sure did. Let's get breakfast.' Although after seeing the welts, food was the last thing Maura wanted. 'Afterward, you can start helping the kids. That is if you feel up to it.'

'I can do the work, Miss Mo. Don't worry.'

They returned to the kitchen and Meg took the chair next to Tully.

Maura's heart swelled to be able to bring the brother and sister together. She'd saved two more from a life not worth living. Here they had a chance to grow up happy.

Young Sister Anne-Marie entered the kitchen with Juliette and Meg's attention went to them, her brown eyes softening. She pushed back her chair to get up but met Maura's gaze and slid back in. A baby could sure make people react in strange ways. Most certainly Meg had felt compelled to go to the child.

But that was easy to understand. Juliette was such a sweet baby. She'd even affected Calhoun.

While Sister Angela led the blessing, Maura took stock again as she swept each face at the table. From the five Johnson brothers, to the Harrison twins, and the remaining nine others all were special. This was her calling. Each one needed someone to save them. To love them. This was what she was born to do.

Though she accepted that, her heart still cried for Calhoun and his warm kisses that turned her knees to jelly and melted her insides.

Her love for him would always remain a part of the fiber of her being. As constant as the moon, the stars, the heavens.

She might not ever see him again in this lifetime, but she'd stored every detail of him in her memory. His dark, wavy hair that brushed his collar, his intense black eyes that could see inside her heart, and the cleft in his chin that lent character to his face and dazzle to his smile. Yes, he was her first – and last – love.

Outlaw or lawman. He was known simply as Calhoun.

TWENTY-EIGHT

As the afternoon waned, Maura counted ten new mattresses ready to be slept on. They weren't as full as most, but no one would complain. After they had enough for all, they could always add more stuffing. Though she was tired and every muscle ached, she'd had a very good day.

Meg had proven herself. She'd done everything anyone had asked plus more. She'd really taken to Juliette and the baby to her as well it seemed. Juliette had cooed and touched the girl's face when she'd held her. The two just seemed to bond. They really couldn't afford the extra mouth to feed but Maura couldn't turn the girl away. Her father needed to be horsewhipped within an inch of his miserable life.

Just then, Maura spied two of the five Johnson boys sneaking into the chicken coop. 'Oh no you don't. Get out of there!' No telling what they had in mind but it wouldn't be good.

'Shoo!' Emma being closer rushed to them before they could do any damage.

The youngest no more than six looked up at Emma through a fringe of hair. 'We was just goin' to collect the eggs, Miss Em.'

'We've already gathered them for the day,' Emma answered, picking him up and holding the chicken wire up for his ten-year-old brother. 'There will be no more until tomorrow.'

'Why don't chickens lay eggs twice a day, Miss Em?' the older boy asked.

Uncle Max ambled by. 'Good question, son. Why do geese fly in a "V"?'

The ten-year-old shrugged his shoulder. 'I dunno.'

'When you know the answer to that, you can move on to chickens.' Uncle Max pointed to the other kids playing chase. 'If I was you, I think I'd go join them.'

'Yes, sir,' the boy mumbled.

Maura's gaze swept to the sweet Harrison twins clutching their ragdolls and playing hopscotch with Sunny. All seemed content and contained – for the moment. She turned and hurried inside to help finish supper.

The wonderful aroma of stew met her. It would be filling and delicious. Tomorrow she'd have to go hunting for game. A deer would feed them for a month. But that would take luck. And she'd have to be extra vigilant. Danger was all around them and she felt it in her bones that trouble would soon come visiting. Often in the late-night hours, she felt it closing in. She never got comfortable enough to sleep until she'd checked the doors and windows multiple times to make sure they were locked and the children were secure.

Uncle Max wandered up. 'Keep a close eye on our kids, Maura. I saw a flash of something at the edge of the woods. I think we're still being watched and the campsite I noticed when Calhoun was here is being used.'

The hair on Maura's arms stood. 'Calhoun thought they'd move on when he left. But they haven't. What are they wanting?'

'Who knows?'

'This waiting is getting on my nerves. I wish we had more men here. Do you think we might hire some?'

His brown eyes held worry. 'And pay 'em with what? All our money has to go for food.'

'True. Do you think we should try to train Tully to shoot?'

Max shook his head. 'That boy has all he can handle. Angie and Bernie would come near picking up a shooting iron.'

Maura's gaze found the oldest sisters riding herd on the children. 'You're probably right. But for now, it's just us.' She sighed. 'I have to get supper on.' She rested a hand on Max's shoulder. 'Thank you for everything you do. You're a huge help.'

He ducked his head, then looked away. 'Just don't want anything to happen to any of you.'

She kissed his cheek. 'Don't think it goes unnoticed.'

Clutching her wool shawl tight around her, Maura hurried across the play yard, stepped into the kitchen, and tied on an apron. Bernadette had beaten her inside and was busy peeling potatoes. 'What can I do, Sister Bernadette?'

'Make how you say . . . corn bret.'

'Oh, you mean cornbread. I might have to sift the weevils out, but we'll do whatever we must.'

'*Oui.*' The unflappable sister's warm smile put joy in Maura's heart. 'It's good.'

The two women began to hum as they worked side by side.

Sister Angela entered and stopped. 'Beautiful. Happy people. Happy *enfants.*'

'I think so too,' Maura agreed, glad she'd hid her sorrow well. It did no good to wear a long face or frown. Best to cover the coming trouble.

Yet Calhoun was never far from her thoughts. She wondered where he was, what he was doing. And if he thought of her.

The afternoon shadows were growing long by the time he neared the orphanage. Still, Calhoun had to pass by the place where he'd hidden the loot, so he made the decision to stop. It wouldn't take long, and it would ease his mind to know it was still there. He reined up at the large boulders he seemed to remember and dismounted, scanning the area.

Parts of it looked familiar but horrific pain had dulled his vision. He didn't recall the brush growing halfway up the rock pile. This couldn't be it. Still, he searched for the crevice he'd stuffed the loot into.

It wasn't there. This wasn't the right place.

Disappointed, he used all his strength to crawl back on the horse. He'd have to do more thinking. But first he had to get to Heaven's Door. It was near. He could feel Maura drawing him with the smell of her sweetness, the taste of her honeyed lips.

How could he leave a second time? A week ago, it'd almost killed him. Next time it would.

Dios Mío, as the Spanish population would say. My God was right. He didn't stand a chance. Leaving would kill him and so would staying. Not only him but Maura.

After a week away, his first glimpse of the place he held dear was like a balm for his soul. No one had yet to call the playing children to supper. He sat for a moment unmoving, taking it all in.

Gunner noticed him first and ran, barking his fool head off. He ran in circles around the horse.

Sunny squealed at the top of her voice, 'Mr Calhoun!'

Suddenly, he was two and three deep in kids of all ages. 'How are you all doing?'

'We missed you.' Sunny touched his leg, his foot still in the stirrup.

Henry grinned up at him, the gap showing missing teeth was in full view. 'Mr Calhoun, we got eggs from the chickens! We really did!'

'That's excellent, Henry. Let me get on to the barn. Have you had supper yet?'

'Nope,' little Alphie said.

'That's good. I'm starving. I'll be in directly.' It was a miracle they moved and he could pass through. They'd for sure run to tell Maura. Well, he had no choice but to face that.

In the barn, he unsaddled and fed the gelding, dread growing. Things would be different now – awkward – since Maura had spoken of her feelings. He'd make it as easy on her as he could.

After feeding and bedding the horse down, he turned to leave with an anxious sigh. But when he stepped out of the barn he collided with Maura. A quick grab kept her on her feet.

'I'm sorry. I wasn't paying attention.' He met her cornflower blue eyes accented with dark edges around the circles and swallowed hard. The red in her hair seemed more vibrant. She was more beautiful than any woman had a right to be.

'I'm fine,' she said low. 'I'm glad you're back.'

He chuckled. 'Didn't expect me this soon, I'm sure.'

'I never thought I'd see you again. At least not for a while.' She stood in indecision then asked, 'Will you hug me? I really would like a hug.'

'Of course, I will. Anytime. Sorry you had to ask.' He pulled her close and folded his arms around her slim body.

She buried her face against his chest. Calhoun closed his eyes for a moment, savoring the feel of her in his arms and breathing in the soft fragrance that clung to her clothes.

'I'll try not to make you ask for hugs when we're alone,' he murmured into her hair. 'But if I forget, poke me.' He let her go and stepped back. 'I found my brother's body and buried him, then I found Rupert Donavan, the leader of the gang. Maura, he's planning to raid this place and says he'll kill everyone here. I had to come and warn you.'

She inhaled sharply. 'Why? We have nothing.'

'Donavan still wants me and thinks there's buried treasure here. He's willing to do anything to find it.' He rubbed her arm. 'We have to get ready for him. I'll speak to Max after supper and we'll come up with a plan. Don't worry. We're going to stop him and his men.'

'How?' she whispered.

'Not sure just yet, not enough to give you specifics.'

'I . . . this is crazy. How many men does he have and how soon will they come?'

'Too many. They were building some kind of outlaw post. I think they'll finish that first. But I expect they'll mount an attack within the next week or two.' He put an arm around her waist. He'd told her enough for now. She was scared and rightly so. No use making it worse. He picked up his saddlebags and threw them over a shoulder. 'Let's go eat. I'm starving and I want some of your coffee. You've spoiled me, you know.'

'I have?'

A smile formed on her lips, grateful he could put it there. As they walked, Maura told him about Meg coming and what she'd said about her father.

'She's such a sweet girl and just needs half a chance. Such a change has come over Tully to have his sister here.' She glanced up. 'Are you listening to me?'

'Every word. I'm glad you took her in. She needed a good home.' If he ever met that poor excuse for a father, he'd make the man regret his miserable life. 'I need a word with Max if I can get it.'

'He promised to take supper with us. I think he'll keep his word.'

'Good.'

They reached the door. He dropped his hand from her waist and held it open for her. The loud babble of voices instantly stopped. He removed his hat. 'I'm sure glad to see you all.'

'Thank you for coming back, Mr Calhoun.' Sunny slid out of her chair and took his hand. 'Will you sit by me?'

188 Linda Broday

'No, I want him to sit here,' Henry insisted. 'We got man stuff to talk about.'

'Sorry, Henry. Sunny asked first.' He followed her to a chair. There was a slight scuffle between Alphie and the youngest of the five Johnson brothers as both boys tried to steal the seat on the other side of him. 'Let's settle down, kids. Miss Mo and Sister Angela are frowning. You can all take turns.'

The door opened and Max walked in, taking his usual spot at the end closest to the exit. Calhoun nodded to him and got one in return. Relief filled the older man's eyes.

The coffee, stew and cornbread really hit the spot. He kept glancing down the table at Maura and winking. Of course, she blushed so he accomplished what he intended. All too soon, the meal was over. He gathered his saddlebags and motioned to Max. They crossed the compound for privacy.

Once the door of Calhoun's quarters was closed and he lit the fire, he told Max everything he'd heard. Max sat in silence, staring at the flames.

Calhoun spoke quietly. 'Donavan is dead serious. Men like him don't back down. He's coming.'

Finally Max spoke. 'Do you think he really believes there's treasure here? Or is it something he's hatched up to gain more men?'

'Does it make any difference?' With warmth spreading through the room, Calhoun removed his coat. 'Who knows what he believes? The man is crazy and eaten up with greed. Human life holds no value for him.'

'We agree on that. How many did you estimate in the gang now?'

'I counted a dozen but that might not have included ones I didn't see.'

'Damn.' Max stood and leaned his lanky frame against the wall next to the fireplace. The flickering flames brought out the silver that danced in his long brown hair. 'What are we going to do? You got a plan?'

'Nothing beyond fighting like hell. You?'

Silence engulfed them. The only noise was the crackle and pop of the fire.

'We need some dynamite,' Max murmured. Looking up, he met Calhoun's gaze. 'I might have a friend of a friend with ways to get some. But we'll need money.'

Calhoun thought about the loot. If he could just find it . . . 'I have a little. How much we talking about?'

'A hundred should buy enough.'

'Give me a couple of days.' Calhoun's thoughts whirled. 'I figure Donavan's gang will attack at night and probably by the front door of the chapel. That's the easiest way in. We'll block the back way with wagons. If we conceal pockets of black powder all across the front, we might get most by the time any get inside.'

'Black powder's cheaper.' Max shook his head. 'That'll take one of us being out there to set them off though. Sticks of dynamite we can light and throw and that would get rid of quite a few.'

'We'll whittle them down to size a little at a time.'

'Still, that's two against twelve seasoned gunfighters.' Max fished tobacco and papers from his pocket and began rolling a cigarette. 'Maura's a pretty good shot and Emma's fair, so that makes four.'

Pitiful odds.

'What about that new girl? Meg. We need to find out if she's fired a weapon. A lot of kids grow up hunting for game.'

'Not a bad idea. I'm wondering about the sisters and their feelings on guns. Want a smoke?'

'No thanks. The sisters can help in other ways like blocking the doors and arming them with skillets. A cast iron skillet can knock a man out.' The conversation he'd overheard between those two members of the gang floated around in his head. 'Max, there's something else.'

Max lit his cigarette and took smoke into his lungs. 'Ain't there always?'

'Killing isn't all on those outlaws' mind. They talked about having fun with your nieces before they put a bullet in them.'

Max stilled. 'Over my dead body.'

'Mine, too.' Just the thought of anyone laying a hand on those two ladies in that way brought Calhoun's back teeth clamping together so tight it hurt. 'I'll tear 'em limb from limb if they try.

Those devils better hope to God I'm dead or I won't hesitate one second in sending them to the fiery pits of hell.'

Steely resolve wrapped the threat that he fully meant to enforce, no matter how he had to do it. He wouldn't rest until they no longer had breath in their bodies.

From the dark expression in Max's eyes, he shared that sentiment.

The quiet man smoothed his beard. 'Once a long way back, I caught up to a man after he'd kidnapped my neighbor's pretty wife and tortured her in ways you can't imagine.' Max's eyes clouded with the memory, and he barely spoke loud enough to hear. 'I took my time with him.' Max paused. 'Left him barely alive, then fed him to the alligators two days' ride from here. I'm planning the same for anyone who even thinks he can hurt my nieces. If they do . . .'

Max didn't need to finish. Calhoun already knew the unsaid part.

The man's threat hung in the air drawing a shiver up Calhoun's back. 'Amen,' he ground out.

TWENTY-NINE

The following morning, the weather had a chilly bite in the air. Typical for a Texas fall. One day up and the next down, very unpredictable. It didn't much matter to Calhoun. He didn't have a choice. He had to find the loot. The lives of everyone were in his hands and he had no time to waste. Donavan was fired up to find either buried treasure or the loot they'd stolen from him. Or both.

The greedy outlaw wanted it all and was determined to get it.

Calhoun was fairly certain by the feeling in his gut that the loot was still where he'd put it.

Only where? He'd thought about it until he'd given himself a headache last night.

Maura said she'd found him at the edge of the woods where the Mission San Francisco de la Espada property butted up against the trees. So it had to be somewhere around there.

There was no sign of Max when Calhoun went over to the kitchen for coffee and breakfast, playing with Gunner every step of the way. The dog loved to retrieve sticks.

What sort of guard dog would he make? Would he even bark at a stranger? Gunner might be the kind of dog that licked an intruder to death.

Calhoun cleaned his feet outside the door, took off his hat, and went in, finding the cozy room empty of children. 'I'm either early or the kids have already finished eating.'

'You beat them.' Maura poured coffee and set it down in front of him. Dark circles sat under her eyes. 'It doesn't look like you slept much either.' She took the seat next to him.

'I lost something and it's important that I find it.' He took a sip from his cup. 'Miss Maura, you know the way to a man's heart.'

'Is that right?' Despite the news that must sit heavy with her, she smiled. 'I'll try to remember that. Would you like breakfast? I made you two eggs.'

'Ah, those priceless eggs. I'm flattered. What about the kids?'
He laid a hand on top of hers.

'They're getting flapjacks with sorghum that Max surprised
us with, so they won't mind. What do you have planned for
today?'

'I need to ride out for a bit but I won't go far. I was wondering
something. Can you tell me exactly where you found me that
day?'

'Well, maybe not exactly. I went out the kitchen door and
straight across into the trees. I didn't veer up or down. I remember
that clearly. I sense it's important.'

'I've been trying to piece together fragments of memories.
That thing I lost had to have been around there.'

Emma walked in and went to the coffee, pouring herself a
cup. She'd entered so quietly.

'Did you share my news with your sister?' He took a sip of
his coffee. Emma was such a pretty girl to have to suffer torment.
He still wished he could run across the people who cut her hair.

'Yes, I told her about Donavan. We share everything and she
needed to know.'

'I agree. Max and I spoke well into the night and think we
hit on a plan. Not ready to talk details yet though. We're still
working on ways to defend this place. Do you know if there's a
trapdoor leading below ground? Back during constant attacks,
most places like this had one.'

'Why yes! We found a trapdoor, but the room below isn't in
the best of shape. Plus, it's kind of small.'

'I think we might need to get it ready. We'll need to hide the
children and nuns when the shooting starts.'

'That's a great idea. Emma and I will start work on it today.
We can't do anything outside anyway.' She rose. 'I'd better get
ready for the starving children and pour the milk.'

She no sooner got up than the kitchen quiet was assaulted by
the onslaught of hungry children. Led by Sister Angela, they
formed a line until they reached the door. Hollering, they ran
past the petite nun and scrambled for chairs close to Calhoun.

He laughed and grabbed his coffee holding it up as they jostled
the table.

'Why is everyone so excited?' he asked.

'It's flapjack day!' Alphie answered.

Tully grinned. 'We get sorghum too!'

'Is that right?' He glanced away and blinked hard. How could a father hate a child like Tully? The boy was exactly the way God wanted him. 'Tully, have you caught any more fish yet?'

'Nope. Won't let me.' The boy looked around for his sister. Panicking at not seeing her. 'Where's Meg?'

'Why don't I go look for her? OK? You just sit right there.' Calhoun got up and went into the hallway that he was told led to the sleeping quarters.

He kept going and found her with Juliette in one of the private bedrooms.

The girl's pretty brown hair was combed in a becoming style, curling around her shoulders. Her dress was a bit too snug and barely buttoned, but it was probably all she had. Her lowlife father had neglected her. Calhoun wanted to haul off and hit something. There was no retribution for men like him. Poor kids.

The tender way she held the baby touched him. The gentle care was like that of a mother.

What did he know about young mothers? Feeling like an intruder on her privacy, he started to look away when he caught her murmuring to the child.

'I'm sorry, Juliette. I'm so sorry.' A tear escaped and she hurriedly brushed it away.

That was odd. He wondered if Maura had heard Meg apologizing before and knew why. It wasn't his place to say anything, him being a man. She needed a woman's attention. He decided it would wait until they ate.

He turned around and went back to the kitchen. Meg entered shortly after and took her chair next to Tully. The boy said something and grabbed her as though fearing she'd disappear again.

Meg gently patted his arm. 'I'm fine, Tully, I was just tending to the baby is all.'

Maura brought milk around, filling the glasses and Emma began serving plates of flapjacks. He got a plate of eggs with flapjacks and dove in. Midway through the meal, the three-year-old at the end of the table spilled her milk and started crying.

Maura's gentleness in soothing the child and calmly cleaning it up brought a lump to his throat. She deserved to have kids of her own. He prayed she'd get some one day.

All too soon breakfast was over. He stood and told Maura he was leaving.

She leaned closer and kept her voice low. 'Don't be out in that wind too long. If you want some coffee to warm you up when you get back, find me. I don't mind making more.'

'Appreciate it.' He yearned to kiss her, but this wasn't the time or place. 'Maura, I found something odd with Meg this morning.' He told her what he'd overheard. 'There could be nothing there but I wanted to mention it.'

'I've noticed how attached she'd become to Juliette. I'll see to it. Hurry back.'

With a nod, he turned up the collar of his coat and went to saddle his horse. His feet crunched on the frozen ground. Gunner caught sight of him and ran over. With three short barks, he leaped up midair, his tongue lolling out. Calhoun picked up a stick and threw, wishing all the problems and worries of the world could be fixed by chasing sticks.

Finding that loot could mean the difference between life and death for a whole lot of people. Animals too.

Maura waded through the kids in the playroom to where Meg rocked Juliette. 'Would you mind coming with me for a minute?'

'OK, Miss Mo.' She handed the baby to Sister Anne-Marie who was hovering near.

Maura took the girl into the bedroom she shared with Emma. 'What is it, Miss Mo?'

'You were overheard saying you were sorry to Juliette. Sorry for what, dear?'

Meg flushed with embarrassment and began to cry. 'I'm sorry. I didn't know what to do.'

'Have you recently had a baby?' Maura asked gently.

The girl was silent and looked down. 'Yes.' She raised her eyes. 'I'm sorry I didn't tell you. Please don't make me leave. I beg you.'

The girl's terror brought tears to Maura's eyes. She put her arms around Meg and held her for several moments murmuring soothing words, then drew her to the bed. 'Let's sit. You don't have to be afraid. I just need to find out what's going on. No matter what it is, you have a home here. OK?'

'Thank you, ma'am.' Meg folded her hands in her lap.

'When did you give birth?'

'Three or four weeks ago, I think, to the best of my recollection.'

'Do you still have milk?'

'No, ma'am. It's gone.'

'OK, now I need to ask something very important.' Maura wiped Meg's eyes. 'Is Juliette your baby?'

Again, with lowered head, she hesitated, wringing her hands. Finally she spoke, still looking down. 'Yes. My father was threatening to kill her so I brought her here to keep her safe. At home I tried to hide her, only she wouldn't be quiet. He was so mad when he found her. He called me names and beat me so bad I feared for my life.'

What a horrible man. Maura took Meg's hands. 'I'm glad you brought Juliette here. She's a precious child. And I'm glad you sought shelter with us.' She paused, her thoughts whirling. 'A baby needs to be with her mother. We'll find you a room where you can have some privacy.'

'I'd like that, ma'am. Thank you so much.'

'Very good. I'll have to tell the sisters and Emma but they'll understand.' Now came the hard question. 'What about the baby's father? Is he someone you know?'

'No, ma'am.' Fresh tears rolled down the girl's face and her lip quivered. 'This stranger caught me while I was doing the wash one day and dragged me . . .' Her voice broke. 'The pain was bad. I screamed. He knocked me out. When I came around, he was gone. I put on what was left of my clothes and snuck into my house up to the loft where I slept. I told my father I was sick.' Meg gave a shuddering sob. 'He was drunk anyway.'

What a nightmare for such a young girl to go through. There was so much evil.

'I'm truly sorry, Meg. So sorry.' She held the girl against her. 'I wish I could make all the hurt and heartbreak go away. You're safe now and you're with your baby daughter.'

After several minutes, Maura spoke. 'Go back to Juliette. It's almost feeding time. I'll find you another place to sleep.'

'Thank you for understanding, Miss Mo. I'm used to anger. Kindness is strange to me.'

'Get accustomed to it, dear. Kindness and compassion are all you'll get here.' Maura turned away and blinked hard. 'I'll get Emma and we'll make you a private room. Juliette will stay with you.'

'To have her back . . . you don't know what this means.'

'I think I do. Now go get her and I'll get busy.'

They left and went separate ways. Maura found Emma in the kitchen with Uncle Max.

'I'm glad to see you make it over, Uncle,' Maura said. 'Want some breakfast?'

'Maybe in a little bit,' he answered. 'Seen Calhoun?'

'He ate and rode out. Said he had to go find something he lost. Whatever that means. We talked about clearing the secret room below the floor so we can use it to hide the children and sisters if we need to.'

'That's a good idea,' Emma said. 'We have to make ready.'

'Wonder why I didn't think of a secret hiding place? They all used them in places like this when they were under attack,' Max growled.

Maura turned to Emma. 'Can I have a word in private?'

The two went out into the hall. Keeping her voice down, Maura told her sister about Meg. 'You and I need to locate a small room just for her and the baby.'

'It'll have to be inside here and not out where Uncle Max and Calhoun sleep.' Emma's brow wrinkled in thought. 'There's a small storage room we can clear out that would be large enough for a bed and a few other things.'

'Great. That'll work. Let's go look.' They hurried next to the room off the kitchen that was filled with tons of rotted, dusty castoffs from former days when the monastery was a place of refuge for the poor and downtrodden.

Emma glanced around, her hands on her hips. 'This will be fine, don't you think?'

'I certainly do. And I love that it's right off the kitchen. The heat will keep them warm. But what to do with all this? Seems we're just shuffling things around like a shell game.'

'Most needs to be thrown away.' Emma stepped into the kitchen for Uncle Max. 'Uncle, we need a moment.'

He scooted back his chair and came to the storage door. 'Don't tell me you girls have plans for this space?'

'Yes, we do. It's important.' Maura patted his arm. 'Do you have time to help us haul all this out? It's really not any good and we need to empty this room for Meg.'

'You girls find more things to do,' he grumbled.

Maura patted his arm again and kissed his cheek. 'I know. But you love us anyway.'

'Yep, there's that.' He sighed. 'Let me finish my coffee and I'll pile it down by my workshop for now. There might be something here I can use.'

'Sounds like a plan and we'll help you carry things.' Emma wiped her nose and left a streak of dirt across her face.

Maura knew they'd both be dirty by the time it was said and done but she didn't complain. Little mama would have her own room. It was the least they could do to make the poor girl's life more bearable.

Calhoun stood back a short distance from the tree line and thought. He needed to go back to that night and remember every detail. The problem was . . . he'd been in agony and losing blood. He could barely put one foot in front of the other. Still, lives depended on him.

He closed his eyes and let his mind drift back.

They were running for their lives and he kept urging his gelding faster, holding tightly to the reins of the loaded pack horse. Then came the sharp crack of rifles and bullets exploded all around them. Yelling, screaming, the thunder of hooves and the loud bursts of what seemed like hundreds of rifles spitting their deadly missiles – the noise had been deafening. The projectiles had fallen around them and some found their mark.

Sweat broke out on Calhoun's forehead despite the cool wind. Pain ripped through his side as it had that desperate night. He shuddered in agony.

Then stillness came and he realized he rode alone with the

pack horse. He remembered coming to a stop . . . no that wasn't right. He'd fallen off, too weak from blood loss to hold the reins. He had lost consciousness and when he came to, the horses were gone and the loot lay on the ground.

Calhoun opened his eyes and moved back a good twenty yards more and scanned the area for large boulders. Maybe he was too far left. He veered off to the right about twenty yards or so and still found no sign of boulders. He retraced his steps and went left even farther back.

The trees seemed to part and a pile of huge rocks rose up in front of him. There! He hurried over studying them, looking for a wide crack between two.

He'd stood on the ground so there was no need to climb up. Halfway around, he spied the flat rock that had acted as a lid. He moved it aside and there nestled into the space were two burlap sacks. He paused for a moment, gratitude washing over him.

Filled with relief, he lifted one out.

It would be foolish to remove them with Donavan about to attack. He opened the sack and took out four hundred. That would be enough to get everything they needed for now plus replenish their food supply.

Hiding the sack back in the hole, he slid the rock lid back over them and hurried to his horse.

He still had lots to do, and his leg was killing him. Calhoun needed the warmth of Heaven's Door and Maura's smile.

THIRTY

Over the next two days, Calhoun and Max busied themselves securing Heaven's Door as best they could,
clearing brush away from the windows in order to see
better and also reduce the possibility of fire plus nailing the
windows shut so no one would get in that way. They had yet to
purchase the explosives because the man they sought to buy
from had gone to Austin.

Maura's nerves were frayed from worry and this horrible wait.
She jumped at every noise. It helped to keep busy and there was
always something to do. A blessing for sure.

Meg and Juliette had settled into the warm room where they
had privacy. Sister Anne-Marie had been a bit out of sorts for a
day or two since she'd seen it her duty to care for the baby,
but after hearing Meg's sad story had latched on to little
three-year-old Sally. The toddler always needed extra care and
Sister Anne-Marie needed a purpose.

That night after putting the children to bed, the adults talked
at the table about divvying up guard duty.

'Between the two of us, I think Max and I can do it.' Calhoun
leaned back in the chair, stretching his long legs under the table.
'There's no need for you women to keep watch in the cold.'

Upset that she couldn't help, Maura eyed him sharply. 'Do
you think I can't handle it? I insist on taking a shift.'

Max's gravelly voice sounded. 'He didn't mean it that way,
niece.'

'I didn't. Thank you, Max,' Calhoun said calmly. 'I just wanted
to spare you the cold. Is there a law against caring?'

'Of course not. But I still want to do my share. Heaven's Door
is mine and Emma's responsibility.'

'Maura, I certainly won't object if the men want to take on
the guard duty.' Emma glanced around the table. 'We don't ask the
men to take care of the children. I don't see a problem.'

'Emma, Calhoun is still nursing his injuries and the cold rain we've had doesn't do them any good. And Uncle Max . . .'

Their uncle shot them a stare. 'What about me? I ain't too blamed old.'

'Well, you're no young pup either,' Maura said defensively.

Sister Angela pushed back her chair. 'I help.'

'No!' The word exploded from all six gathered around.

'No, Sister Angela.' Maura patted her hand. 'You do everything in this place. We don't need to add guard duty to the list. Uncle Max, Calhoun and I have it covered in three shifts of four hours each. That's an easy stretch and no one will miss a lot of sleep or freeze. Agreed?'

She hated to cross the men, but she felt strongly about this.

Calhoun looked ready to slug someone. 'I've never seen a more stubborn woman. If that's what you want.'

'It is.'

Before they left the kitchen, they decided Max would take the first shift, Calhoun the second and Maura the third. At least for this night. They could switch in the coming days.

Maura would take the three to seven a.m. slot. Everyone went to bed except Max who went out to his designated post.

When three a.m. rolled around, Maura was dressed warmly and armed. A nearby owl hooted as she went to relieve Calhoun. Clouds obscured the moon and she jumped when Calhoun emerged from the darkness. He seemed more apparition than human and for a moment she fought the urge to run.

'All's clear,' he said low.

'That's good. We're not ready for them yet.'

'We will be,' he assured her. 'Max and I will get the dynamite and black powder tomorrow.'

'I'm relieved. I've been so worried that they'll catch us unprepared.'

Calhoun reached for her and she leaned into the shelter of his arms. 'I want this to be over and no one get hurt.' Her voice was low and Maura prayed he didn't detect her fear.

'Me, too.'

'Thank you for coming back, Calhoun.'

'I couldn't stay away. I care too much for the people here.

And you. I've never seen a place like Heaven's Door and it's very special.'

It made her happy that he'd become so attached to them.

'I'm glad. We've become very attached to you, too.' In fact, the old mission wasn't the same without him. She blinked hard and patted his chest. 'Go get some sleep.'

He covered a wide yawn. 'I believe I will. But first, I need to taste your lips.'

Tingles of anticipation rose, and her stomach quickened. She tilted her head and closed her eyes, barely breathing. The first touch of his mouth on hers weakened her knees. The steadying hold on his coat kept her from falling as her heart raced double time.

She wanted to stay in his arms forever. Just like this.

Calhoun slid his hands up the column of her throat and rested under each jaw. Deep emotion filled the kiss and brought tears to her eyes. This was meant to happen. Out of all the men in the world, this one was sent to her.

The thought made her tremble and sent delicious waves curling along her spine.

All too soon, he ended the kiss, murmuring against her mouth. 'One day, I'm going to do this proper, lady, make you an honest woman. Take note of that.'

The vow hung on the slight breeze and she didn't want to move, didn't want to break the spell that bound them together.

'Don't make promises you can't keep,' she reminded him softly.

He pulled back, a crooked smile curving his mouth. 'Lady, I'll keep this promise no matter what. You just wait and see. I'm going to make you moan my name.'

'Oh, you will?' she teased. If only she knew what his name was, she'd do it now.

'Yes, ma'am.' He yawned again. 'I'd best go.'

'Before you fall asleep at my feet.'

'Hey, I wouldn't mind that.' He brushed a kiss to her temple. 'But a bed might be more comfortable.'

'That it would.'

He turned and walked away. Maura followed his tall form with her gaze, admiring his perfectly formed backside. Then she settled back under a live oak tree keeping those inside Heaven's Door from harm.

The shift passed peacefully. But along toward dawn as the sky began to lighten, a rustle reached her ears then the clop of hooves. She sat up straighter and gripped the rifle. A small, mule-drawn cart came down the narrow lane and pulled to a stop in front of the stone chapel. A petite woman wearing a dark shawl over her head climbed down. She stooped over and walked with a limp. She went around to the back of the cart and removed a box. She carried the box to the chapel steps and set it down, then went back for a child's rolling hoop and a pile of quilts.

Maura leaned her rifle against the tree and moved forward to catch the visitor when she came around the cart. The woman jumped half out of her skin. The scarf on her head hid most of her facial features so it was hard to judge her age. She was barely five feet tall, if that.

'Don't be afraid, ma'am. We've been finding things left here and were curious about whom to thank.'

The woman's dull eyes grew large. 'I didn't mean no harm.'

'You didn't cause any. Everything was something we needed here at the orphanage. We're truly grateful for all of it. But why did you leave the items so mysteriously?'

'Folks are scared of me. Call me a witch. And worse.' She touched her head-covering and hesitated several moments before removing the wrapping to show her face.

Maura sucked in a breath. One whole side was a massive scar with small growths on it. Now that she could see her face, the woman was only around forty or so. 'What happened to you, ma'am?'

'Born like this. I can't live in town. I'd be persecuted to death.'

'I'm truly sorry.' She knew how mean some people could be. 'Do you live nearby?'

'I have a little house way back in the trees. I sneak up in the tree line and watch the children play. They bring me such joy. I wouldn't hurt a one of them.'

'I know you wouldn't.' What a lonely life. Hers and Emma's didn't compare.

'Nothing I brought here was stolen. It was all mine. The pup came from my dog's litter. Everything was mine.' She glanced down. 'I'm not a thief.'

'I would never think that.'

'There's a few toys in the box over there and a hoop that children love to run and play with. My sister's two used to love spending time with me so that's why I have these toys. And books too. They're doing me no good now. They're grown. My sister got run off by her husband.' She looked down at her hands. 'I don't have a soul left.'

'What is your name?'

'Eula Mae.'

Maura rested a hand on her stooped shoulder. 'Eula, would you like to come be with the children sometime? We'd love to have you and they won't care about the way you look. Please? I hate to think of you all alone.'

For a moment, hope flared in the woman's dull eyes. 'I don't know.'

'Just think about it. We have an infant who loves to be rocked.' If that wasn't enticement enough, Maura didn't know what was. 'You'd be welcome here at Heaven's Door.'

'Heaven's Door is a mighty pretty name.'

'The children named it and it stuck. We love it here. So peaceful.' Only now a band of outlaws was about to attack and kill them all. They wouldn't come in the daylight though. Like skunks and rabid animals, they lurked in the black of night. 'Would you like to come in for a cup of tea to warm you?'

'I need to be going. You've been very kind.' Eula covered her head and face with the shawl.

'Wait, can I hug you first? I don't know about you, but I really need one.'

Surprise, then longing, clouded Eula Mae's eyes. At her nod, Maura put her arms around the disfigured woman and held her tight. Strangely, she hugged Maura back and that told of her deep longing to fit in somewhere with someone. The clean fragrance of Eula's freshly laundered dress with patches surprised her. The woman hadn't let her disfigurement stop her from bathing.

'Thank you for coming. I hope we'll be friends. I sure can use one.'

Eula's eyes filled with tears. She tried to speak but was too choked up to get them out. Giving up, she turned to her cart and climbed up.

Maura waved as their mysterious benefactor trundled down the lane.

Her heart broke for another lost and lonely soul. She was going to work at coaxing Eula Mae over to join them. She'd just have to keep an eye for a figure in the tree line. Maybe the woman would agree to be a substitute grandmother or aunt and the children would feel they had some family.

In turn, Eula could rejoin the living – or at least this small part of it. Where it was safe.

But was it really?

THIRTY-ONE

C alhoun rode with Max to the far side of San Antonio after skirting the town. They had to avoid the sheriff since he still wanted to arrest Max. Quite some distance off the beaten path, they pulled up in front of a modest home tucked back in the trees. A barn and corral sat next to it.

'I'm glad you knew the way because I never would've found it.' Calhoun started to dismount when a pack of snarling dogs ran from the brush. His horse skittered nervously, its eyes rolling back with just the whites visible. 'Max, you better get the owner out here or we'll have a mess on our hands. These horses are ready to run. It's all I can do to hold mine.'

'McGee!' Max yelled. 'Call off your dogs! McGee!'

A man wearing a Scottish tam-o'-shanter ambled out in a green and blue plaid skirt. What did they call those things? Oh yes, kilts. An odd piece of clothing if you asked Calhoun and nothing he would ever remotely consider putting on.

McGee scratched under one arm. 'Dogs! Down! Git now!'

His accent was a bit on the thick side, making it hard to understand him. The dogs however seemed to have no such difficulty and disappeared around the house, much to Calhoun's relief. He and Max dismounted.

Max shook McGee's hand and introduced Calhoun.

'Nice to meet you.' Calhoun clasped a calloused hand. He'd seen a kilt on a man a few times but still found it odd. In Texas, a man didn't need anything that would blow up in the wind. He needed something covering his rear.

'Would ye be of the Scots, Calhoun?' McGee asked.

'I really don't know, sir. My folks didn't speak of our ancestors much. They were too busy trying to make a living.'

'I don't know about mine either.' Max glanced toward a barn at the side of the house and a few horses in a rickety corral. 'We came to this country to put the past behind us.'

'Aye. I knew some McTaggarts in the Scottish Highlands.'
McGee finally must've sensed they wanted to get on with business. 'How much powder and dynamite do ye need?'

'Whatever we can get. I'll have a little extra for your trouble.'
Calhoun just wanted to get on with it and get back. He always
got a bit nervous with strangers, not knowing if he could trust
them.

With a nod, McGee led them to the barn, but instead of going
inside, they went behind it. The man reached into a pile of leaves
and lifted a trapdoor. 'Down here.'

They followed McGee into the dark interior where he lit a
lantern.

'Hey, aren't you afraid this whole place will blow with that?'
Calhoun shot a nervous glance to the barrels and crates stacked
everywhere.

'Relax.' Max patted him on the shoulder. 'McGee's been doing
this a long time. Besides, he doesn't deal with nitroglycerin.
A big difference.'

'The lantern is weak.' McGee's Scottish burr seemed to have
gotten thicker. 'We shan't tarry long.'

They made their purchases and Calhoun paid him along with
a little bonus. They then loaded it all into their saddlebags.

'Nice doing business with you.' Calhoun shook McGee's
hand. 'Appreciate it.'

'Wish I could come help ye. I love a good fight.'

Max stepped forward and hugged the man. 'Next time we'll
have a long talk about the home country, old friend.'

They mounted up and headed into town.

'I want to stop at the mercantile for a few things, Max.
And you?'

'There's a pretty woman I used to love visiting. I think I'll
stop in and say hello. She's never seen me sober. And it's a
good place to keep out of the sheriff's sight.'

Surprised about Max's woman, Calhoun smiled. 'That sounds
like a good idea. It won't take me long to select my purchases,
so I figure we can meet up at the edge of town. You can't afford
to get locked up now with the imminent attack coming.'

'Sure don't need to land behind bars,' Max agreed.

They rode along in silence a bit. Calhoun enjoyed the warmth of the sun soaking into his bones. Finally, he looked over at Max. 'Mind answering something?'

'What's that?'

'I've noticed you haven't touched the bottle in a week or so and wondered what changed. Or did you just run out and haven't gone for more?'

'I didn't know you paid that close attention to my habits,' Max growled and squinted at him through one eye. 'But then I reckon a man like you has to if he wants to stay alive.'

The statement was anything but casual. Max knew too much and that wasn't good. But he wasn't the kind to go around talking about what he knew.

'I'm not the only one who's noticed. Humor me.'

'Well, I'll tell you. I haven't had the devil on my back as strong. It's strange how those kids can change a man and make him see things in a different light.' Max stared off in the distance. 'I want to be the kind of man they see when they look at me. Little Alphie is like my own kid. Follows me everywhere and smart as a tack. You know what I'm saying? Those kids make me feel good inside.'

Calhoun nodded. 'They've changed me too. I pity anyone who hurts them. Funny. I think they've had an effect on everyone.'

'I've seen it. That Sister Anne-Marie was scared to death of her own shadow and hid in a kitchen closet. Barely came out to eat. Beats all how she's laughing and playing with the children now. And the nuns' English has improved.' The horses clopped along and the town was coming up. 'Yeah, those kids are something.'

'Did you ever have any of your own?'

'One. A son.' Max paused and his voice dropped. 'I'm to blame for him filling up a grave.'

This was something new, him talking about the past. Max never did that.

'Anything you want to get off your chest?'

'He was five and curious about everything. I'd ridden into town for supplies. While I was gone, he found an extra gun I kept in a drawer.' Max bit back a sob. 'He . . . he accidentally shot himself. I'll never forgive myself.'

'It wasn't your fault.'

'Yes, it was. I knew to put it up high but I left it in that drawer. What a fool.'

Guilt could sure twist a man up inside. Calhoun knew. If he could only go back and make some changes his brother would still be alive.

'That was the end of my marriage. A week later, my wife packed up and left. Haven't seen her since.' Max blew out a breath and reached into his shirt pocket for his sack of Bull Durham and papers. 'I lost it all. Lucius said I deserved what I got.'

'What does he know? No one made him God.'

Max barked a laugh. 'He made himself. Just ask him.'

They parted ways at the town limits and Calhoun trotted on to the mercantile and tied up.

It took a little time to make all the selections, but by the time he finished, he bought some new clothes for himself, Meg and Tully and a little something for every single person at Heaven's Door. The hardest part was finding the right surprise for Maura, one that would make her understand how special she was to him. By the time he'd finished, the pile was pretty tall but he was satisfied with his purchases.

The clerk stared. 'Are you sure about all this, mister?'

'Yeah. Don't worry. I have enough to cover it.'

It was an excellent use for that stolen money.

Satisfied, he asked for a burlap sack to put it all in since his saddlebags were full. He tied the bag to the pommel. He filled a second bag with a large ham, bacon, sausage and other needed food and tied it to the horse on the other side. He could transfer some to Max when they met up.

If things worked out and Max still took the first shift, he had plans. Anticipation built and curled against his spine. He'd light the fire in his room before he went to supper. No, on second thought, maybe he wanted it cold. Calhoun grinned. That would be a reason to snuggle.

He left town and found Max waiting at the edge.

'Did you buy out the store?' The man took one of the sacks.

'I got a few things for everyone and some meat. Those kids don't get enough meat and they need it to grow. Also got Tully a shirt and pants. What he's been wearing is downright pitiful. Everyone needs a treat now and then to put a little joy in their lives.'

'I reckon they do.'

They rode in silence for a bit and were almost to Heaven's Door when Max spoke in that gravelly voice of his. 'I'm not gonna ask where the money for all the explosives and purchases came from. Not any of my business.' He glanced over at Calhoun, squinting one eye. 'Is it stolen money?'

'Now, Max, that's my worry. You know the orphanage is forever short of food and those poor kids don't have anything. If this can brighten their day and put a smile on their faces . . . let's just say I'm OK. It's being used for good.'

'I won't argue that point. No, sir.'

With the afternoon sun on them, they put the horses into a trot. The children came running when they rode up, happy as all get out to see them.

'Hi, Mr Max,' Alphie hollered. 'I missed you.'

'I missed you too, boy.' Max reached down and lifted him up in front of him on the saddle. 'Did you do anything fun today?'

Calhoun propped his arm on the pommel and watched the pair, thinking about what Max had told him.

Alphie grinned up at the man he worshipped. 'I sure did. God left us some toys in front of the chapel. Lots of things for us to play with.'

'You don't say?' Max trotted ahead to the corral.

Henry patted Calhoun's leg. 'Guess what?'

'You grew a mustache and Miss Mo made you shave it off.'

The boy died laughing. 'No. I lost another tooth. Miss Em said if I put it under the pillow it'll turn into a penny by morning. Just think. A whole penny of my own.'

The fact that one penny made Henry feel rich brought a lump to Calhoun's throat. Life wasn't fair. Nothing about it was fair to these orphans.

'It's true, Henry,' Sunny piped up. 'My papa used to put my lost teeth under the pillow and by morning I had some money. Once I got a whole nickel.'

'I'm gonna work on all of mine and see if they'll come out.' Henry opened his mouth and started wiggling one.

'Better think about that, Henry,' Calhoun warned. 'How can you eat without teeth?'

'Oh yeah, I'll think of something.'

One of the Johnson Five tried to jump on the back of the horse.

'Don't do that, son. Let me go on to the barn.' Calhoun moved slowly through the onslaught of kids.

If not for Emma and Sister Bernadette, they'd have followed behind him.

The men removed their saddles, then brushed their animals down and fed them. Maura arrived as they finished. Max picked up one of the burlap sacks and went on ahead leaving them some privacy.

Maura stood close as though not sure of her welcome. 'You slept through breakfast then rode out before I had a chance to tell you I met the mystery woman whose been leaving gifts.'

'That's wonderful and I want to hear more, but first I want to kiss you.' He gently pulled her into his arms. 'I have a powerful thirst for you.'

The scent of the fresh air and sun-drenched sheets encompassed him. He nibbled along the seam of her lips before kissing her long and deep.

This made Calhoun's world all right. All the worry, the trouble and the weariness of riding all day melted away. Her heart thrummed against him, keeping time with his. As though it always had.

A little mewling sound came from her mouth, then she pulled back enough to murmur, 'Calhoun, your delicious kisses make me melt inside. I want to stay just like this forever.'

'Those kids won't let you. Besides, we need to eat and guard against intruders.'

'I know.' She sighed. 'But I've become very addicted to you, mister. I need you.'

Smiling, he leaned his head to one side, looking at her. 'How bad?' he teased. He nibbled behind her ear. 'This bad?'

He left warm kisses down her throat. 'Or how about this?'

'Everything you have I want.' She took his face in her hands. 'I'm very serious.'

'So am I.' He drowned in the blue depths of her eyes. 'Lady,

I have something planned for you after supper in my room. Max will be on guard duty.'

'I'll be there.'

'Good.' He threw his saddlebags over his shoulder and handed her the second burlap sack. 'Wait just a minute.' He reached into his trousers and pulled out a nickel. 'Put this under Henry's pillow tonight.'

'He'll be so thrilled.' She slipped it in her pocket. 'Thank you.'

'We have to try to make these kids feel special in some way.' Then he put an arm around her waist and left the barn with her filling him in on mystery woman Eula Mae.

Calhoun inhaled the deep fragrance of the Texas land and knew he'd never felt this depth of peace before. With himself. And with life.

THIRTY-TWO

After stashing the explosives behind a locked door, Calhoun called all the squealing children around and passed out the gifts. Max stood off to the side watching. 'These are from me and Mr Max because we wanted to put smiles on your faces.'

'Is it Christmas?' The question came from one of the shy Harrison twins who always looked down in the mouth.

'Nope. Not Christmas yet. These are just-because gifts. You see, Mr Max and I were talking about how much you mean to us and we decided to show you.' Well, part of it was true anyway. He ignored the shake of Max's head.

After giving the children a toy, colorful hair ribbon, or hairbrush, Calhoun turned to the nuns. He handed each something practical: needles, colorful yarn, and items for sewing. Emma got a decorative comb to pull her hair back.

Maura watched it all, a confused look on her face. She seemed a bit angry.

He went to her. 'Don't worry. I'm giving yours to you tonight. I didn't leave you out.'

'I'm simply wondering where all this came from. Who are you, Calhoun? And what are your ties to Rupert Donavan?'

'Donavan is an enemy and I pray to rid the world of him one day. I bought these things because they are greatly needed.' He brushed her cheek with a fingertip and spoke softly. 'I had the money, and this is the way I wanted to spend it.'

She shook her head. 'The money I found in your trousers when you came couldn't buy all this.'

'I had some stashed. It's what I lost and went for when I rode out only I'd forgotten where I'd put it.' He turned to look at the excited kids. 'Look, I didn't rob anyone.'

Maura studied him for several heartbeats. 'OK, I believe you. This has been quite a day for the children with Eula Mae bringing toys and now you. Tully looks so happy with his new clothes. You've made such a difference in these kids' lives.'

'All I wanted to do.' He watched the scene, his heart filling with warmth. 'Maura, very soon these children will be fearing for their lives as bullets fall around them. Some may even die. They'll have this moment to remember and know they are loved. That they aren't throwaways. That someone cares.'

'Beautifully put,' Maura murmured. 'Thank you for loving them and caring.'

'Always.'

Max hollered out, 'Calhoun, show them the rest!'

'Coming, Max.' Calhoun took Maura's hand, and he lifted the second burlap sack. 'Cooking meals will get a little easier for a while with this.' He handed the sack to her.

She reached in and started pulling out the ham, bacon, sausage and all. Emma and the sisters gasped.

Sister Angela clasped her hands together. 'Praise be! God heard our cries!'

'Look at all this food!' Emma exclaimed. 'I've never seen so much except in the mercantile.' She strode to Max and kissed his cheek then hugged Calhoun. 'Thank you both.'

'You're very welcome. Miss Emma, I think you get prettier every day. If you keep this up, some gentleman is going to come and whisk you right off your feet.'

'Oh, Calhoun. Bless you for saying so but I'm too old to believe in fairy tales.' Emma put an arm around Maura. 'But my sister seems to think handsome princes still exist.'

'Yes, I do.' Maura met Calhoun's gaze. 'I most certainly do.'

'Now, Miss Maura, I might just try to live up to that.' He watched her cheeks get rosy and thought he'd never seen a prettier woman in all of Texas. If things worked out . . . No, he wouldn't count on that. He kept far too many secrets from her. If their relationship stayed on course and deepened to a serious level, he'd have to do some confessing. He had too much respect for her to continue under false pretenses.

Only by then, she'd probably slap his face and send him packing. He wouldn't blame her.

They talked and laughed a little more, then as the sun hung

low in the sky, the women took the bounty he'd bought and went in to prepare supper.

He loved the lightness of this moment and listening to the laughter. But a big black storm was heading straight for them and would leave nothing but fear and sadness.

Even as he stood there, he felt it rolling across the land, that huge, dark, evil monster.

And he didn't know if he had enough strength to stop it.

Everyone's immense lightness carried over through supper. The children chattered nonstop of the toys and new clothing and how happy they felt. Even the baby had a new blanket and Gunner a juicy bone to chew on. Calhoun had thought of everyone.

Maura wouldn't let herself worry about where the money had come from. It truly seemed a gift from God as the children claimed.

All she could think of was making her way across the compound to Calhoun's quarters. He'd made several silent promises with those beautiful dark eyes of his that were always so unreadable. But today, he'd dropped the curtain covering them and she'd seen enough to give her hope.

Yet, she wasn't fully giving herself permission to believe she had the future she sometimes dreamed about. To believe and have everything fall through as it always did would devastate her.

Once the meal was over, Max went out to stand guard. Maura hurried to clean up, then removed her apron and made sure her hair was pinned up neatly away from her face. Her hands trembled a bit as she dabbed a drop of perfume behind her ears. The light fragrance of lilies encircled her seeming to mimic anticipation of what the night might bring. Perhaps Calhoun would gift her with whatever he'd bought and that would be all.

But maybe . . . She wouldn't let herself complete that thought. She'd had far too much disappointment.

Maura threw a wool shawl around her shoulders and crossed the compound to his room.

He opened the door at the light rap. 'I'm glad you came. I was afraid you'd back out.' He ushered her inside and took her shawl, draping it on the back of a chair.

'It's chilly in here.' She glanced toward the weak flickers in the fireplace.

'Sorry. I just lit the fire. It'll be warm soon. Have a seat.' He pulled out a chair for her then went to get a package lying on the bed. 'While I was in town today buying gifts for everyone, I got this for you.' His boot heels sounded on the wood floor and he dropped the brown-wrapped package in front of her.

'Calhoun, you shouldn't have done this. I have all I need.'

'But what about your wants? Don't they count too?' he asked softly, the cleft in his chin deepening with a smile. He pulled out the other chair and sat.

'I've never let myself fancy nice things. Saves being let down and bitter. I cling to happiness despite the storms.'

'That's commendable. Still, I bought this gift for you and you alone. I beg you to accept this token of deep affection.'

'Then in that case, I have to, don't I?'

'Indeed.'

Maura tugged at the brown mercantile paper and beautiful blue fabric shot through with silver thread spilled out. 'Oh, Calhoun!' She jumped to her feet and held the dress against her, smoothing the soft material. A tiny row of delicate lace accented the modest neckline. 'I've never seen a more stunning dress. It's simply gorgeous.' She twirled around, the light garment billowing out.

Calhoun chuckled, drawing her gaze. Then an expression she couldn't distinguish crossed his face and she stopped. 'What?'

'You look like one of those children unable to contain her excitement.'

'Blame it on this dress. I feel like a princess.'

'Because you are, Maura.'

Suddenly self-conscious by the way he looked at her, she folded it up. 'I've never owned anything so fine.' Leaving the folded dress on top of the paper, she lifted her blue eyes. 'Thank you, Calhoun. It's truly magnificent.' She drew a shuddering breath. 'And it cost far too much.'

'Sorry to burst your bubble. The dress was marked down to nearly nothing. The clerk said it had been hanging in the window for nigh on to a year because the women shoppers thought it too plain.' He leaned back in the chair, his hands behind his head. 'San Antonio women have odd thinking. I knew it would be perfect on you with your beautiful hair and blue cornflower eyes that can see way down into a man's soul.'

'Not quite that far.' Maura didn't know what to do now. Should she politely thank him again and march out with the dress and go back to the mission? Or stay? But for what? This was strange, unfamiliar territory.

A solemn expression on his face, Calhoun stood and closed the space between them. She felt small next to him.

Holding her gaze, his dark eyes softening in the dim light, he silently took the pins from her hair. The mass of long tresses cascaded down her back, spilling over his hands like the whisper of a hope. She closed her eyes for a moment, as some strange desire surged through her veins, knocking her off kilter. Before she had time to adjust, he ran his hands through the long strands, low groans rising from his throat.

She raised her lids and stared into his dark orbs that held so much emotion. 'Calhoun.'

'Nothing can compare to your loveliness. I mean that. Nothing. You truly take my breath.' He bowed at the waist and extended his hand. 'May I have this dance, Miss Maura?'

With his manners and handsome features, he could easily be a dashing prince.

Maura's heart fluttered. 'Here? I've never danced in my life. Besides, we don't have any music.'

'I'll hum a song I know. The dance is simple. Just stand in one spot and sway.'

'Then I have to try.' She fitted her hand in his and placed the other on his shoulder. He didn't know this fulfilled one of her secret fantasies. Here with no one to see her make a fool of herself, she took a deep breath and relaxed. He hummed a song with a nice melody and the sound transported her to a ballroom in some castle. She was dancing with one of the most attractive men she'd ever seen.

In his arms, she felt safe and protected. A languid warmth spread through her and she leaned into the cocoon he'd created, resting her head on his shoulder. She swayed back and forth against him, imagining they were in some fancy place.

'See? I knew you could do it,' Calhoun murmured against her temple. 'You're doing fine. Having fun?'

'I am. Of all the things I regretted most not getting to do was dancing.'

'I'm glad I could fulfill a dream, pretty lady.' He began to hum again. After a few steps, he spoke. 'The first time I opened my eyes over there on the bed and saw you through my pain, I knew you were something very special. I thought surely a woman like you was taken. Imagine my surprise when I learned of your circumstances. But it made me happy to know you were free.'

His warm breath ruffled the loose tendrils of hair around her face. Maura closed her eyes and sank further into his embrace. He released her hand and wrapped both arms around her.

'I watched you with the children and noticed how they adore you. I knew why. Even when you're displeased with them about something, you're always kind, always caring.'

Continuing to sway back and forth, she scowled and glanced up. 'You shouldn't pay such close attention to such things.'

'Why?'

'Because I'm no one to admire. I have my faults and plenty of insecurity. Sister Angela and Sister Bernadette, now those are truly admirable women.'

'And so are you. I know from experience the kind of woman to look up to.' He kissed the tip of her nose. 'Nuns are supposed to be kind and compassionate. You've had no teaching yet still practice grace and humility, despite the shameful way folks treat you, shunning you and Emma like they have. Your own father is barely civil.'

'It's no big secret. I just treat everyone as I would want them to treat me.'

'I need a kiss in the worst way. I hope you don't mind.' His voice was thick.

She tilted her head in invitation and Calhoun wasted not a moment in claiming her lips. She sagged against him, slipping her arms around his neck. His dark hair brushed her skin like the softest goose feathers.

This was where she always wanted to be. With him. In his strong arms.

Quivering with want of this mysterious thing teasing her, Maura leaned back, searching his eyes. Her voice was low and steady. 'Don't ever let me go, Calhoun. Who you are matters nothing to me. I know all I need. I can't read the direction of your heart, but I'm certain of mine. I've already confessed my love and it's grown even stronger since. I'm . . .' She let her voice trail, unsure of saying more. She would not beg. A woman had her pride.

He tightened his hold on her, his full lips just inches away. 'I have no intention of letting you go. Stay the night.' He left a trail of kisses down her throat, the ends of his dark wavy hair lightly sweeping across her skin bringing delicious quivers. 'Please,' he murmured, his voice husky.

'I have no desire to leave. I have to feel your touch on my skin. In fact, I need that. I have this fire inside burning me alive and I think you, with all your assumed experience in these matters, must know what it means.'

'I do believe I might.' He scooped her into his arms and headed for the bed.

THIRTY-THREE

Morning dawned and for a moment Maura didn't know where she was. A warm hand rested on her stomach. The sleeping male beside her and her legs lying so possessively on his sent her memories flooding back. She jerked herself upright and looked around for her clothes.

'Going somewhere?' Sleep had roughened Calhoun's voice and made it deeper.

'I missed guard duty. Poor Uncle Max spent the entire night guarding us.'

'No, he didn't.' Calhoun yawned and rubbed his eyes. 'I relieved him at midnight. You were sleeping like a rock, so I slipped out. I didn't wake you for your shift either.' He tiptoed two fingers down her bare back. 'You look so beautiful when you sleep and the worries of this place and caring for the children slip away.' He pulled her down and nuzzled her neck and behind one ear.

'Let me up. I have breakfast to help with. Whatever will the sisters say if I miss it? They'll be sure to raise eyebrows. And Emma . . . I don't know what to tell her.'

'The truth?'

'Of course, but can I make her understand? She'll lecture me.' The thought of that and having to explain her absence to everyone brought on panic. 'Please, let me up. I need to go and you need to get some sleep.'

He released her and she rose, flinging on her clothes. She shot a glance at his tousled hair and bare chest and heat flooded over her. How she yearned to crawl back into the spot next to him. But she couldn't.

'Thank you for last night. It was much better and far more satisfying than imagining what making love would be like.' She slipped on her shoes, wet her lips, and searched for what she had to say. 'I don't regret a minute. If this is all, if you ride out and never come back, I'll cherish the memories to my dying day.'

He threw back the covers, seeming to give no thought of his naked body, and padded to her. 'I wish I could make the right promises, lady, but I can't. It would be wrong and I won't do that to you.' His kiss held urgency and she clung to him for all she was worth, welcoming every bit of tenderness he could give.

When he ended the kiss, she stared up at him in wonder and amazement. Could it be true that Calhoun, this one brave man, would stay and introduce her to even greater passion?

Maura gently touched his face, studying him. 'I never knew it would be like this.'

'Me either. You're the most amazing women I've ever met.' He dropped kisses on her nose and eyes before settling on her lips.

A decade of hoping and praying only to see every prospect dashed raised caution. As much as she wanted it, he wasn't going to stay. She had to protect her heart.

'We'll talk later.' She pushed out of his arms. 'I have to go. Get back in bed before you freeze.'

'Yes, my love.' He lightly swatted her behind as she headed for the door. 'I'll be over later. I plan on becoming a nuisance.'

At least until he left again. And he would. She saw it in his eyes.

A noise outside the door prompted her to hurry. She grabbed her new dress off the table and slipped out quickly, not giving whoever it was a chance to see Calhoun in his all togethers.

She turned and collided with Emma.

Concern lined her sister's face. 'Maura, I was worried about you. You didn't come to bed last night.'

'I . . .' Calhoun's response to her question about what to say came back and she swallowed the lie. 'I stayed here. And before you start in on lecturing me, I know what I'm doing.' She paused, wetting her lips. 'I love Calhoun even though he's not staying. I'm going to grab what little I can. Emma, women like us are never going to have the whole pie – only a piece.'

Emma sucked in a quick breath and hugged her. 'Of course, I'm happy for you. I wish you only the best. You know that.'

'Thank you. My head is spinning, but yet, I'm cautious. We've both had the rug pulled from under us far too often.' The picture of Calhoun lying in bed, wearing nothing but a sinful smile, popped into her head.

Please, dear God, let this be for real, change his mind and let him stay. I beg you.

'Yes, we have. Sisters Angela and Bernadette asked where you were.' Emma linked her arm through Maura's. 'I said you were still out on guard duty.'

'Thank you. We have to look out for each other.'

And so her morning started. Maura laid the dress on her bed and dove into work. But the memories with Calhoun kept popping up at the most inopportune moments and it was a struggle to make any headway on her work. Others would catch her staring off into space and ask what she was thinking about.

Maura would smile and say, 'Nothing. Nothing at all.'

The day turned out calm and warmer than it had been. Early afternoon the children were outside playing and Henry was showing all his friends the nickel under his pillow that morning. After Calhoun had gotten up, had coffee and ate, Henry showed him, proud as could be.

'You know, I might have to pull some of my teeth too,' Calhoun joked, winking at Maura. 'Either that or take out a loan from you.'

Henry's face fell but he looked up at his idol. 'If you need it, I guess you can.'

Calhoun ruffled his hair and winked. 'No, keep it. I won't take your money.'

Mighty relieved, the boy ran out the door.

Maura reached for Calhoun's hand. 'Thank you for the coin. You made Henry feel special.'

Her heart took a tumble at his grin. He had such a fondness for these orphans.

A bit later, Calhoun was out in the yard discussing the matter of defending the orphanage with Max. Maura's gaze kept straying to the perfectly proportioned man she loved.

She'd spoken to the two men about the black powder they'd bought. Now they had to decide where to make lines on the ground away from where the children were. Some already lined pots in the front of the chapel so they could easily toss in a flame and ignite them. Both Calhoun and Max wore their guns at all times which made her feel safer. She understood the necessity.

War was a horrible business and she hated the very thought of maiming and killing. Yet if they wanted to survive, they had to be ready for that. Sometimes you had to fight to exist.

She scanned the woods where she'd found Calhoun and wondered if the outlaws would come that way. The faint outline of a person caught her eye and her heart lurched.

Eula Mae?

Or was it one of the gang watching? To be watched gave her chills. She rubbed her arms and hurried to find the men.

Both looked up when she approached. She quickly told them about the figure in the trees. 'I can't tell who it is. Maybe it's the mysterious woman Eula Mae but I can't be sure.'

'We need to check it out,' Calhoun said. 'Max, if we come at them from the side, they won't see us until we're on them.'

Max nodded. 'Good plan.'

When they started to move off, Maura grabbed Calhoun's arm. 'I'm coming.'

His dark eyes swung to her. 'It's too dangerous, Maura.'

'What if it's Eula Mae? You'll frighten her and send her running. I don't want that. She's frightened enough.' When they hesitated, she added, 'Please. If I see it's a man, I'll head back. And if it's Eula, let me go alone.'

Max blew out a breath. 'All right. But you listen to us.'

'And stay behind,' Calhoun added.

They moved around to the front and slipped into the woods there, cutting through the trees at a fast clip. As they got closer to where she'd seen the figure, they slowed and moved quietly. Both men had drawn their weapons.

Maura strained to see ahead but trees blocked her vision. Onward they crept. Finally, Calhoun turned to her and spoke low. 'Wait here. We're going closer for a look.'

She opened her mouth to protest and he added, 'If it's the woman, we'll come for you.'

At a quick jerk of her head, they moved away, melting through the trees like vapor. She strained to see something. Anything. Listening. Waiting.

It seemed forever before they reappeared with guns returned

to their holsters. 'It's a woman,' Calhoun reported. 'Go ahead. Has to be your friend. We'll head back.'

Relieved, Maura strode out of the tree cover and began to whistle a tune to let Eula know she wasn't a threat. She was just taking a stroll on a beautiful fall day. She just prayed Eula would stay put until she got there.

About twenty yards ahead she saw Eula and waved. 'Hi, neighbor! It's Maura from the orphanage. Isn't this weather pretty? I just want to soak up the sun.'

Eula Mae didn't reply. Neither did she scurry off, so that was encouraging.

'Do you remember me?' Maura asked.

'The lady from Heaven's Door. I was watching the children run and play.'

'They are a sight to behold all right.' Maura smiled and mentioned an incident that had made her laugh. 'Eula, would you like to come say hello to them?'

'I'll scare 'em.'

'I don't think so. They're really quite intuitive, so much that sometimes it surprises me.'

A red bird flew down from a tree and landed on Eula's shoulder. It just sat there a minute and went on its way. Just like a dear friend stopping to say hello.

'Eula Mae, that was amazing.'

'Weren't nothing. Happens a lot. I reckon they know I won't hurt 'em.'

'Kids are the same way. They know safety from danger. Please, just come and say hello.'

Eula glanced toward the children, longing on her face. 'Maybe for only a minute.'

'Can you walk that far?'

'With help. Can you find me a sturdy walking stick?'

Maura scanned the area and discovered a short piece of limb about two inches around. She picked it up. 'I think this will work and you can also lean on me. When you get ready to go home, we'll take you in the wagon.'

'I would be obliged,' Eula replied.

They slowly made their way across the wide expanse of the compound. When they neared, the children came running

with Gunner. The dog was spinning in circles, looking like a
furry top.

'We have a visitor.' Maura put an arm around her new friend's
shoulders. 'This is Miss Eula Mae and she a little lonely living
all by herself.'

'She looks like my grandma!' Alphie exclaimed, taking Eula's
hand. 'Hi, Grandma, I'm Alphie.'

Sunny laughed. 'She looks like mine too. She can be a grandma
to us all.'

'That's a wonderful idea, Sunny.' Their welcome brought a
lump to Maura's throat. The children didn't even see the disfigured face or her hunched back. All they seemed to notice was
their need for some kind of family and how easily a perfect
stranger could fill that role.

Eula smiled and laid a hand on Alphie's head. 'You're each
such beautiful darlings. I loved watching you laugh and play. I
would love to be your grandma.'

'Aunt Eula!' Tully hurried toward them as fast as he could.
He arrived out of breath. 'Aunt Eula, I've missed you.'

'Tully, you don't know how happy I am to see you.' Eula
hugged him.

'Do you two know each other?' Maura asked. What were the
odds of that?

'Tully is my sister's boy. He used to stay with me quite a bit.
That's why I had those toys that I brought. From the time he
was born, he always bore the brunt of his father's temper.'

'Meg's here too, Aunt Eula.' Tully's face was one big smile.

Eula turned to Maura. 'Is that true?'

'Indeed it is.'

Happy tears filled Eula's eyes. 'I feared her father had killed
that child. He flies into horrible rages.'

'She's safe now. Along with her baby girl.' Maura stepped
aside to let Meg and Juliette through.

With a wide smile and eyes glistening, Meg hugged her aunt
and introduced her to little Juliette.

By then, Emma and the sisters had come to see what the
ruckus was about and Maura filled them in.

Sister Angela made the sign of the cross. 'Praise God! De lost
are found.'

'Celebrate.' Sister Bernadette's round cheeks took on a rosy hue.

Emma shook Eula's hand. 'I'm very happy to meet you. This does indeed call for a bit of celebrating. Will you please stay for supper?'

'I'm . . .' Eula glanced at Maura. 'I need to get home to feed my animals before dark.'

'Of course.' Maura saw the panic on Eula's face. 'Maybe this might be too much too soon. You can eat with us another time. Thanksgiving is coming soon.'

'And I will.'

Calhoun and Max wandered up to complete the crowd and Maura grew warm under Calhoun's gaze. She moved to his side and slipped her hand in his. Her world had completely changed in the blink of an eye. She wasn't the same woman who'd arrived with sixteen ragtag orphans.

But the change wasn't only confined to Maura. Everyone at Heaven's Door had received a transformation. The children wore smiles now. They had a grandma and Tully and Meg had been reunited with their aunt.

Maybe the biggest change was in Eula Mae. Her dull eyes had brightened to the color of a morning sky and the dark fear lining her face was gone.

If it wasn't for the constant threat of attack hanging over them, this would be the happiest time of their lives.

THIRTY-FOUR

Eula Mae spent the afternoon watching the children play, reading a book to them, and rocking sweet Juliette. Maura loved the peace that had come over the disfigured woman. Then Calhoun hitched up the wagon and Maura and him drove her home.

The dwelling was hidden from sight, shielded by a thicket. If you didn't know it was there, you'd miss it. It was small and in need of repairs, but Eula had kept it up as much as she was able. Calhoun promised to come and fix everything in his free time.

Twilight fell around them as they bumped along the road. Sitting next to him and wrapped in the warmth of his companionship, Maura rested her head on his shoulder. 'My heart is happy, Calhoun. I'm so thankful that I could give Eula Mae some peace.'

'She's a sweet lady. I'm sure she's suffered greatly for her disfigurement. Callous people are quick to see the worst and not care their words wound sensitive folks.'

'Seems they always pick on the most vulnerable.'

'It's always been that way, darling.' He draped an arm around her shoulders.

Everything inside Maura stilled. She was unprepared for that word. Things were moving too fast and sweeping her along without any time for thought.

She lifted her head and sat up, turning toward him. 'Calhoun, I love being with you and what we shared last night made me happier than I ever thought I had a right to be.'

'I hear a "but" coming.' His face showed confusion. 'I thought . . .'

'I'm not coming back to your quarters tonight. I need to tend to my commitment to this orphanage and that means taking my shift at guard duty.'

'I don't mind taking both our shifts.'

'I know. But I don't want that. This is all so new to me, and I want to take it slower and explore everything that comes with it. I'm twenty-eight years old and waited all my life for you to come along. I want to savor this new experience like a meal I get after going without food for half a lifetime.' She took his hand. It had strength and could be soft and gentle, build things, and handle a gun with ease. 'Please say you understand.'

'I'd be the lowest kind of man if I didn't. I see your point to take it slower. We can go at whatever speed you want. Just please don't shut me out.'

She gave him a bright smile. 'As if I could even if I wanted. You are the man I've waited for and I intend to keep you for as long as you'll stay.'

A smile finally broke across his face. 'We'll see. No promises.'

Relieved of that weight, Maura put her head back on his shoulder. 'Fair enough. It's going to be a nice fall night. It's about time for a full moon. Big, glorious moons make me think of romance and kissing.'

'Do tell.' He pulled the wagon to the side of the road. 'Maybe we should fix that.'

It took no urging from her. She sighed happily as he pressed his lips to hers. He still wanted her despite the restrictions she'd laid down. She seemed like a baby taking its first steps on wobbly legs and trying not to fall on her face.

A swarm of flutters in her stomach made her a little lightheaded.

Oh, how tempted she was to feel his bare skin, his muscles and sinew under her fingertips again.

But there was time for that and more.

Unless Rupert Donavan descended with his gang and ruined the future she could suddenly glimpse in front of her.

How Calhoun managed to persuade Maura into switching guard duty with him he'd never know. But he had a feeling in his bones that tonight Donavan would launch an attack. It stood to reason that it would come before dawn. That's when most folks slept the soundest.

An owl hooted nearby and startled him half out of his skin. He drew his gun in one swift movement.

He was getting jumpy. He holstered his gun and glanced up at the clouds suddenly covering the full moon. 'What are you waiting for,' he whispered. 'Get it over with. But you'd best be prepared for a fight like you have *never* seen before.'

And if everything fell just right, he had a dose of justice waiting for Donavan for killing his brother.

His twin's face, rigid in death, swam in front of his vision, bringing shards of pain.

'You will pay for that, Donavan. I swear by all that's holy.'

Pulling up the collar of his coat so it brought a bit of warmth to his ears, he grabbed his rifle and did a turn around the front checking the pots of black powder. Then the dynamite hidden under low bushes here and down the road at the turn off. Using this up here would be a last resort. Everything looked ready.

If the attack came, he prayed everyone would remember what to do. They'd already explained to the children what to expect and to go as quickly as they could to the trapdoor. He and Max had taken them down so it wouldn't be quite as scary. They'd also impressed upon the kids the importance of silence. In the event that the adults would lose their lives, the gang wouldn't find the nuns and children.

A low warning began to vibrate under his skin. This same feeling had come over him the night he was shot and nearly died in the brush. It had to be an omen.

The sky made a subtle shift in color from black to dark gray. Calhoun sat on the ground, his back against a tree trunk. Memories of making love to Maura drifted through his head. He could still taste her lips, still hear the tiny moans that slipped from her throat. And the satiny texture of her skin. To spend a lifetime loving her was his fervent wish.

But that depended on the path of their destiny.

He'd never wanted to keep a promise more than the one to marry beautiful Maura. If she'd still have him after he revealed the answers to his secrets. The chance she wouldn't had been one of the main things keeping him quiet for this long. He didn't know if he could take her rejection.

To never see her, kiss her, hold her again would destroy him.

The faintest sound of what sounded like galloping horses

reached him. Had he really heard it? Or had it been his imagination?

He got to his feet, crooked his head and listened. A moment later, it came a bit louder. Something was coming very fast toward him. Horses. Lots of horses. The hair on the back of his neck stood up.

Max. He needed to go for Max but there probably wasn't time. He guessed the shooting, if and when it came, would have to suffice. He wouldn't want to cry wolf and feel like a fool.

He silently walked a little distance down the narrow path that led from the road, careful to stay in the thick growth. Now the galloping hooves were clear and coming ever closer. He turned and went back to his spot in front of the chapel.

To his great surprise, Max met him. The man was rolling a cigarette. Except for a small tremor in his hand, he was calm.

'Did you hear those horses?' Calhoun asked.

'Yep. Been expecting them and I know you have, too. That's why you persuaded Maura to trade shifts.' Max had a rifle in the crook of his arm and twin guns at his hip. 'I feel them in these old bones.'

It shouldn't have been a shock given that Max once rode on the wrong side of the law. Outlaws were a breed of their own. They knew how each other thought and acted. They seemed to have a built-in warning system, honed by years of running from the law. That made them good at evading capture. Too damned good. They could smell a lawman miles away.

Max finished rolling his cigarette and handed it to Calhoun, then started another. 'I woke Maura up and told her to get ready. Also put Gunner inside. Locked him in a bedroom.'

'Excellent thinking.' Calhoun stuck the cigarette between the top of his ear and hair where he could easily grab and light it.

When Max got his own rolled, he did the same. He rolled them each a second one for backup. 'Maura's used to being her own boss, so she probably didn't listen, but I told her to stay inside and pick off as many as she could from there.'

Though Calhoun didn't feel at all like laughing, he chuckled at the very thought of Maura abiding by that order. 'I hope you didn't waste your breath.'

'Probably did.' Max was silent a moment. 'My wife had quite a bit of sass herself. I miss her.'

Max's sadness covered them both like a wet cloth. Speaking of regrets naturally crossed a man's thoughts in moments of thick danger. Calhoun didn't know what to say that would help so he offered no reply.

Several moments later, Calhoun glanced up. 'Time to go down to the road and pick some off before they get up here. Don't you think?'

'It would be the smart thing to do.'

'As the remainder of the gang make it here, I'll move up and get them from behind.'

At Max's nod, Calhoun set off at a fast clip. By now, the horses were probably a quarter of a mile away. He arrived at his position, breathing hard, but got settled into the thick brush where they'd hidden the dynamite. He had a good view.

The gang of outlaws arrived much like an explosion of evil that spread out to cover everything and everyone. The riders hadn't expected to be met by a storm of dynamite and gunfire though. Calhoun took out several riders before they could even draw their weapons. He wasn't sure how many due to the darkness but at least one or two lay dead. In the yelling and disarray, some dove off their horses and scrambled for cover.

For others, once the moment of surprise passed, they veered off into the trees on horseback and disappeared into the night.

They had to be cutting through the woods. With rifle in hand, Calhoun hurried toward the orphanage.

Up ahead came the sound of gunfire and he knew Max was getting some shots in. As Calhoun got close, a blast of dynamite shook the ground. Along with it came screams of pain.

A few more down. If they didn't panic and picked them off a few at a time, they'd win this fight. They'd not give up, that much Calhoun knew. There was too much at stake. He'd fight until he no longer had breath.

He reloaded the rifle as he ran. As he reached the chapel and got Max's location, he gave an earsplitting yell and released a barrage of gunfire with his Colt and quickly reloaded.

One of the attackers galloped by on horseback and fired.

Pain pierced Calhoun's shoulder. Gritting his teeth against the burning throb, he returned fire but missed. Lighting a stick of dynamite, he threw it into a clump of bushes where one of the gang had sought cover. The blast took care of the man's compadre as well.

Calhoun quickly swung to another target and another.

But still the gang kept coming. They'd multiplied since Calhoun had counted them in that box canyon. They must really want the stolen loot and the buried treasure awfully bad. Donavan had a reputation about promising things but not delivering. But sadly, it appeared the chance he might keep his word this time had helped in recruiting efforts.

The battle raged with as many shots coming from inside as out. If they could keep it up. But four against no telling how many were horrible odds.

Calhoun lit another stick of dynamite and threw it. 'Come on. I've got lots more!' he yelled.

One of the men on horseback galloped up to the chapel doors and tossed a flaming torch.

Now they were going to try to burn the place. He couldn't get to the women and children inside. Please save them, he prayed.

The wooden door caught and went up in an inferno.

Suddenly, Calhoun realized Max had stopped firing. He must've gotten hit. For all he knew his friend could be lying somewhere dying.

The gang must've sensed the tide had turned and began advancing, forcing him back.

It was time for the black powder in those pots. His cigarette almost out, he sprinted past one and ignited it. The blast knocked him down, but it pushed back the advancing gang.

If they could just make it to daylight . . .

He hoped the sisters were praying because they needed a miracle. He reached into his pocket for the second cigarette and lit it. Rising from where he'd fallen, he lit several more pots of black powder and sticks of dynamite. The gang retreated beyond reach and seemed content to wait him out. They knew he'd run out eventually. Max still hadn't fired a shot which wasn't good. The light the flaming chapel door gave off revealed a figure lying where Max had been.

'Calhoun, are you all right?' Maura called from a window where she'd broken out a pane of glass to shoot from.

'I'm fine.' He glanced at his bloody shoulder. One little lie didn't count. Not when he had a slew of big ones. In the lull, he reloaded his Colt.

Come on sunrise. Give him some light.

Several of the gang galloped by on horseback and mounted another attack. Like wild dogs, they smelled blood and moved in for the kill.

One of the women screamed from inside and Calhoun's heart stopped. Some of the group must've gone around and gotten in through the kitchen.

Heaven help them.

Max lying dead or wounded and Calhoun wasn't in the best of shape with fire still raging in his shoulder. With his assumption that rotten men were inside trying to make good on their threat, hope was dwindling along with ammunition and explosives.

The barrel of a gun poked into his back. 'Breathe and I'll blow your head off, Calhoun,' Rupert Donavan growled.

THIRTY-FIVE

'Are you sure you have who you think you do, Donavan?' Calhoun's mind whirled even as the man took his gun. He had to buy some time.

'Who are you trying to fool? I know you, Jonas.'

'Or am I the twin brother? Huh? We looked exactly alike.' Calhoun slowly turned and faced the confused gang leader. 'We were both there that night.'

Finally, Donavan snarled, 'I don't care which one you are. I kill you and you're both dead.'

'But what about all that money you took from the Frost National Bank? I'm the only one who knows its location. Isn't that what you want?'

'Hell yeah, I want it. It's mine.' Donavan's greedy eyes glittered in the flames of the burning door.

A woman's scream came again.

'I'll tell you where I hid it if you'll take your men and leave this place right now. Deal?'

'Well now, I ain't gotten the other things I came for.'

'What's that?'

'To see you dead. And to get the buried treasure I know is here.'

'You can't have everything,' Calhoun pointed out. 'Best take what you can get. A greedy fellow like you needs a lot of money.'

'Then there's the matter of not trusting you. You could tell me anything and have me chasing my tail.'

Calhoun shrugged. 'A chance you'd take, I guess. Everything comes with risk.'

Inside the chapel, came yells and loud voices. Breaking glass. A child's high-pitched scream and a man's deep voice. He had to get in there somehow before he lost the ones he loved.

A dark shadow crept up behind Donavan. The person didn't act like one of the gang. No, it was someone else. But something had happened to Max.

Just as Calhoun was about to make a swing into Donavan and hope for the best, the shadow spoke. 'Drop your gun.'

Donavan's eyes widened. He hesitated and the shadow nudged him with the barrel of a pistol.

'I said drop it.'

The gang leader finally followed the order. Calhoun grabbed it and turned to the shadow. 'He has one in his boot. A knife too.'

Rupert Donavan swore a blue streak and started to comply then made a sudden move and turned, firing. Orange fire spat from the shadow's weapon. Donavan gave a cry and went down.

With their leader on the ground, the handful of the gang still breathing turned tail and leaped on their horses.

'I don't know who you are, mister, but thank you.' Calhoun looked and the chapel fire lit up the man's face.

Lucius Taggart.

'I didn't do it for you,' Lucius answered, slapping handcuffs on Calhoun. 'You'll stand trial for crimes you committed, Jonas.'

'Look, both of your daughters are in that chapel and it sounds like they're in a bad way. Unless you put a bullet in my chest, I'm going to help them. Furthermore, your own brother is lying somewhere on the other side of these steps. He may be dead or dying. Undo these cuffs and let me see to him and the ones inside. I give you my word I won't run.'

Though reluctant, Lucius released the iron bracelets. 'This is just temporary, for my daughters' sakes. Make sure they're OK. But run and I'll track you down like a wild animal.'

'Thank you. If you can see to Max, I need to get inside to the women. One of the gang is in there with them.'

'Go.'

Calhoun wasted no time in running around to the kitchen door. It lay in splinters off to the side. Hurrying in, he raced toward the chapel area. Smoke was thick and he could barely see.

'Maura! Maura! Please answer. Please don't be dead.'

'Calhoun! I'm in the children's playroom,' she hollered. 'Oh God, I'm glad you're safe. I was so worried.'

Calhoun's knees went weak with relief that she was alive. He ran down the hallway coughing from the smoke. At the door of the playroom, he froze in amazement. Tully, two of the Johnson brothers and Henry had an outlaw face down and were sitting on his back and legs. Gunner was chewing on his arm and releasing fierce growls. One sleeve of Maura's dress was ripped off. She was helping Emma off the floor and tending to a cut on her sister's arm.

'You are a sight to behold. Did he hurt you?'

'No, I'm fine. Luckily, the kids came up out of the trapdoor and tackled him.' Maura caressed his face with her fingertips. 'I was so scared.'

'Makes two of us.' Calhoun pulled her into his arms and hugged her tightly. 'I wasn't sure I'd ever see you again. The gang was probably double the amount I thought we'd face, and like rats, they kept coming and coming, no matter what we threw at them. Maura, your father saved my life.'

'What? How?' She stared at him with wide eyes.

'Lucius appeared as Donavan was about to pull the trigger and kill me. I guess he heard the shooting and knew we were in trouble.' He brushed a strand of hair out of her eyes. 'You can ask him those questions but for sure I owe him my life.'

'It's surprising that he found time to care about anyone other than himself.' Maura rested a hand on his chest. 'Is Uncle Max all right?'

'I don't know. Your father went to check on him while I came in here. Max is either wounded or . . .' Calhoun glanced at the boys before finishing, 'Or something.'

'I have to go see. I won't be able to bear it if he's . . .' She let the sentence trail.

'Has anyone seen my glasses?' Emma asked.

'I'll find 'em, Miss Em.' Henry got off the outlaw and searched the floor. He finally spied them. 'Here they are, Miss Em. They's broke.' He handed them to her.

One of the lenses had a big crack and one of the earpieces was missing. 'Thank you, Henry.' She put them on even though they were lopsided. 'Go see to Uncle Max. I'm fine. I'll let the sisters know it's safe to come out with the kids.'

Calhoun grabbed the outlaw and jerked him up. 'Thank you, boys. You did a fine job.'

'Get them away from me,' snarled the lawless man. 'I'd rather be in jail.'

'That's good because that's where you're headed.' Calhoun herded him out the back and around to the front. There he ordered him to sit cross-legged on the blackened ground. 'Move and I'll shoot you.'

Lucius had handcuffed one of Donavan's hands to his foot. The man wasn't going anywhere but he gave them all a black scowl.

'Uncle Max!' Maura ran to her uncle lying in the bushes. 'You're hurt.'

'Not so you'd notice. Maybe a teensy bit,' Max answered, glancing around.

'They're gone, Uncle. The attackers left and we're all alive.'

'Imagine that,' he answered weakly.

Lucius Taggart bent over Max and helped him sit up. 'It's nice to see you alive. How long's it been? My recollection is several years.'

Max rubbed his head and blood had soaked one sleeve. 'At least that, Lucius. Now I don't feel much like talking.'

Calhoun clasped his friend's hand. 'Man, I'm happy to see you, Max. We survived. Despite the odds we made it.'

'Yep. We sure did.' Max again glanced around. 'Did you happen to see a little boy out here? He's about five years old.'

'A boy? No.' A strange quiet settled over Calhoun. He exchanged a glance with Maura. 'What was he doing?'

'The kid laid a hand on my shoulder and told me it wasn't time. I swear, he looked like my boy. He said not to worry, that I'd be all right and then he vanished. The weirdest thing.'

It had to be Max's son. There was no other explanation that Calhoun could see.

'You've always been a bit touched in the head, Max,' Lucius said. 'It's all that rotgut you drink. You've pickled your brain.'

'Father! Stop it.' Maura put her hands on her hips. 'You don't know what you're talking about. I won't have you speaking to Uncle Max that way. Now apologize at once.'

When Lucius hesitated, Maura added, 'If you don't, you can leave right now. I positively won't stand for this even if I never see you again.'

'Seems I spoke out of turn, Max. Sorry.' Lucius swung to Maura. 'That make you happy?'

'It'll do,' she said. 'Now, help get Max into the orphanage.'

She turned toward the fire. 'It looks like it's about to go out. Thank goodness the chapel is made of stone.'

'That saved it.' Calhoun put a hand on her back. 'We'll have to make new doors for the front and back but if that's all I'd say we escaped lightly.' He handed her his gun. 'Will you keep an eye on these two while I help get Max inside?'

'It would be my pleasure.'

Dawn broke and colored the sky a soft pink that took a person's breath. It was great to see following a night of hell.

Lucius gave Calhoun a warning scowl as he approached with Max as though to say he hadn't forgotten about his pledge to take him in. Calhoun ignored him and hurried to Max's other side, and they made faster work of getting the man to the nearest bed. It appeared Maura's doctoring skills would get honed a little more.

Maura had closed the wound and was focusing on bandaging Max's arm when she heard the door. She paused and turned. 'Oh good, I'm glad it's you, Calhoun. I don't want to see Lucius.'

'He's outside. I hitched the wagon up and we're taking the outlaws to the sheriff. How are you, Max?'

'About as you'd expect after being shot but give me a few days and I'll be fine and dandy. Little Alphie is really worried about me. Can you maybe fill in for a bit?'

'That's the thing, Max.' He met Maura's blue eyes. 'Seems Lucius is intending to hand me over to the sheriff along with the outlaws. I think my time here has come to an end as all things do. I just came to say I'm glad we met.'

'He's what?' Panic widened her gaze. 'He can't. I won't have it. Uncle Max, you just lie there a minute. I'll be back.'

She stormed past Calhoun and out where her father sat in the wagon, the back loaded with outlaws. 'Get down! I want to speak to you.'

Lucius sat like a rock, not even looking at her. 'Then I'll climb up there, but we are going to get some things straight here and now.'

'You've always been high strung, Maura, like your mother. There was no reasoning with her.' He climbed down and stood in front of Maura.

She was so angry she'd balled her hands into fists. 'First of all, don't speak about my mother. She was the best part of you, and you never had sense to know it. Why are you taking Calhoun to jail? He and Max saved us from a gang of cutthroats. Does that not matter to you? He could've ridden out, but he stayed, and he fought like the devil so that we might live. Does that sound like a bad man to you, one who deserves to be hanged? Answer me!'

'Men can pretend to be anything. You know nothing of the world, Maura. No matter what you wish to pretend, he is Jonas Calhoun, a bank robber, thief and murderer. And yes, after a short trial, I intend to hang him.'

'There you go!' shouted a bound gang member from the wagon. 'He's the same as us.'

'Over my dead body.' She licked her dry lips, searching for words to convince him he had the wrong man. 'I know him far better than you ever will. I've lain by his side, I've given him my body, and I love him more than I ever thought possible to love any man. He gave me kindness and gentleness like I've never known. Emma and I certainly got none from you. I intend to marry him and spend a lifetime by his side. Who knows? I may even now be with child as we speak.'

'You're making this up.'

Calhoun stepped to Maura's side and put an arm around her waist. 'What she says is true.' His dark eyes stared into her upturned face. 'I love your daughter and God willing, intend to spend the rest of my days proving it to her.'

Lucius scoffed, 'What would a man like you know about love?'

'You don't know me,' Calhoun said quietly. 'Stop judging me.'

Maura faced her father. 'He's the finest, most honorable man I've ever known, and I won't listen to you tear him down. To hang him right here before you even know the truth. I wish I could say that you have even half his honor, courage and decency.'

His face stony, Lucius dismissed her with a wave of his arm. 'You see what you want to see, daughter.'

'I grew up with you, remember? A child knows when she's not loved.' Maura inhaled a trembling breath. 'I used to yearn to crawl into your lap and snuggle, but you preferred to caress your stupid rope. You have an unnatural obsession with it.' Maura raised her chin. 'I don't need you now. I learned to make it on my own.'

Lucius finally looked down at his feet. 'Yet, I kept the outlaw Donavan from killing Jonas. Does that not count for something?'

'It does and I thank you for that. Please drop this folly of taking him into town. I beg you. I've seen into his heart, and I know he's not the man you claim. He's a deputy US marshal and has the badge to prove it.' She could see the lines of Lucius's face softening. 'If you ever want a sliver of a chance of meeting your grandchild, you'll cease this craziness and let us be.'

'You leave me little choice.' Lucius raised his gaze. 'I did love you and Emma. I always loved you. Didn't know how to show it.' He glanced away and seemed to struggle. 'I know the least painful way to hang a man, but I didn't – don't – know how to be a father. That's why I stayed gone so much. It made me uncomfortable and seemed best if I disappeared. I'm sorry.'

Finally, an apology after all these years.

From the back of the wagon, Donavan shouted, 'Awww, that's sweet, Hangman! Let's go. I need a doctor.'

'Hold your horses!' Lucius answered. 'You'll get there.'

'So, what will it be?' Calhoun asked. 'If I'm staying, I need to gather up the dead and get them ready by the time you get back. They're going to start stinking soon. And I need to make two new doors before nightfall.'

'Then do what you have to. I'll be back soon to load up the dead.' Lucius put a stiff arm around Maura and climbed into the wagon.

The hug wasn't much but Maura realized he had to start somewhere and had made the effort. That was huge.

She turned to Calhoun. 'I have to get to Max and finish up with him, then I want to look at your arm.'

'My arm is fine. It's already stopped bleeding. I think I only got grazed.'

'Men.' She grinned. 'Then I'll start breakfast. I'll call you when it's ready. I wish you had some help, but we can't let Tully do it. It would be too difficult emotionally for him to handle such a task.'

'I agree. He's only a child in a man's body. I can do it myself; it'll just take a little longer.' He bent his head for a kiss and strolled off whistling.

Maura let out a contented sigh and watched him.

THIRTY-SIX

That night, after a day spent cleaning up and fixing the ruined doors as best they could until he could build new ones, Calhoun was resting on his bed. He stared up at the ceiling, his thoughts in a jumble. He had to tell Maura the truth, no matter the cost.

He wouldn't go any further with this secret between them. He loved her too much.

Sure, she'd get angry, but he only prayed she'd forgive him and see the reasons why he kept quiet.

However, things could go the other way and she'd order him to leave. In that case, he'd ride out, his heart breaking, and never see her again.

A light knock sounded, and he went to the door to find Maura. 'I was just thinking about you. We need to talk.'

'I felt a need to come for some reason. I noticed something troubling you through the day. If you're having second thoughts about marrying me, I understand. I bring a lot of unwanted baggage.'

'No, it's not that at all. Please don't think that. But you might after I clear my conscience. Sit down.' He pulled out a chair for her then sat opposite. 'I hardly know where to start but I suppose with my name. Your father is right.'

Maura gave a little cry. 'You're Jonas Calhoun?'

'Yes, and I was a member of Rupert Donavan's gang. But I never murdered anyone in cold blood, no matter what Lucius said. I got caught up in Donavan's schemes before I knew it.' Jonas Calhoun lifted her hand and held it gently. 'You see, I was standing on the gallows with your father with a rope around my neck when Donavan galloped into town. He shot the rope, freeing me. I leaped on the back of his horse, and we hightailed it out of town.'

He paused a moment, getting his thoughts in order, daring to hope she could forgive him. 'The funny thing was, I hadn't done anything before that except drift into town. The sheriff said I was J.A. Cody who was wanted for murder and robbery. I kept saying I wasn't him, but no one would listen.'

'Why?' Maura asked. 'You were telling the truth.'

'The sheriff was collecting a big reward for Cody's capture so he was ready to say anything, even tell a lie.' He turned Maura's palm up. The calluses spoke of her immense strength in taking care of not only herself but her sister and now orphans too.

'That's horrible! And disgusting.'

Calhoun placed a soft kiss in her palm. 'But, that's the way some lawmen are and that's not an isolated incident. So there I was caught up in a mess with Rupert. He said I owed him and maybe by all rights I did. I rode with him and his men on quite a few jobs. He robbed everything: banks, trains, stagecoaches, even waylaying unsuspecting travelers. He didn't care and he left plenty of bodies in his wake.'

He released her hand and stood by the fireplace, staring into the flames. 'I'd been trying to find a way to escape long before my brother Cutter came the night I was shot. Cutter was the lawman and said he was getting me out. We planned our getaway for midnight after the gang was asleep and Cutter rode off. He came back at midnight, and I was waiting. Only before I got on my horse, I decided to go back for the loot from the last bank robbery to hurt Donavan. I didn't even know what I was going to do with it. The thought hit me to exact some revenge for the people he'd killed. I didn't want him to profit from the robbery. That's when everything went sour.'

'Oh Jonas, why did you go back? It wasn't important.' Maura went to him and laid her head on his good shoulder. 'You swung at the hornet's nest and got stung bad. I can guess what happened.'

'I made a noise and woke everyone. But I jerked up the bags of loot and ran back to Cutter. We threw it on a third horse and lit out like the devil was chasing us. They wasted no time in following and emptied their guns at us. They got Cutter and I kept riding.

'Maura, he gave his life because he wanted to free me.' He glanced down at her feeling so unworthy. 'Seems he made a deathbed promise to our mother and tried to keep his vow. He paid dearly.'

'So many things make sense now – the badge, the empty bank bag, Cody's wanted poster. Where is the loot?' she asked quietly.

'I hid it in the crevice between two large boulders in the woods not far from where you found me.'

'And that's where the money came from to buy explosives and the windfall from the mercantile?'

'Yes. I only took four hundred of it.'

Hurt filled her eyes and she pulled her hand back. 'You lied to me every step of the way, Calhoun. You didn't trust me or anyone else.'

'I was trying to find a way out of my mess. But I hurt you and that's the bottom line. I don't know if I can ever make that right.'

'I don't know either.' She turned her stiff back to him. 'Our relationship is based on a lie. Everything was a lie. How can I trust you again?'

'Not everything was a lie.' Deep loss enveloped him. His quiet voice shook with emotion. 'I love you, Maura, and that's the God's honest truth. It's the kind of abiding love that carries a couple through whatever life throws at them. What I feel is unshakable and lasting. You're everything good and kind and I would rather die than betray you.' His heavy sigh filled the thick silence. He dropped his hands to his side. 'I'll get my horse and leave.'

When she said nothing, he gathered up his things and went out the door. He'd gambled and lost and his chest hurt like he'd been kicked by a team of mules. He hurried across the compound to the barn for his horse. Where he'd go, he had no idea and the bad part was he didn't care. Dropping his load, he reached for his saddle.

Footsteps sounded on the dirt floor and he swung to see Maura. Tears streamed down her face and her voice was thick. 'I can't let you leave. You said you love me?'

He couldn't look at her, afraid he wouldn't have the strength to walk away one more time. Why had she followed? He lifted the saddle and threw it over his horse's back, then leaned on it, still keeping his eyes from her. 'What do you want?' he asked hoarsely.

Maura moved close and her sweet fragrance drifted to him. She cleared her throat. 'I knew there was a chance you might be the outlaw Jonas and not Cutter and I thought I'd prepared myself for the possibility. I told myself it didn't matter who you were.'

Calhoun turned to face her. 'But?' he asked softly.

'I'd rather take you as you are than to live with this emptiness. You made me dream and see that maybe we could have a future.' Maura wiped her tears. 'When you save someone's life, they belong to you forever. You're mine and I'm not letting you go.'

He grinned. 'Is that a fact?'

'It's an old proverb or something. I'm afraid you're stuck with me, buster.'

One step and he took her face between his hands, staring deep into those blue eyes. 'I can't think of anyone I'd rather belong to.' He ground his lips to hers, drinking of her sweet goodness.

She meant more to him than his own life. Without her, he didn't want to keep breathing.

The kiss shook him to the very depths of his soul. Maura was all that mattered. His breath was ragged when they broke apart. 'I vow to you by all that's holy that I'll never give you reason to doubt me about anything. I swear that.'

They took his belongings back to his room, discussing their future.

'The question is, what do we do with the stolen loot now?' Maura asked.

'I could return it to the bank anonymously.'

Maura's eyes twinkled. 'That sounds like a job for the sisters. Let them take it and if folks badger them with a lot of questions, they can launch into excited French. What do you think?'

'Perfect solution. They could say they found it. Who would accuse three nuns of robbing a bank? I just hate that we have to give it back when there is such a need here. That's the part that troubles me. These kids need it.'

'Dear, you forget that it's the people's money, not the bank's and part of that might be someone's life savings or a widow depending on it to live out her days.'

'You're right. You're a very smart woman with a heart of gold.' He lifted her hand to his mouth and kissed her fingers. 'And my moral compass.'

'I love it when you talk sexy. But, you can't go through life as Jonas.'

'Jonas died the night of his escape. To honor my brother's memory and all he sacrificed for me, I think he'd approve if I took his name.'

There was one sticking point he'd have to eliminate that tied him to the lie but he wouldn't bother Maura with that now. Cutter had told him that he was deep into some kind of trouble with a powerful rancher and the man was holding something over Cutter's head. Somehow, Calhoun had to fix that and cut the last tie in order to be safe.

'Then, you can step into the job as well, Marshal. Emma pegged it from the start. Who would know you aren't him? You look the same and I'm sure you're very good at bringing in bad men.'

'I guess you're right. I'm a deputy US marshal.' He grinned. 'How about that? Cutter would be very happy.' He hooked an arm around her neck, fiddling with the buttons of her dress. His deep growl held the same kind of wanting that burned inside her. 'Would you like to celebrate?'

'I believe I would, Marshal Cutter Calhoun. I crave your tender touch.'

The next morning, Cutter rode out and came back a short while later with two burlap bags.

It's strange but she would never think of him as Jonas. That didn't fit this man.

Maura went to meet him, her heart swelling at the sight of the tall figure sitting proudly in the saddle. He seemed truly grateful for a second chance to live a good life. So was she. She'd waited so long for someone like him to come along. Cutter was a fine man with a kind heart. He loved her and cared for the children as though they were his own.

He dismounted and left a searing kiss on her lips.

'I've told the nuns we had a task for them, but I wanted you to be here when we share what it is. I also told Emma and Max.' She put an arm around his waist. 'Do you mind sharing your story with the sisters? They need to know the truth and what's at stake for you and all of us.'

'I have nothing more to hide. I'll gladly answer all their questions. Let me transfer these sacks to the wagon and I'll be in.'

A short while later with Emma watching the children play, they gathered around the long kitchen table.

First, Cutter told his story then Sister Angela nodded and spoke. 'What you want us to do?'

Maura took over. 'Take the sacks into San Antonio to the bank, not the sheriff. Ask to speak to the bank manager and tell him that somehow the money ended up at the orphanage. Remember to ask for the bank manager. Explain how Donavan and his gang were going to attack and we had to spend four hundred of it to buy explosives to defend ourselves and the children.'

Sister Bernadette nodded sagely. 'Our *petits enfants*.'

'Tell how the outlaws did in fact attack and we barely escaped death but he's been arrested and in jail now. Anytime they start asking a lot of questions, launch into excited French. You don't know anything except the need to return the money. You're trying to do the right thing.'

Sister Angela nodded. 'We say, "Praise God" and "God is Good" many, many, many times.'

'Many.' Sister Bernadette clapped. 'God send answer.'

Maura smiled and began to relax the breath she seemed to be holding. They understood and would be the best for the job. 'Yes. That's perfect. I just regret that we can't keep some of it for the orphans.'

Sister Angela rested a hand on Maura's shoulder. 'God send money. We pray for it.'

'Sisters, thank you so much.' Cutter hugged them. 'You've been angels to me and to these children. It's easy to see why everyone loves you.'

Shy Sister Anne-Marie got up and clasped Cutter's hand. '*Tu es un homme bon.*' Then the girl who'd dedicated her life to God pulled him down to kiss his cheek.

'She said, "You are a good man",' Sister Angela translated.

For the shy sister to say anything to Cutter was amazing. Maura loved the change in her. So many adjustments had happened since they first met.

'I guess you need to be going,' she said. 'The sooner the better.'

'We take money back. *Oui.*' Sister Angela ushered them outside.

The oldest Johnson boy of twelve ran out behind them. 'I'll go with them.'

Maura glanced at him. 'I don't think so.'

'What if someone robs those ladies? I'm big for my age and can pass for fifteen. Please,' he begged. 'That's a lot of money.'

Cutter turned sharply. 'How do you know they'll be hauling money?'

'Yes, how, Earl?' Maura tapped her foot.

The color drained from Earl's face. 'I sorta heard you talking. I wouldn't want anything to happen to these sisters. I like them. A lot. And what if the wagon breaks down?'

The kid made a lot of sense. But was this just a ploy to get to town and then do God knows what?

'What do you think, Cutter? Do we let him go?'

'Why not? Wouldn't hurt anything and he could be a deterrent for thieves.'

'So, I can?' Earl asked.

'Go ahead.' Maura placed her hands on his shoulders. 'You are not to let them out of your sight for one minute. Stick to them like glue and don't think you can run off once you get to town.'

'I know. I promise I won't leave 'em.' Earl ran and jumped into the wagon, giving each nun a hand up.

With Cutter's hand on the small of Maura's back, they waved as Earl drove the wagon out. 'I sure hope and pray this works and kills all thought of you being Jonas.'

If not, she didn't know what to try. All she knew was she'd gladly die for this man who'd shown her how to love and a glimpse of the bright future shimmering in the distance.

Cutter was working on new doors for the place and Maura was supervising the children when the sisters and Earl returned from town. Earl was sitting so tall on the seat and grinning to beat all. He seemed to have reached a new level of maturity.

Maura waved. Maybe she needed to give him more responsibility. It seemed to have worked wonders.

He helped the sisters down then hurried to Maura. 'You should've seen these ladies. They really did great and the banker was so thrilled to get the money back that he gave them each twenty dollars. They were waving their arms and God blessing this and God blessing that to beat all.'

Calhoun arrived to hear and grinned. 'I'm glad it's done.'

'And that's not all, sir.' Earl's voice was in that change between boy and man and kept going high and low. 'Sister Angie told the banker in no uncertain terms that Jonas is dead so they should stop looking for him. She told that to the sheriff too and shook her finger at him.'

Maura laughed. 'I can see her now. Thank you for going, Earl.'

'I wouldn't have missed that show for anything.'

The sisters carried a basket laden with food and stopped to pass out something to the children before coming on.

'He take money,' Angela reported. 'He know we mean business. He give twenty dollar.'

Sister Bernadette joined in. 'We buy food and candy for children.'

Maura wound her arm through Cutter's. 'That's wonderful. Thank you for taking care of this matter. We have so much need here but at least we got a little out of our good deed.'

'God reward.' Sister Angela glanced around. 'God not forget us.'

'Well, I wish I had your faith.' Maura tilted her head at Calhoun. 'Is your offer of marriage still good?'

'It sure is. Name the place and time, darlin'.'

'Tomorrow at noon we'll find us a preacher.'

With a whoop, he picked her up and whirled her around much to the children's delight. Soon they were all dancing in the yard.

They made so much noise, Emma and Max came out to see what was happening.

'We're going to have a wedding, Uncle Max!' Maura exclaimed laughing.

Max chuckled. 'Well, it's about time. I always knew you should be together.'

Maura thought back to the bleak days of the past when all seemed hopeless and was glad she never gave up. Nothing was lost or impossible as long as a body kept hope in their heart – not only with her and Emma. While she knew Max would always fight his demons, she knew that he'd try his best to win the battle with the bottle. He'd already done amazingly well and she was so proud of his progress.

A little later she found Cutter gazing at the old mission that was now an orphanage.

She slipped beside him. 'A penny for your thoughts.'

'I was just admiring the new door. What do you think?'

She gasped, noticing that he'd painted *Heaven's Door* on the new wood. 'It's perfect.'

'I think so too, my beautiful Maura. There's magic here. It truly is Heaven's Door – a door to a paradise that's beyond my wildest dreams. I'm very glad I found this place.' He put an arm around her and squeezed, pressing a kiss to her temple. 'But mostly I was looking at you. I'm the luckiest man alive, my love.'

EPILOGUE

T hree months passed and Maura and Cutter settled into life as a married couple. He stepped into his brother's job and had captured one of the meanest outlaws the west had ever seen. When he'd delivered the man to jail to await trial, the sheriff gave him a piece of good news.

'Hey, Cutter, do you remember that big rancher down at Uvalde who was making a lot of trouble for you?'

Calhoun froze. Had the man managed to convince everyone that Cutter was disreputable? He glanced at the door and judged the distance in case running seemed the better option. Everything inside him stilled.

'Yeah, Sheriff, I remember.'

'Someone found him dead yesterday. Shot through the heart.'

'You don't say? Hope they don't blame me.'

'Relax. They already caught the killer. Thinking of giving him a medal.'

Calhoun chuckled, relief flooding through him. The last piece that could tie him to the lie and ruin his new life was dead and buried.

The newlyweds were working toward getting their own small piece of land but for now they lived at Heaven's Door. Maura was overjoyed to discover she carried Cutter's baby and prayed it was a boy. But a girl would be just fine, too.

The orphan children were growing like weeds, especially baby Juliette. She was holding her head up good, rolling over and holding her toys. Every milestone was celebrated.

Even so, ever since the night the outlaw gang attacked and the children had to hide in the little room beneath the floor, they wouldn't stay out of it. The dim area that was off limits was a mysterious world to explore.

One day, Maura missed Sunny, Henry and their group of friends and found them down below the floor playing with bags of shiny silver rocks.

'You know you're not supposed to be playing down here, don't you?' Maura scolded. 'Remember what I said?'

'Look, Miss Mo. Ain't these pretty?' Henry held one up for her to see.

'It's very pretty. Where did you get those?'

'We dug 'em up,' Alphie said, looking mighty proud of himself.

'How many bags did you find?'

'Three.' Sunny grinned. 'They're buried treasure.'

'Yep.' Alphie nodded.

Was it true what the outlaws said about treasure being inside the old mission? She didn't know what silver ore looked like but this could be it. Excitement swept through her at the possibility.

'OK, Uncle Max and Mr Calhoun need to look at these. Put them down and all of you march up out of here.'

With glum faces, they did as they were told and Maura went to find Cutter who'd just returned from a few days away. As a deputy marshal, he'd hunted down an outlaw and locked him up. He looked rather pleased with himself and the job he'd stepped into.

'Sweetheart, the children found some rocks down under the floor. Will you come and take a look at them?'

'Sure. They're probably nothing but I'll check them out.' He finished hammering on a bench he was building and went to find Max.

Minutes later, the men went down and came back up wearing wide grins.

'It's silver ore,' Cutter announced. 'I never would've believed that rumor.'

'Jim Bowie's lost treasure,' Max added. 'I can't believe it.'

When Sister Angela heard, she made the sign of the cross. 'God reward. Praise be.'

The two men lost no time in taking the bounty to Bandera, fifty miles away. Hopefully, word wouldn't reach San Antonio and bring hoards of greedy men. They returned with five hundred dollars cash out of the thousands they deposited in a bank.

'We have enough to make this the best orphanage in three states,' Cutter announced at supper that night. He saluted the children. 'Thank you for finding it. You all get new clothes.'

'Hurrah!' Earl shouted amid the din of excited voices. 'And shoes?'

'Yes, and shoes.'

That night, Cutter held Maura close, running his hands over her silky skin, then resting them on her belly where his son grew. 'I can't contain this love I have for you. It's the strongest feeling I've ever known.' He inhaled a shaky breath, a tidal wave of emotion forming tears in his eyes. 'I'm still reeling from all my good fortune. New life was born from hopeless despair. Thank you for being my wife.'

She kissed his cheek. 'I wouldn't want another husband and father for our child. Life didn't pass me by and I'm not too old to know love. We have all our tomorrows waiting for us and I can't wait to start living them. With you.' She caressed his face and leaned toward his waiting lips.

AUTHOR'S NOTE

The story of historical figure Jim Bowie and his lost silver has always fired my imagination and I couldn't help making that a part of my plot. Bowie moved to San Antonio, Texas in 1828 and by 1830, had become a Mexican citizen. Members of the Lipan Indian Tribe came often to town to exchange silver for food, medicine, etc. and that piqued Bowie's interest. He struck up a friendship and they showed him their silver mine located somewhere in San Saba County, Texas. They let him work the mine and keep a few sacks of silver but then they turned on him and he barely escaped with his life. He buried the treasure and before he could return with a group of men, the Texas War for Independence broke out. He died at the Alamo and the location of the silver mine and the sacks he buried was forever lost. Many have searched for the mine believed to be near Menard, Texas but no one has ever found any trace. It makes a colorful Texas Legend for sure.

True fact: Jim Bowie did spend some time at the Mission San Francisco de la Espada and fought in a battle waged there at the beginning of the War for Independence. The mission was built in 1731 by Spain as they tried to hold on to their land holdings. It became a refuge for Native Americans who lived there and worked in the fields. Over the years it went through periods of abandonment and today, although some of the buildings are in ruins, the church section has limited services on Sunday. I thought it was a great place in which to set an orphanage.